THE HOUSE

OF

WRITERS

M.J. NICHOLLS

Sagging
Meniscus

Printed in the United States of America.
Set in Williams Caslon Text with LaTeX.

ISBN: 978-1-944697-06-8 (paperback)
ISBN: 978-1-944697-07-5 (ebook)
Library of Congress Control Number: 2016936259

Sagging Meniscus Press
web: http://www.saggingmeniscus.com/
email: info@saggingmeniscus.com

For Nicola

Table of Contents

The Corridor of Opening Lines   1

This Lexicographically Limber Universe   5

The Vertical Victor   7

Cal's Tour: *High-Quality Literary Fiction*   9

This: *1*   17

The Trauma Rooms: *1*   19

Books no longer in print   23

Mhairi: *1*   25

A Better Life: *1*   29

The *Farewell, Author!* Conference: *1*   33

Cal's Tour: *Middlebrow Fiction*   35

Puff: The Unloved Son: *1*   43

This: *2*   45

The Trauma Rooms: *2*   49

A Commission Gone Awry   53

Mhairi: *2*   61

A Better Life: *2*   63

The *Farewell, Author!* Conference: *2*   65

A Blast of Kirsty   69

Writer Portraits: *The Great(est) Opaquist*   73

Cal's Tour: *Scottish Interest Books*   77

This: *3*   87

The Trauma Rooms: *3*   89

Puff: The Unloved Son: *2*   93

AD FROM SPONSORS   95

Mhairi: *3*   97

The Jesus Memos   99

A Better Life: *3*   103

The *Farewell, Author!* Conference: *3*   107

I opened the wrong door   111

This: *4*   113

The Trauma Rooms: *4*   115

The Basement   117

Mhairi: *4*   121

Cal's Tour: *Science Fiction*   123

A Better Life: *4*   131

The *Farewell, Author!* Conference: *4*   135

Things to do before writing the next paragraph   141

Puff: The Unloved Son: *3*   151

Mhairi: *5*   155

Writer Portraits: *The New Writer*   157

This: *5*   161

The Trauma Rooms: *5*   163

The Corridor of Cheap Commodities   167

A Better Life: *5*   169

The *Farewell, Author!* Conference: *5*   173

Mhairi: *6*   177

I said thanks Mum   179

Cal's Tour: *Romance*   181

AD FROM SPONSORS   189

Your idea of literature   191

This: *6*   193

The Trauma Rooms: *6*   195

Puff: The Unloved Son: *4*   199

A Better Life: *6*   201

The *Farewell, Author!* Conference: *6*   205

Mhairi: 7   209

Alice: A Fictional Serviette   211

Cal's Tour: *Toilet Books*   213

This: 7   219

The Trauma Rooms: 7   221

Writer Portraits: *Movements*   225

A Better Life: 7   229

The *Farewell, Author!* Conference: 7   233

Mhairi: *8*   237

Writing into the future   239

This: *8*   245

The Trauma Rooms: *8*   247

C.M. Horvath's Almost Girlfriend   251

A Better Life: *8*   255

The *Farewell, Author!* Conference: *8*   259

Bizarro Tim   263

Mhairi: *9*   265

This: *9*   267

The Trauma Rooms: *9*   269

A Better Life: *9*   273

The *Farewell, Author!* Conference: *9*   275

The Two Poems of Archie Dennissss   279

AD FROM SPONSORS   283

This: *10*   285

The Trauma Rooms: *10*   287

Writer Portraits: *The Beekeeper*   291

A Better Life: *10*   297

The *Farewell, Author!* Conference: *10*   299

The Corridor of Closing Lines   301

THE
HOUSE
OF
WRITERS

The Corridor of Opening Lines

MY nodes have been compromised. You think it's simple, eating this oatcake? "George, how about we change tack and coerce the gorilla?" This isn't the last we'll hear from Iolande! Put a sock into the mixer and thank me afterwards. The afternoon was tired, stale, and pointless, like the complete works of Jhumpa Lahiri. Can't we *eat* them? I am the most accomplished theremin player in the universe and I don't need a single word of validation. Potted kettles are not black. In a totalitarian state there are seventeen variations to observe: consider the limpet and the squirrel and the oboe. He ate

THIS iphone is crunchier than we expected. Black pots are not kettles. Assertions made in wet weather are not proper assertions. "Idiotic capering is prohibited." The results were positive, the consequences negative. Fiddling expenses is encouraged in local governments provided the items claimed are flammable. Slurp from an ashtray, sip from a soda siphon. Is this mere mindless surrealism? Do electric sheep dream of androids? Mick Jones awoke one morning humming "Lost in the Supermarket." "Where is the safest place to

WELCOME TO

herself and she ate himself and a small decorator coughed in the middle. That string arrangement is *beautiful*! "Hmm," Lorna said as she brushed cookie crumbs from her skirt. This novel ends in the first sentence. Who needs cleverness when you have randomness? I was feeling unsatiated so I phoned the doctor who told me I needn't feel unsatiated so I hung up. Show me a man who's read the complete works of Evelyn Scott and I will show you a dyslexic parrot. "Are you going to dip that chainsaw in limeade or *what*?" Goodbye! The reader died at 3.45am last night. You open your mouth to speak and realise there are no mouths. Bitterness is the best thing ever. Help a Spartan? Pauline stretched in her king-size bed and thought, "Damn! I hate luxury." "Fire up the

T

H

E

H

O

U

S

E

O

F

store this balalaika?" Year-long swear words rarely make for effective comebacks. I am a normal male aged 34 I like fencing rabbits crosswords real estate and princes at weekends I wear rubberwear and speak in a dialect beyond comprehension. Charlie's sister was tired of eating Charlie so she salted a chip instead. Later, as he sat on his balcony eating the corpse of J.G. Ballard, Dr. Robert Laing reflected on the unusual events that had taken place. Undertakers rarely die. Dieters rarely undertake. Zebras crossed the pond and James considered the changes in his life so far while snakes hissed outside his verandah. Kettled blacks are not pots. Vertical invasion or horizontal? Drugged and stupid and megaphone!" Ian instructed. The wettest nation in Yugoslavia is France. "Is this art or brainmush?" the critic questioned. I cannot write this novel until all the noodles in China are free. I would *love* to begin this novel—say on 10th July? Goddamn it, not another verruca! Adelaine regarded the spelling error and decided to shoot the hostage. Everyone dies, or do they? The orangutan, beshitten and bemused, considered the advantages of investing in BSkyB. Tagliatelle—myth or reality? "That's a very statesmanlike apple you're holding there, Andy," said Sid. Stealth ululation is the secret to success. Every time a dream comes true, a salamander dies.

W R I T E R S

free! The chlorine aficionado lounged on a pouffe. "Racist language has not yet been invented," Rory muttered. A rap musician and a toreador decide to split the rent 50/50. Zebra crossings make me cross, as they do everyone else. Channel Four news exploded. It is a fact universally acknowledged that a single woman in possession of no fortune must be a Jane Austen fan. "Are *you* serious?" the serious man asked. Inside the shed there lived a cubit. Bedeck the halls with bits of Holly. For sale: a sieve: used once. You have reached the end, and now you must begin. Is the next sentence the worst thing ever written?

THE HOUSE OF WRITERS

This Lexicographically Limber Universe

ARE you skilled with words in an age when words are sqaunderously piddled down so many unthinking drains? Are you a spinner of yarns, a whirler of sagas, a rotator of epics? Do you take pride in the sibilant syllable, the luxuriant noun, the plosively placed preposition, in sentences that sing like angels in a cosmic opera? Does your heartbeat dance to the flick of the cursor? Can you fill a blank page with enough razzle-dazzle, fuzzbox, and too-rah-rah-ray to make the everyday reader spurn his duncehood? Perhaps your parents have praised your spooky fictions about inventive slashers and cunning killers, loved your vivid descriptions of sleazy cities, sorry tinkers, hoary winters, or smiled at the way you make your people hum with life using only twenty-six squigs. Perhaps you're an inveterate artist with forty unseen novels fraying and yellow in your drawer, lonesome for the light, or an amateur hobbyist ready to party with the professionals, or a defeatist who cynically smote his penman's dreams for a cushy deadheaded life as a ScotCall phone monkey. You dudes, in all your multitude, have reached *The House of Writers*. We strip the sorrow from screams and send you spinning into dreams in ecstatic and awfully inky twirls. Who, and wherefore, art us? Here we are—we are here! We are a forty-storey structure situated in the peaceful Crarsix wilds, twenty minutes off the Aldercrux sliproad past the Gibson Museum, only forty minutes from the secluded marshes of the former ComFuPlex (now a stock-dump farm). We promise every employee the means and motivation to take on the challenge of making it as a writer in the genres available, to survive in this hostile climate, in this lexicographically limber universe presided over by call centres, fast-food futures, and the realistically near threat of

5

a deoxygenated atmosphere slowly extinguishing the human race. By browsing our prospectus, we hope you will find many boons and booms to bring you closer to our face, and when you arrive, ready for the fresh intake of change, you will find everything you ever believed unimaginable will manifestly overtake your so-deeply entrenched cynicism. Still not convinced? Perhaps these parting lines from J. Frank Glazo, author of over three thousand novels, will convince? "The House has turned me into a totally different person—a successful one." Say howdy to your future. Say *bienvenue* to the new you. *The House of Writers.*

The Vertical Victor

THE House of Writers has undergone several structural metamorphoses, firebombing mishaps, and mismanagement disasters before becoming the vertical victor of today and tomorrow. The building was opened on Nov 3rd 1989 and designed by Anglo-Norwegian architects Portia Entwittle and Limber Alsöö who, in their own words, were "after a sort of filthy pigsty aesthetic." Originally a housing scheme designed to accommodate rehabbed paedophiles and pederasts and keep them at remove from Aldercrux town, the building became a popular spot for—to quote Limber—"acts of fragrant and abundant rear-ward fucking." A group of activists, Paedofinder General, singled out the tower block for a firebomb attack during the media "nonce-bashing" campaign of 1999, and the building fell into disuse over the new millennium when the residents were relocated or buried. In 2008, the computer manufacturing firm ComFuPlex opened their largest warehouse in the UK on Crarsix farmland, and the tower block was renovated for use as a separate office facility (costing almost twice to renovate than erecting a new one—we're happy the accountant was drunk). A relatively uneventful thirty years (in Crarsix) passed. By Jan 2038, ComFuPlex had become the UK's leading manufacturer of computer software—Apple and Microsoft the main contractors—until a short-sighted engineer made a mass-mistake resulting in a mass-meltdown. In a Microsoft CEO's words: "The squinty-eyed preening vanity refused to wear specs while engineering and missed a crucial screw and screwed up crucially, sending the West back to the Palaeolithic period, or 1972—same thing." In other words, a design flaw was replicated in every machine made after 2035, and complications with the internal cooling mechanism (or "fan") and various far-too-technical-to-explain motherboard hiccups and crackles led to every computer in the country uniformly exploding after four years, forcing every business to revert back to arcane filing systems and telephone use. ComFuPlex dumped their useless stock in the surrounding fields upon bankruptcy, and local inventors occasionally "farm" through the rubbish to create new contraptions. In the wider world, over the last fifty years literature became an increasingly niche pursuit—the public nibbled on narratives via filmphones, TV-lenses, and other technologically implausible means to force youngsters away from digesting texts. By 2040, writers were perceived in society as intellectual snobs and treated with casual contempt by the public. To clamp down on hate crime, the Tories introduced Artists' Licenses, whereby every work was made to conform to two rigid dicta: 1) Make it wholly understandable to even the dumbest, most bumbling alien. 2) Make it funny and light and utterly unthreatening to even the most delicate flowers. Literature went underground, forcing literary artists and experimenters into the wilderness (in some cases, literally roaming forests writing their seditious works under trees), until two redundant husband-and-wife entrepreneurs (Marilyn Volt and James Teaver) leased the building and opened House to straggling writers desperate to ply their craft. Soon, exiles from the country signed up to head our diverse range of genre-programs, accommodating the needs of a select but loyal readership throughout the country. Thanks to an agreement with the local government, The House is exempt from the Artists' legislation, since our readers are private, and we provide an essential service in rounding up straggling scribblers who would otherwise be criminals or suicides.

Cal's Tour

High-Quality Literary Fiction

My upbringing in a council house in the knobbly bits of Aldercrux, with a sister keen on stapling my slacks to the desk, pouring cream down my collar, and ritually tongue-lashing me every time I sat down to write, prepared me for life in The House. The First Floor is a hearty face-slap for those tied to utilities like three square meals, water, electricity, and a moss-free place to urinate. All dolled-up like a decaying aesthete's mansion (think Des Esseintes), the writing space is a Victorian drawing room with dusty chaise longues (feat. lion's head armrests), high-backed demi-thrones, Arthurian tables rakishly ravaged by ink-smeared papers, and bowls of rotting fruit (mostly yellow-blue kumquats). Beside the bookcase, packed with every grandisonant hack who ever tortured the semicolon, one finds the staff—four louche fops sprawled in chairs wearing double-breasted dinner coats talking excitedly in accents that hop between affected RP, Anglo-American, and Indo-Greek. As Elgar says: "Four destitutes posing for a Cruikshank etching."

Henri Plover, or the "Indominatable," as he styles himself, is unofficially in charge, but the philosophy on this floor is loaf before you leap—*sit down and sink in think before you sit up and sink in ink*—so no one is really the boss, proper. Henri is a recklessly smiley fellow with weedy centre-parted black hair, bibulous cheeks, and a belly like pork suet—the über-uncle—while London is the grandpa: a plump senior with stately grey prickles and oddly pink lips, always willing to raise his tankard to show off his shiny Proust-faced cufflinks. Marco is skinny and swarthy and says very little

9

(I never spoke to him once, but you may find the key to unlock his quietude), while Elgar is pale and blonde and all about the cheekbones and startling heft of shoulder-to-finger Victorian bling. "We're thoroughly decent chaps," London says, "unless you happen to interrupt us." I made this mistake on my first day and they've never forgiven me.

A typical day in the department? Typically untypical. Early morning is time for the "entrapment of *ipsissima verba*," i.e. to reflect on the correct words, eating Madeira off the plated face of Alice, sipping sherry from the head of Queen Elizabeth I, and flicking through Burton and Cervantes to absorb their essence. Be prepared for nutritional hell. My first, and only, meal was servings of rock-hard Madeira, my mornings spent pounding fistfuls of crumbs into shape for my lunch and dinner, chugging back belly-burning sherry to keep myself hydra-intoxicated enough to blot out a few notions. Around eleven, the chaps retreat to wax their particulars and buff their non-specifics (don't ask), and you will have some time to read (to impress—*À la recherche du temps perdu*) and dream of healthier meals. "A memory of things repast," as Henri says. In the afternoon, you will learn to "napalm the *locus communis*," i.e. to write HQLF sentences (see Henri's Master's Class). The evenings are yours. If you can find the House's caretaker Mhiari, try to blag a block of cheese or lamb, because life expectancy on this floor is limited until you can trick your body to tolerate the S&M diet.

The department is in disrepair. When you step out the lift (at the time of writing the lifts are functioning—but prone to plummets and floods), you will step onto a damp red carpet, strewn with half-smoked briar pipes, tubs of moustache wax, unread back issues of *The Lancet*, burst blazer buttons and farmyard cufflinks, into a corridor sweating through a layer of florally offensive wallpaper, where a tacky pyrite dado rail runs along the wall, forming a sort of tributary for the sweat as it puddles onto the carpet in a shiny hue of beige. Tacky chandeliers filled with moth carcasses, old couscous and socks hang precariously from the ceilings, several weeks off an extravagant accident, while untarnished portraits of the usual suspects hang crookedly on the walls: Henry James, Marcel Proust, Joseph Conrad, Thomas Mann. Never walk anywhere in your socks unless you like the squelch of sweat or icky toes. As the smallest department, they make the least money and have the narrowest readership, so can't afford maintenance or edible food or running water. As to your sleeping quarters ("fourths of sleep," as Marco says): a four-poster Victorian bed with an oaky brown canopy patterned with sleeping lions and snakes, framed by ruby-coloured curtains with furry hems and tassels with sheets of purple silk. (Slick with damp, usually, with several strategic buckets placed round the bed to catch falling drips.) As to interior décor: a tatty leather couch with an obese Manx named Madeleine lying sprawled over a throw rug with phoney Egyptian hieroglyphs, dreaming of days when its kind prowled the world as kings, and all manner of pseudo-spiritual clutter on the shelves and mantelpieces—purple gourds stuffed with potpourri; candles scented like lentils; dream-catchers, thought-trappers, soundbiters, and mindlickers; Zodiac calendars with pencilled Latin exclamations (*salvum me fac! cunctis nos adjuvet!*); and stacks of paperbacks from Henry James, all broken-spined and underlined.

Observant recruits will spot the many oil paintings of a stern-looking bald man with ruddy cheeks. This is Paul Andrew Donall, the single benefactor (reader) of HQLF works—a retired mineral magnate who made millions in the Persian Gulf War selling oil to both sides at twice the price. As a seventy-nine-year-old dandy of private means, he has sought to improve himself by reading "brullunt books" and has kindly patronised the dept. with one-fiftieth of his fortune. The writers take guidance on their content from Mr. Donall and tailor their prose style to meet his requirements—fortunately, he favours the long convoluted sentence, lively with many digressive clauses and semicolons, that over the course of three pages ceases to have any parsable meaning, like the late Henry James. He demands a "sturry fur ma pur wee brain tae fulla" (a followable story) but also wants sentences that reach beyond his intellectual powers, while flattering his intelligence by seeming to have a meaning only he can understand. He favours sentences whose meaning is almost entirely cryptic, as though a private Donall lexicon, not unlike the works of Gertrude Stein, only less odious. A man of changeable moods, he once fired the entire dept. minus me, hiring them back a week later! He's easy to see: a shrivelled prune in a chequered beige blazer and tartan breeks, sporting a cane and miners' bunnet, with a cravat and pocket hankie horribly prominent. His accent is brusque salaried Glaswegian, his speech the frenzied Gatling of a man no longer required to make himself understood. The writers dance around him like tinkle-toed toadies, fussing with plates of Madeira and sherry and pre-softened Edam! (Best policy: keep shtum when near.)

My first week was a steep learning curve, fraught with smudgy first drafts, damp rooms and vitamin deficiency. At nights, I lay under my heat-insensitive mattress shivering while Marco (my roommate) stayed up until 3am cooing over his early novels, lulling me to sleep with theatrical renditions of Butler Fortescue's most outrageous admonitions, punctuated by startling cries of "Peerless!" or "Magnifique!" whenever sleep dared to interrupt the programme. Every morning I dozed on a chaise longue, hallucinating water and roast dinners, nodding along as the fops commented on my work so far, reading the worst passages with patronising chortles and my strongest with solemn gravity. "Such ribald ravings of masterful magniloquency!" London said. "These sentences are thick with the clichéd indecision and a recherché juvenescence of Flaubert!" Edgar said. "What outrageously precocious attempts to unite the psychopathomaniacal interzones of Turgenev with the cacopornoformalogical hinterlands of Dostoevsky!" Marco said. I massaged my migraine. Learning to please these chaps is something you will have to teach yourself.

What of the books? Consult the following categories:

1. Novels about princes reflecting on their affairs with servants and prostitutes.
2. Death-bed reflections about princes and their affairs with servants and prostitutes.

3. Monologues about privileged childhoods in Monte Carlo and the impossibility of reuniting the 1920s *Kammerspielfilm* movement with neo-German Expressionist aesthetics.
4. Unpunctuated confessions from dying poets about their unholy lapse from pure formalism into the grubby intellectual mire of vorticism.
5. Books where characters fetishise their furniture for hundreds of pages in homage to Des Esseintes' decadence.
6. Pompous, pseudo-philosophical tracts written by sexually tormented hermits who asphyxiate themselves in plastic bags.

A short list of their recent novels: *Four Score & Seven Dreams, The Manners of Manny's Manor, Rendezvous of the Baden-Baden Butlers, The Duke of Bliss, Who Stole My Kites?, Prince Heimlickt's Adventures in Angioplasty*, etc.

Henri's Master's Class

Here's my brief Master's Class in High-Quality Literary Fiction for any new recruits to test whether they possess the verbal legerdemain to sign up for our programme. Let's start with a syntactically simple sentence:

I dropped my pencil on the carpet.

First challenge: increase, twofold, the dramatic quotient of this event. Every minor happenstance for our narrators has some significance, personal or metaphorical. If they pick their nose, it must be reflective of the struggle of the Byzantines to defeat the Ottomans in Constantinople; if they brush away dry skin, it must be emblematic of man's struggle to find ontological certainty in an indifferent cosmos, etc. If they sneeze in public, the embarrassment must drive them to wild fits of despair, to suicide or murder, and so on. Try now to heighten the drama of that sentence. Our example:

I dropped my prized, cherished old pencil onto the murky, stained, and horrible carpet.

Here, we contraposed the preciousness of the pencil with the beastliness of its destination, and deployed multiple adjectives for cumulative exaggerative effect. Second challenge: imagine this scene as the most dramatic tragedy that has ever befallen any man. Try to squeeze every scintilla of drama and emotion out of this falling pencil. Exaggeration is our speciality; don't be afraid to overdo it! Our example:

To my unfeasible horror, I dropped my prized and cherished pencil onto the murky, stained, and horrible carpet, and collapsed howling in hysterics at the injustice of a world where such terror and dread could befall such a man as I.

Now, to show you the level of artistry at work, here's this sentence as it appears in one of our published novels.

To my unquenchable and unfeasible horror, I stood outside myself watching myself, as if my body had floated into a separate consciousness outside my own, hovering outside me like some demon, my pencil describing a 45° arc as it tore itself from my hands, revolving in horripilating loops like the rings of Hell in Dante's Inferno, searing my heart with fire and hurt, pulling me down to the depths of despair as in Mirbeau's Torture Garden, *as my treasured and beautiful pencil, the passion of my heart and my very life's blood, my one and only love, came crashing to the floor like an orchestra in the fires of Abaddon, swallowed up by the interminable, tormenting flames of the remorseless carpet.*

Study the sentence carefully. Read it aloud. Do you see the unnecessary, emphatic verbal repetition (epizeuxis), dramatic exaggerations about corporeal states to create a false sense of profundity, the overly precise description, literary references in similes, and an emotional overstatement of the importance of the pencil? If you think you can make sentences like this, we're waiting for you in the HQLF department.

A Word from the Team

HENRI: Pray mercy! An intruder! How strange that nature does not knock!
MARCO: Keats?
HENRI: Dickinson.

MARCO: Blast!

HENRI: Greetings, writers! Enter, entrer! Viens ici et dégustez un sherry sur la banquette!

EDGAR: Henri, my dear lush, what can those rapscallious hopefuls expect from us in the HQLF department?

MARCO: A new name, for a start!

HENRI: We run the High-Quality Literary Fiction department, erstwhile known as the Henry James Peninsula for Polished Prose Perfection, or the Marcel Proust Sanatorium for Seriously Shimmering Syllables. Step aboard our abode! If you are a passionate purveyor of the anfractuous artistry of the Lord Henry James, the winding words of priestly Marcel Proust, or the epithymetic lyrics of Saint Vladimir Nabokov, this is the floor for you. Here you will work alongside our team of highly skilled logolepts and verbivores to produce novels fit for the finest most finessibly erudite hands and minds.

EDGAR: Well said.

HENRI: Remember when Cal (James McIntyre!) came to work for us, his prosaic and proletarian appellation was preformed into a prettier gnome de plum, pending our ponderous and philosophastering peregrinations? I posited Calltonius Inchcome-Hundepheffer.

LONDON: Me, Callismus Avenus-Ephebus.

EDGAR: And I, Callimachus Serrismus-Darvu.

HENRI: How silly!

MARCO: Tell them about our books!

EDGAR: Dear boy, do you take me for a mattoid?

MARCO: No, but you're most certainly a fustilugs!

EDGAR: Slander!

HENRI: Chaps, please! You'll petrify our future Masters!

LONDON: Shall I tell the readers about my latest epic? My protagonist is a dastardly duke writing a novel while cancer devours his bowels. I had the most eerily plosive gastrointestinal cramp during composition and this discomfort is reflected in the wild stenographic rhythms of my prose. Shall I read you an excerpt? I like to read my old books exactly one year after publication, to de- and reconstruct the Himalayas of my artistry.

EDGAR: Stop him!

LONDON: *"I steered my prized stallion along the promenade, terpsicho-really light-tripping upon the gauche gravel outside the hideous edifice of Ghastly Manor—"*

HENRI: Good grief!

LONDON: *"I had tripped the light fantastic at Count Ebenworth's ball, but now I trembled at the night so drastic, as the various rectosigmoid horrors surged anew in my cavities, and another wrenching night swaddled in the arms of pain and suffering awaited me—"*

MARCO: My conchas, my auricles!

LONDON: *"Retiring to the oak-brown depths of my boudoir, my pills arranged like so many tormented sinners as etched into the incomparable artefacts of Hieronymus Bosch, I faced the night with the grim assiduity of a matador gazing into the eyes of a rampaging bull as it limbered for an attack and—"*

EDGAR: Leaping Lords! Zounds, man! Cease! Desist!

LONDON: There's no need to be pigglewiggles.

MARCO: You made that word up.

HENRI: You're all pigglewiggles! So, patient readers, if you fancy frolicking with the chaps and myself, please send an application to Marilyn at The House. We hope to be hearing from you soon!

LONDON: Every burden is a gratitude, and made to be shaken off.

MARCUS: Shakey?

LONDON: Diderot.

MARCUS: Blast!

This

I

I AM writing this novel about The House of Writers on the twelfth floor. I am supposed to be working on a steampunk adventure set in a Hoosier brothel in which the locomotive drivers have gone on strike. But I would rather be writing this novel. I call this a "documentary" novel as the structural mode is fragmentary, hopping up and down the floors, flitting between first- and third-person narrators as one might find in a television doc. The term applies to works where the characters are based on real people and real events are reported in fictional form, a famous example being Truman Capote's *In Cold Blood* and an obscure example being Alan Burns's *The Angry Brigade*. The reportage in this novel ranges from autobiographical narrators (Cal McIntyre is based on me, both in terms of naïve impishness and asexual allure, although as a narrator he is a mere reporter), to direct snatches of dialogue overheard, stolen memos, emails, papers, and dramatisations of stories I have been told by loose-lipped liars. All this adds up to a skewed representation of a shambolic organisation. Structuring this narrative in a linear manner would be a gross misrepresentation of what life is like in this building. In fact, I had to restrain myself from including pages of people simply screaming at the top of their lungs, despite the prospect that might have been somewhat amusing and more "experimental" than the lump you have before you already. I will be popping up now and then to address the reader (who?) and tell you various things about my personal life that you were often curious about but didn't have the gumption to quiz me on.

The Trauma Rooms

I

ERIN lost her stapler. She interrogated Gam Aintpol, whose stapler theft had taken on mythic status in the northwestern corner of the office, shaking his skeletal frame until the truth seeped from his nose (snot implied honesty), and raided the cupboards, drawers, and hidden partitions, encroaching into the western corner of the office, where Rain Beezquix tongue-lashed Erin for her violation with the phrase "sheer brasserie and chronic gall," seeking to show her magnif off-the-cuff way with words, and failing. She ventured into the fire-exit corner, finding a door with a Munch scream motif—a convenient decoy for a massive stationery hoarding—and stepped into a sub-corridor with a long stretch of doors on either side. It seemed improbable so many cupboards could exist in such a narrow portion between the main floor and the back stairs, but she didn't have time to question the architectural quirks of The House, she was seeking a stapler with which to bind her first three chapters for her reader, Boril Soxmond from Bulgaria. She opened the first door where a manic man in a robe launched himself at her.

"Am I the BOLDEST AND BRIGHTEST VOICE OF A GENERATION?! Can I have . . . can I have . . . have the Pulitzer now?" His scabbed fingers dug into her shoulders and she stood stunned by the door. From the bathroom, a man in clothes appeared.

"Max! Release that woman! Max, you are the most significant British novelist on the scene since Martin Amis. Your voice is a breathtaking original. You have taken the novel to fresh and daring

19

new places, and have a thrilling career to come," the dressed man reassured the manic one, cooing him back to his wall-mounted bed where he sucked his thumb and muttered the words the dressed man had uttered.

Erin was taken to the bathroom, where the dressed man revealed himself as a doctor treating a rare kind of trauma caused by an overexposure to hyperbolic praise from critics during his patient's early days as a writer.

"Max's dad was the editor of *WeWuvBookz*, the most influential book website in the world at the time, and had arranged for his son to be praised up and down as the Next Best Thing. Max became dependent on the four or five pages of praise in the inside of each book and on the back and front covers, and when his dad was run over by a tractor, Max's fame dipped and reviewers labelled him a flash-in-the-bedpan and other such insults, causing a complete mental breakdown. He took to running around in the nude screaming "I am the voice of a generation!" and other slogans. No idea why he stripped off to do this, it's something the mentally ill never do except in books."

"Sorry for barging in. I had no idea this place existed. I was looking for a stapler."

"This is one of the ten trauma rooms. Each room houses a different trauma victim. I tend to each of them."

"Oh. Good."

"I find that—"

Before he could utter what he found, Max burst in naked in a second panic.

"Am I good? Am I good? AM I ANY GOOD!?"

"Max! You are a . . . talented, verbally inventive, outrageously funny, and heartbreaking talent on a par with . . . Norman Mailer. Help me out here, please," the doctor whispered to Erin.

"Erm, all right. You're a fantastic writer."

"IS THAT IT?!"

"No, more than that. You're a—"

"She means you are a voice vibrant with warmth and humour.

20

Your sentences pirouette like ballerinas across the page, your language is at once rich and accessible, erm . . . you construct complex metaphors and dazzling similes, and your use of zeugma is second to none in the history of literature."

"—sensational wordsmith, I was going to say, absolutely, categorically, worthy of the Booker, the Nobel, and the Pulitzer all at once."

"Steady."

"YOU TAKING THE PISS?!?"

"No! I mean that your talent will one day earn you those awards, probably. You are brilliant but at a realistic level, people don't resent you because you have this Godlike skill for writing, they love you because you are simultaneously intelligent and down-to-earth . . . the common man and highbrow critics adore you."

"You see, Max? You are loved and respected for your abilities. You are the frenetic and fizzing spokesman for a lost generation."

"Yes. Frenetic and fizzing . . . "

"Let's head back to bed."

"Frenetic and fizzing . . ."

"Sometimes he has nightmares as his head hits the pillow. This can happen three or four times before he settles down for the night. One of the hardest patients I have had to treat. I have pasted reviews around his room and sometimes he is content to sit rocking back and forth reading these for hours. A sad case. I can't seem to devise a solution to his trauma. Short of rediscovering his success, there is little I can do. We know he will never become a best-selling novelist again in his lifetime. Such a shame."

"What is his surname?"

"Grain."

"Yes. I remember his novels. Terrible."

"Oh yes, the most despicable piffle. His father ruined him. Now that you are here, perhaps you'd care to meet our other patients? One of them was loose earlier, so might have nabbed your stapler. Shall we?"

"Erm . . . I suppose. I need my stapler."

"Yes, that's it. Let's head to the second room," the doctor said. Erin didn't appreciate the manner in which he placed his arm on her shoulder, to lead her and hold her back from a possible retreat, but without her stapler, she was bereft—her Bulgarian reader would not read sample chapters in loose leaf form—so she ambled down the ink-scented corridor to meet the second of the ten crazies.

Books no longer in print

Dᴏɴ'ᴛ *You Forget About Me: The Unauthorised Simple Minds Bi-ography*; *Poltroon's Advance*; *The Little Green Lie*; *Imaginative Quantities of Fractal Rings*; *Don't Look Back: A Brief History of Sodomy*; *The Everlasting Story of Norah Jones*; *Poltroon's Defeat*; *How to Talk About Apps You've Never Downloaded*; *Gorgeous George's Last Stand*; *Eat Me!: Michael Bentine's Guide to Underrated Snacks*; *Nick Hornby's Top Forty Albums*; *Whatever Happened to the Chuckle Brothers?*; *I Am the Beautiful Strangler*; *Muzak vs. Silence: A Debate*; *The Huge Blue Truth*; *Fourteen Perspectives on Dan Brown's* Inferno: *A Study Guide*; *Do Frenchmen Eat Custard? (And Other Utterly Random Questions About Our Coastal Cousins)*; *The Bald Superstallion: An Unofficial Colin Mochrie Handbook*; *Horatio's Nutcracker*; *A Concise Overview of the Scottish Novel*; *Buttered Hysteria*; *Six Perspectives on an Abomination*; *Bored in Bethlehem: The Pilgrim's Guide to Livening Up That Epiphany*; *Gargoyle Gilbert's First Fall*; *Eden Prison: Various Angles on Paradise*; *Kristal's Visions*; *It Don't Mean a Thing if It Ain't Got That Swing: Guidebook for First-Time Hangmen*; *H from Steps: The Trial and Imprisonment of Britain's Biggest Paedophile*; *Nick Hornby's Top Forty Singles*; *The Official Guidebook to* Badgers, Badgers! We Love Thee!: A Hexagrammic Musical; *Just William!: The Unofficial William Hague Biography*; *The Ultimate Guide to Traffic Signs in Peru*; *Godard is Not Great: How Jean-Luc Poisons Everything*; *Interdenominational Darts: A Player's Manual*; *Cereal Murderers: The Shocking History of the Kellogg Twins*; *Nick Hornby's Top Forty TV Shows*; *Je ne suis pas un animal: Un Guide de* L'homme-éléphant; *Year of the Purple Artichoke*; *Swastikka Masala: A Guide to Nazi Curries*; *Whiffy the Wondersnake Strikes A Gain!*; *Guerillas in the Mist: The Disappearance of the South Vietnamese Army*; *Islamabad or Islamagood?: A Religious*

Forum; Alice Never Lived Here: Why the Films You Love Don't Exist; Hmm-Yup!: The Complete Hansen Story; Nick Hornby's Top Forty Nick Hornby Novels; Todd Number: A Disappearance; Sick in the Shtetl: Coping with Jewish Ennui; Only Kidding!: The Secret War Diaries of Adolf Hitler; A Beer and a Bonk: The Complete Guide to Scottish Nightlife . . .

Mhairi

I

B EFORE I became Queen Momma of The House, I lived in the poorest quarter of Stockport—a town outside Manchester known for its fantastic cocaine and heroin distribution networks and the most addicted populace per capita. I worked in a seafood restaurant, serving lobster thermidor to balding perverts prone to inserting their tongues and noses into whelks to simulate cunnilingus; in shoe retail, squeezing the plump feet of odoriferous spinsters into ill-fitting stilettos; in a swimming pool catching bloodied bandages in nets and rescuing infant rotters from drowning; in a homeless shelter, fending off inebriated attacks and tempting invitations to have vigorous tramp-sex in their rooms. When the homeless shelters closed down under a new government initiative (the homeless were to perform a town-wide sanitation service in exchange for a night sleeping in corridors and doorways) I too was among the jobless masses and to remain there for longer than I had conceived after graduating from my English Literature degree.

The Bulldog Brethren (TBB) had won the 2039 English elections and set about implementing their "policies," the first of which was to drive out the remaining immigrant population and the un- and under-white elements polluting British professions. To cope with these hopeless times, I fell in with a band of nihilists who introduced me to the pleasures of heroin and cocaine, and I became an addict within two weeks. We hung around in disused office blocks listening to Peter, Paul and Mary, inserting ourselves into the 1960s counterculture in a doomed attempt to imagine what such carefree living might have been like—contriving pleasure-visions of riding pink clouds into portals of infinite love and understanding . . . ending up in viscous fogs being attacked by Alsatians and wolves while TBB leader Neil Himes blustered us to death with his threats of people with tanned complexions working in British curry houses.

To fund the habit, I took a position in their Intelligent Persecution Unit, performing acts of abuse on long-settled immigrants to "suggest" a return to their own countries (in most cases, "their own countries" meant nations in which their grandparents hadn't been born or lived). I was instructed to poke them in public (a repetitive torture technique designed to irritate them on trains or buses or in queues or lifts), to have loud conversations with strangers about how brilliant Britain is doing without its immigrant population, or onto more disgusting behaviour such as posting (British) shit through letterboxes. I had taken up heroin to escape the state of the nation—TBB had created mass unemployment due to culling various industries and opening up sweatshops on the Isle of Man to replace most of the low-skilled work available. My generation had no hope of finding work. I ended up having to perform these disgusting duties in order to receive my unemployment benefits.

I spearheaded a resistance campaign, compiling leaflets on what the immigrant population had done to drag England from the economic marshes, and what the absence of immigrants was going to mean for the future of the nation. TBB, noting the increasing drug problem, decided to replace state benefits with state-supplied heroin (6-MAM content diluted—about as effective as snorting talcum powder). I was in the position of being homeless, under the thumb of the government's useless smack that still provided enough for a minor kick but left one gasping for more, and performing their dirty work. TBB had bred a generation of obedient ratlike drones willing to persecute immigrants for their latest fix. Things turned violent (as was TBB's intention) and soon there were murders and witch-hunts from crazed junkies dying to get their veins on diluted heroin. I decided it was better to burgle homes and beat up white people to get my hands on money, with which I could attend a rehabilitation programme. These were run underground, since the TBB didn't want the youth population to recover from heroin while it kept things under control and proved profitable.

I soon recovered from this and headed into ScotCall to take my chances at The House.

A Better Life

I

Upon completing *Kurious Kat Learns About Industrial Waste Dumping* and *Erectile Dysfunction: A Pop-up Book*, I elected to leave The House and head for the sea. I had a notion that there might be a better life for me somewhere out "there." In the past I had read the ScotCall slogan A Better Life For You is Here (Not Out "There") and fallen into their trap. Answering phone calls about the logistics of having sex in a chimney, or how to remove tarragon stains from The Koran, or if the battle of Culloden was ever restaged using weasels, or if the finest word in the English language was "drosophila," or if tea was T-shaped, or if Atlas ever dropped the sky, or if nasal copulation was unhealthy, is not a Better Life unless one happens to have cabbages for brains. I moved to The House having read the slogan "A Better Life Than at ScotCall is *Here*" and settled down to writing four bodice-rippers set on Neptune per week for a cash-rich slob named Jericho—a Better Life in comparison to an earful of Kirstys branding me an incompetent lackey for failing to answer questions about where Tim had hidden the marmalade, or if spark plugs qualified as real plugs, or if air had a smell. I had no intention of remaining at The House forever. I had to take my chance in the wilds and find the sea. I had heard rumours that a commune had sprung up "there" devoted to the simple life where people lived off the remaining land that hadn't been used to store malfunctioning toasters and digi-pets.

I made the decision to flee when slobby Jericho flung a bodice-ripper at my face, refusing to pay for my services due to the paucity of bosoms in the first four pages (I had made the mistake of at-

29

tempting to weave a plot between the scenes of heaving bosoms and bodices being ripped from their wearers). I packed up my clothes (two shirts, two pants) and savings (twelve pounds) and took to the Crarsix roads. I had to make the trip on foot as all buses took passengers direct to the local ScotCall Training and Advanced Brainwashing Centre whether that was your desired destination or not. I would have to be careful to avoid scavenger buses along the hinterland routes, where buses stopped and operatives chased you along the road trying to "coerce" you into signing up as an operative using their arms to "coerce" you into the buses.

The morning of my liberation was overcast. I was grateful for the cold winds so I could wear (and not have to carry) my coat. I headed along the asphalt road towards the first hectare of stock-dump fields. I had armed myself with a bat whittled from my (former) desk to protect myself from the onslaught of rogue digi-pets, electric toothbrushes, and any other menacing hardware-gone-bad that might wish to feast on my throat. The damp weather would keep the attack count low. The summer heat drove these appliances to fighting frenzies as the sun fried their wires and insides. I showed no mercy, warning the surrounding lurkers by crushing a stray digi-cat to smithereens with my bat—deaf to its plaintive pleas as I hammered its wires and whiskers into the dirt and performed the *coup de grâce* with my jackboot. I continued along the road until an electric hand fan whirred up from the disconcerting quiet and tried slicing out my eyes. I swung my bat around crazily, hitting the pest with the force of a baseball pitcher, and pummelled in its rotors once it landed. I flung its carcass into the field to dissuade its family, but two larger hand fans rose up and tried slicing out my brain in revenge. I readied myself for their approach and powered the bat into action, catching them in a quick swivel. I killed the family, moseyed onward in fear, and emerged from the stock-dump fields unscathed.

A furious washing machine lumbered near hoping to ensnare me in its rinse cycle, but I was able to avoid its feeble attack merely by proceeding at my usual walking pace, and looked on amused as it pursued me for a mile, clattering in desperation until its mechanism fried and the door collapsed from its hinges, leaving a molten plasticky lump bubbling on the asphalt. A microwave spat flaming batteries onto the road, two of which singed my trousers. I noticed that several of the appliances had learned to use other less mobile scraps as weapons and that the overall attitude towards humans had become one of outright hostility, even among the appliances designed to assist deaf or blind people. The prospect of sentience among these discarded write-offs was terrifying.

The *Farewell, Author!* Conference

I

I AM Saul Morton and I should be in a box alongside one hundred other writers, instead of this boxroom in The House (which, admittedly, is not much roomier than a coffin), where I now relate the following.

I recall the notorious *Farewell, Author!* conference of 2045, when the last two publishing houses closed their doors, and The House was the one remaining place to which these once-loved scribes could retreat. Due to staff cutbacks, Random House and Penguin Books relocated into one office in the town of Cumbernauld, where office space was cheap due to a recent infestation of an unidentified species of irritant believed to have bred with super-size cockroaches in the back of basement fridges to form a rat-roach cross-breed of some immense repugnance. Created in the mid-1950s to dump the unwanted scum from Glasgow's overburdened slums, Cumbernauld earned worldwide fame for its surrealist shopping centre, where a substation, car park, outbuilding, WC, and old office block had "merged" to form a structure that offered millions a sense of eschatological enlightenment—the realisation that their destinies must be sought elsewhere, as far from the town of Cumbernauld as possible, that escape must come in the fastest time between leaving the shopping centre, collecting their things, and taking the first train free to a better place—wherever being irrelevant, wherever being better. The publishers took the one remaining photocopier that hadn't been taken in the mass liquidation of their assets and set about retaining the reputation of their mutual houses—in past times, some of the most significant literature had been printed there, most of which had been used as fuel for stoves during the

33

brief reversion to medieval times that followed in the wake of the technological meltdown. An ex-Random House author (*Free to Be Dead*, 2029, *Fields of Mould*, 2037, and *Broken Doilies*, 2042), I volunteered to assist in setting up this last hoorah.

Disused supermarket Fossilfoods was the venue for the conference, where the publishers set about toasting their remaining authors, all of whom had to be dropped due to their skinnied budget of four pounds between them for annual expenses. The publishers' task was to recall snippets from the best books published in past times, and to bind these passages together in a valiant attempt to keep the stove-bound classics in their own (a few other people's) recall. There had been a whispered agreement among the authors beforehand that that evening each of them would write their final few words and commit suicide *en masse*. I had shaken hands with each author in turn and made that promise too, despite being only 43 years old, compared to most of the pensioner-age authors in the room.

This depressing event on the loom, I helped Julian Porter and Rupert Broth establish a tone of celebration. I siphoned near-expired Fossilfoods cola into plastic cups and placed pineapple chunks and cocktail sausages on toothpicks. Four chocolates had been found in the storeroom and were placed on a plate for the *éminences grises* to feast upon. A banner had been stapled up over the back wall showing the title of the event in the plural (in a rush Julian pluralised both words, so the banner read *Farewells Authors!*), and a cassette recorder with a mix of classical and party tunes, with Whigfield's "Saturday Night" rubbing up against Chopin's Nocturne B minor Op. 9 No. 3, creating a contrasting tone of mirth and mournful respect for the suicidal night ahead. I tried fixing the crackle-fizz of the overhead lights and shooing the rat-roaches into the storeroom before the authors arrived (and failed). Foods remained in Fossilfoods' unplugged freezers—bags of frozen peas and onion rings floated in low pools of water, various moulds had overgrown vegetables and baked potatoes, and unappealing lifeforms were reproducing in the sweat-and-sour curries and hotpots.

The door opened at 6.30pm.

Cal's Tour

Middlebrow Fiction

An incident with lighter fluid and my duvet (Marco was furious about me publishing a slapstick spoof featuring the Duke of Winchester—"his second cousin four times renovated") nudged me to the second floor, where the easygoing guys and gals let me try out their mode. The Middlebrow floor is a modern office with strictly purple walls and morale-boosting petunias curling in table vases, while pictures of sunsets and sunrises over fields, oceans, and scenic country landscapes with little quotes attached hang between the offices and boardrooms. Most prominent is the life-sized sunset at the corridor's end, blazing the caption: *The sun only shines in the hearts of the hopeful.* As you enter, an enormous smile named Joe will emerge from an office holding a cup with the slogan *Catch your dreams like butterflies* and say: "Hey dude. What s'up?" If he likes you (he likes everyone), he'll lead you towards an open-plan office where unmanly purple pouffes, sink-into sofas with throw pillows, and bean bags are arranged in a circle of eight around five or six desks, crowded with unnecessarily cutesy trinkets like cuddly-toy dogs, baby photos and potpourri bowls.

The others will be sitting on a circular sofa drinking coffee from similarly sloganned mugs: *On the other side of goodbye is hello. Don't milk your spilt tears. Tomorrow is yesterday's redeemer.* From unseen speakers, a fusion of Appalachian and Celtic folk music will soothe your ears. Doreen has a high fringe and a concerned face, Julia no fringe and a very smiley face, and Rick wears his goatee like a chin gazebo. Joe is handsome and happy.

35

Your bedroom is equally mood-lifting: a cosy space where sponge-painted clouds puff up to the ceiling to meet patterned stars in astronomically inaccurate formations. On each cloud (named after an agreeably fluffy concept) is a creamy "dreaming" button. On my first day, I pressed the cloud TRANQUILITY and harp music swirled out a speaker at such a punishing volume, my heart rate shot up to a decidedly un-mellow 1000BPM. I panicked trying to silence the frantic, celestial strum of the harps and pressed the cloud WORDS, whereupon a cast of basso-to-contralto voices chanted: "Hope, Love, Change, Optimism, Power, You," in a loop. I hit (punched) RELAX. A boom of crashing waves, cawing seagulls, and raging storms sounded over the harp and hopeful voices. I hit TRANQUILITY again, only to increase the volume of the harp, and tried holding LOVE, where a gospel choir belted out, "Say the woo-oo-oord, the word is love!" in all their Beatley power. Rick raced through and switched them off, calming me down with a mug of "anti-stress soup" and a hug. Hopefully this won't happen to you!

Ideas are plucked from stories in the newspapers and rehashed into emotionally enriching novels. Every morning over "butterumptiously yummy" (says Julia) brioches and pancakes, they discuss potential bestsellers. Doreen had read in the *ScotCall Herald* about new benefit changes whereby the long-term unemployed were forced to "piggyback" the homeless—carry someone around on their backs, feed and bathe the person, and help him or her perform mobile begging or selling *ScotCall Dailies* on the hoof. These unfortunates had their spines damaged by the obstreperous behaviour of the drug users and alcoholics, and were treated like horses or human rickshaws and bullied into robbing off-licences and stealing food. The minimum piggyback time was eight hours a day. "That would play havoc with the old spine," Rick rightly said. Julia's idea for a novel was to take "an unemployed man—a lovely trained research assistant down on his luck—and make him piggyback a ruffian. Over the course of the book, the two become friends and overcome their mutual class conflicts. Work towards reintegration. Maybe they start a double act as jugglers or street tricksters!" Everyone smiled (except me—I was still shell-shocked from earlier, harps ringing in my ears). "That would warm some cockles!" Joe said.

Doreen's idea: "There's this story about Los Angeles being too hot for the residents and everyone moving north to Alaska. Apparently the plan is to have African immigrants leave their barren countries and take up residence in Los Angeles, form communities there. I considered how droll it might be for them to take over Hollywood. My hero, a young film-maker called Umbütö or something like that, starts making blockbuster films and the Third World debt is slowly repaid when his movies become worldwide successes. Over the course of several films, Third World debt is paid off, and proper cities with shops and houses can be built in these appalling countries. The West learns an important lesson about the value of generosity." Everyone smacked their lips (except me). "Just goes to show, guys, that with a little imagination and creativity, you really can move the world," Rick said.

Morning meetings are followed by an afternoon of writing. At 4.30 everyone "takes a chill and chews a pastry" in the kitchen or reading room—a whitewashed nook where panpipe sounds help mellow the mind, and a tropical tank resides where coloured flatfish duck and dive around lifeless, whiskered catfish, tempting the reader's eye away from his text. There you can browse the department's bestsellers, such as *Lighter Than Luck*, with its tagline "You only get one chance to change your world"; *Stranger Than Loving*, with its tagline "A heart closed to hope is a heart closed to happiness"; and *Tomorrow's Child*, with its tagline: "Hold the meaning of life in the palm of your hand." Here's a helpful beginning/end snippet from that book for those thinking about middlebrow fic structures:

He hated kids.

He hated their biting, squirting, nipping, groping, wailing, screaming, dribbling and drooling.

One morning, his wife told him she was pregnant.

"Abort it," he said.

"We should think about it first."

"I have. Kill the cells. Flush it out."

"Don't be so callous."

"I am not having a kid. End of."

Jane burst into tears and he stormed out the room. He really bloody hated kids.

*

Tim held the baby in his arms. The peaceful creature slept, a soft smile on its lips. Tim felt a warm shudder in his bones.

"My son," he said.

"Your son," Jane said.

He rocked his baby in his arms. He couldn't quite believe he had made this thing, that it belonged to him, that he was responsible for the living breathing being in his arms.

"My son," he said again. Jane stared at him tenderly. This was the beginning.

"Your son," she said, and cried.

What about the meals? No blocky Madeira or sickly sherry here. I entered the dining area on my first evening to find a long-table of nutritional splendour—organic potatoes arranged in steaming pyramids, seasoned with marjoram and mint; bowls plump with chia seeds, goji berries, and cacao nibs; meek plates of hummus and tahini dip; densely packed troughs of whole grain spelt egg pasta, seasoned with chervil and coriander—among others. I met the readers: Mandy, Rhianna and Georgie, three elderly retired ladies, or as Joe introduced them, "ladies of leisure who fund our fictions from their charitably prosperous banks of inspirationally bottomless money!" At the end of the table, I was surprised to see three small black children sitting patiently awaiting orders. "Cal," Joe said, "you might have noticed our little brown surprises at the edge. This is Angela, Arran, and Arnold from Somalia. We adopted them to help us with our stories. They are abused children from the village of Mowhaar. We offer them a refuge here in exchange for stories about their sufferings." Joe placed a potato into the narrow chute that ran along the table, and when Angela told in her thick Somalian accent about the father who beat her and put scorpions in her bed, Joe raised the pulley so the potato rolled towards Angela's plate. Arran told about his abusive mother who starved him for two days and force-fed him lettuce on the third, and Arnold about having to till an entire field before dawn before he was allowed a cup of water. The ladies cooed and applauded, flinging tofu strips or seitan slices into the chute as extra rewards for their bravery. "The way we see it," Mandy said, "the more articulate they become, the clearer they can describe all the horrors they suffered. And the books will be so much more *authentic*."

"Tell us about your hardships, Cal," Rhianna said to me, "and we'll give you a potato!" I told them about how my sister was pretty horrible to me growing up. "Tsk, you won't even get a sprig of celery at this rate," Doreen said. I went on to explain how she used to urinate in my bed. "My goodness! He deserves at least a Scotch egg for that!" Georgie said. And how she used to put ants in my coffee. "A coif of noodles!" Rick said. And dead bees in my hair. "A punnet of couscous!" Doreen said. And a clothes peg on my scrotum. "A muglet of minestrone!" Mandy said. And how she smeared Marmite on my chin as I slept. "A slice of Madeira!" Joe said. I declined. "Oh, have some Madeira, my dear," Mandy said. The room exploded into laughter.

Socialising on the second floor takes place on the "chillaxminster" carpet, where Joe plays peacenik songs on a ukulele, including "When the Sun Goes Down in Your Heart" and "Sunset Over Lake Positive," while Julia and Doreen sew daisies into legwarmers and Rick improvises free-verse poems to warm ooooohs (no matter how terrible!). The children play with dolls and dump trucks in a sandpit, or attend English lessons given by the ladies (who sometimes stay over). I ended up crocheting "lucky" duck feathers into tights or playing the bongos, munching from a bowl of stone-ground sea-salted corn chips and sucking back pints of sparkling Highland water. At my book launch, a vegan buffet had been prepared and a small stage erected for the performance of two colourful tableaux. The Somalian kids were inserted into papier-mâché costumes—a sunflower, petal, and daisy—and moved around the stage like uncoordinated waltzers to trippy lullaby music played on a xylophone, flatly singing non sequiturs like "love of hope in land of freedom" and "we are hope and loving love" in a way that was more disturbing than cute. Doreen and Julia formed a human light show by manipulating the fairy lights wrapped around their long silvery dresses, beginning with a secret strip tangled in Julia's high-quiffed hair: blue winks below the dirty blonde, moving down her shoulders in yellow-green flickers until a psychedelic disco blinked along the two women's bodies, bunched tightly together as though caught in a flamboyant Venus flytrap. Joe explained how the sunflower revolving around the pansy symbolised the four cycles of growth as outlined in the Arnold Vernon *Hope Through Ecology* manual. The daisy is at the centre of the sphere on the index of the sun. Sometimes when the weather permits it the petunia is in the ascendance. I understood very little, but it was tremendous fun. The evening concluded with a reading from my novel. Here's a sneaky peak:

> *The sun set on the final sheddings of his mis-said heart. Walking into the waning moon as it waxed on the dying embers of the city, he entered a new beginning away from the shattered emblems of his old heart. He was putting his old life behind him, like a used-up bacon slicer being taken back to the repair shop a day ahead of the warranty expiring. He gazed into the middle distance, his eyes magnetised to the hopeful sunset, and with a generous lashing of hope in his hope-filled heart, he went forth into the new world, his heart aquiver with expectation, poised and ready to lead a*

*meaningful, socially conscious, revitalising life, and not the
one of degradation and sin he refused to abandon earlier.*

—Cal McIntyre, *Hope Hurts at First* (p.459)

A Word from the Team

JOE: Hey dudes and pomegranates! Take a load off and let me slip you the info. We four fab ficcers write what "they" like to call Middlebrow Literary Fiction, what we prefer to call Morally Replenishing Moral Fiction: this leans less on the negative. We bite into difficult cookies here, like third-world poverty, homelessness, life in slums, childhood trauma, and substance abuse, always with a hopeful, redeeming outlook. It's easy to fall into despair when thinking about these doozy downers, so we give our readers a positive message and a way to chew on these issues that will make them strong and feel hopeful. Hope is the most commonly said word round here. Have you hope? So, my groovy team, what advice have you got for anyone looking to hang with us moral ficcers?

DOREEN: Be up, don't beat up.

JULIA: Ooh, that's nice.

RICK: Get ready to bite into some difficult crackers.

JULIA: Or a cranberry bagel with tropical sheaves and parsley prawns.

DOREEN: Yum, how voogey!

JOE: Never let the sun set in sorrow.

DOREEN: Voogeylicious!

RICK: Miss friends, don't 'dis friends.

JULIA: Bite into hope, not the Pope.

RICK: Board the bus to the terminal of possibility.

JOE: Hug the love, love the hugs!

DOREEN: Voogeywoogie!

JULIA: Put wishes into the cannon of disappointment.

RICK: Praise be to he, she, they and everyone!

JOE: Love is the best, why settle for less?

DOREEN: Voogeywoowoo!
JULIA: Be prepared to be kind.
RICK: Let the stars light the night on your way to what's right.
JOE: Sail the seven seas for one big smile.
JULIA: If I grant you a wish, will you tell me a secret?
RICK: Close your eyes, dream big, and never give up.
DOREEN: Voogeyseeyou!

Puff: The Unloved Son

I

THE adorable ink-cheeked creation of C.J. Watson was insert-ing his fingers into a pipe that in nineteen days' time would flood the entire seventh floor and drown a hectare of single-sided laser-printed manuscripts, two hundred Macintoshes containing over two billion words of unprinted work near completion, and three people. He unzipped his flies to make a urological investi-gation between two corporeal and industrial waste outlets (to see if his winkie might fit into the pipe), only to have his research in-terrupted by a roar of "What ARE you doing! Get AWAY from there!" He responded to the chide by running up and down the office, figure-of-eighting the writer-locked desks while recreating the exact sonic pitch of an Allied bomber as it unloaded on a village of civilians, collapsing on the cream carpet in a harrowing mass of screams and howls as he scooped his insides up and cried "WHY!?"

The writers turned their murderous eyes on C.J. Watson who was too preoccupied with p.108 of the fourth book in her *Firewood* series to notice her son's powerful screams that arrested one's senses and, like all successful war recreations, bludgeoned the viewer into contemplating the horror of mass sacrifice for the propagation of ideological evil. Upon the cease of his howlings, the child (whose adorable name was Puff) leapt up and took on the part of a grieving widow wailing over her husband's corpse, letting rip a long tirade against the sickness of the world and the beastliness of man un-til F.V. Young lost his cool and hurled his mousepad towards the adorable ink-fingered Puff and chased him around the office with his stapler, shouting his regular threat to "seal that little blighter's

43

lips shut." At which point C.J. rounded off her final clause and took F.V. by the collar, warning him: "If you ever threaten my son with a stapler ever again, I will have you scrubbing the stairs in solders." She used that threat each time as she loved the triple-S alliteration. F.V. didn't.

Claire J. Watson had plotted her nine-book-and-increasing *Firewood* series (ex-Firepile, Fireworld, Fireplace, Firehole, and Fire-ice) during her stint as a phone operative for ScotCall. She spent her free time adding complexities to her fantastical world in order to prevent having to start the writing. When more characters, incidents, metaphors, universes, enchanted lands, and themes had been planned than she could conceivably insert into one book she would expand the scope and dream up another handful of plotlines and opportunities for long indulgent description. To distract herself from the looming prospect of writing she signed up to ScotCall dating and fell in pretend love with an operative whose interests included nailing 5K targets, dodgeball, the music of Santana, and sitting on beaches basking in the wonderful sun of the wonderful world created for wonderful us. Being in a relationship with a target-hitting worker meant she had too much free time to sit and compose her novel, so she allowed her pretend love to impregnate her, hoping this responsibility might provide ample distraction from the business of having to write; only her man doted on her so much she had less preparation to do, so she decided to sever ties with the man and raise the child alone. The arguments ate up a certain amount of time. Once the child was born she realised she didn't love it (him) and so came to her senses and signed up to The House to realise her dreams and knuckle down to complete the nine-books-and-increasing before she went mad.

This

2

THE *House of Writers* is the first "proper" novel I have attempted since moving to The House. In my twenties, my writing method involved a form of permanent self-distraction using the internet (a portal to view cats). I would write a sentence (or half a sentence) and click back onto the three or four regular windows I had open and stare at the same content I had seen that morning observing minute variations as the feeds expanded. I became so habituated to writing one sentence (or half a sentence) and clicking onto the web pages I had seen before, looking for distraction opportunities, that writing became an incremental and unabsorbing process and the only solution I had was to develop a form of composition that allowed for aimless digression. I also had to account for the general sloth and sleepiness that overcame me when faced with the prospect of starting anew, worrying that the present day's writing would pale in comparison to yesterday's (with yesterday's paling in comparison to the previous day's, etc.) I had to permit myself to churn out semi-conscious sentences and hope later I might have the concentration to whip them into line as passable constructions.

Often I would bring up Google images of people I hoped one day might respect and admire me. I would drift into fantasies of the novels I would never write and the success I would never have and this fantasising was more appealing than the business of placing words on the page for an unseen audience that might never top more than a handful of people. So the words took longer to emerge from brain to hand to screen due to this trance-like immersion in

fantasies of being the most talented and hilarious writer and come-
dian and musician and actor in the world (with a tormented romantic life and brilliant eccentricities), and the novels became collages
of dreams, resentments, hopes, failed ambitions, digressions, fantasies, and comedic vignettes, which seemed an acceptable form as
far as representing life and individual consciousness went (being as
good a purpose of the novel as any).

Despite these barriers, the novels appeared in quick succes-
sion—*Then* (2015), *Now* (2016), *When* (2017), and *Earlier* (2018)—
until this technique was exhausted and passé among my small cabal
of readers. I progressed to writing "technogeddon" potboilers composed of emails and instant messages, eschewing narrators and ob-
scuring characters/speakers to create a sense of informational over-
load (presaging the meltdown two decades later). These works were
in vogue and I found a wider audience with *(No Subject)* (2020) and
Anonymous Would Like to Chat (2022), the latter composed from
anonymous messages on a chatroom and ending with a series of
murders and suicides. I became complaisant turning a profit as a
doom-monger and tried to write a more positive novel about two
lovers who find each other after fending off various stalkers encountered on dating sites. *The Blacklist* (2024) appeared to lukewarm
reviews so I returned to writing bleak visions of tomorrow. *Bleak
Visions of Tomorrow* (2027) was well-received as one of the ur-texts
of the post-meltdown gen.

After the meltdown and the ScotCall rebranding of the country,
I worked in their publicity department until The House opened. I
fled immediately, and spent an unsuccessful few months in the experimentalists' basement trapping rodents and using their tails as
a makeshift pen (and their blood as makeshift ink) and set to work
hacking out novels on various floors. All I had to do was knock
together semi-readable plots and find unambitious readers to purchase a few copies to survive, although the dispiriting workload
wore me down. I decided it was a miracle to be working at something I love, despite The House having long since killed the pleasure I take in putting words on the page (this novel an exception—it

feels so nice to be writing this sort of thing and not a pornographic western set in a Turkish rodeo). I hope if civilisation rises from its illiterate bog and my oeuvre is reappraised, this novel will be included among my early, visionary works as a late masterpiece.

The Trauma Rooms

2

THE doctor took three short paces to the second of the trauma rooms, located with convenience across from the first, and cautioned Erin about its contents.

"As in the first trauma room to which I took you—"

"Ten seconds ago," Erin said.

"—yes, ten or thereabouts seconds ago, as you correctly evinced, this patient is suffering a mania as a result of critical hyperbole. In this case, he was a ghost-blurber, that is to say, professional writers paid him to write their blurbs and critical comments in praise of various authors. One day, for amusement, he read one of the books he was blurbing and suffered a violent physical and mental breakdown. He is fairly calm these days, so I can let him tell you the remainder of the story. Terence, this is Erin."

"Hello Terence."

A man with the expression of lugubrious schnauzer kicked once too often by its sadistic master offered a limp hand.

"Terry," he said.

"Care to tell Erin what happened when you read that book one evening?"

"I suppose," he said with the voice of a teenager told by his parents that all colleges and businesses had closed forever and there was no money left to support him. "I had been making mega-bucks writing blurbs and critical comments on the back pages of novels. The publishers sent me outlines of the plots, and I salt-and-peppered their words, adding superlatives to increase market value and reader frenzy. Established writers paid to read the books and

49

provide praise contracted their duties to me, and I wrote their lines for a cut of their fees. In those days, for a writer to be published, certain initiation rights were required—the CEO of Penguin liked to sodomise first novelists with a bronze replica of Julius Caesar's penis, while other established writers took turns to urinate in their nostrils—and once in the 'established' club, writers provided a collective backslapping service on their respective books, contracting their duties to people like me: I doubt one of these writers read a book by their contemporaries. I never had any artistic ambitions myself, in fact, I rarely read books published after 1900, I was mad into the Victorians. I had written newspaper copy for several years, but the rise of vicious youths fresh from their BAs and diplomas shunted me from the profession. Anywho, to circumambulate back to the point. Yes, I made a nice living. I could afford to take a lover at last, after years struggling to scrape enough pfennigs together for a pint of milk, and I had the damp in my flat treated. One night, having written the 500th blurb, I opened a can of fizz and settled down to read one of the books—the latest novel by John Green, entitled *Fractured Lovelines*. I need a moment to compose myself before I describe what happened next. Please excuse me."

"That's fine. Take your time," the doctor said. Erin stared on, rapt. In the ten-second pause, she scanned the area for her stapler. Aside from a plastic cup on a side table, there were no possessions in the room.

"So I suppose I had come to believe in my own hyperbole. I never questioned that these books were anything other than works of stupefying wizardry . . . I opened the John Green and read the first five pages. At first, I mistook my stomach pain for the aftermath of a chilli garlic chicken curry I had eaten that night, and powered on past page one, wincing at the knots, until I arrived at page five and vomited blood over the e-reader in the shape of a fractured heart. I doubled over, howling in pain. I could not believe a book could be that appalling. I screamed out: 'I called this book a daring take on a controversial topic! I said this was a brave and beautiful novel to be cherished for decades to come!' I clutched my stomach and screamed. I ran out onto the street, shouting non-sense, assaulting people who tried to help, eventually passing out in a motorway layby, covered in slime and scum, having leapt into a polluted pond to cleanse myself of the foulness that had overtaken me. Then I entered the most horrific dreams, the content of which I am not prepared to speak about and that I will take to the grave."

"We are still working through those," the doctor said.

"All because I read five pages of that John Green novel. If I ever meet John Green, I will hack off his cock and—"

"All right, Terence, remember our lessons on controlling violence."

"Yes, of course."

"He can't be released, you see," the doctor whispered to Erin, "because he still vows murderous revenge on each of the authors he blurbed. This John Green novel has caused him ineradicable trauma."

"I'm not surprised."

"Yes, his books are the most inexcusable waffle. Thank you, Terence, we will be moving along."

"Nice to meet you," Erin said. He nodded with the thankful expression of Kaspar Hauser handed a lump of wax wrapped in cat hair for his dinner.

"Shall we proceed to the third room?" he asked Erin, as if addressing a bemused child, and placed a guiding arm on her shoulder once more. She accepted his overfamiliar touch in the hope of locating her stapler.

"Fingers crossed," she said.

"Yes! That's right. Very good. Onward."

"Yes . . ."

THE HOUSE OF WRITERS

A Commission Gone Awry

To: James L. Horton
From: Derek Haffmann

Dear James,

I am the MSP for a town in West Region called Linlinger. We are a small locale with a proud foot in the manufacture of swan ornaments and raisin crackers. I half-read of one of your books (*Pandora's Bucks?*) and I would like you to write a novel with me as the protagonist. I am not a vain man so I do not expect your depiction of me to be wholly flattering, although as a Member of ScotCall Parliament I expect you to exercise discretion when it comes to describing my role in the power structure and the facts of my personal life (however fictional). I will pay you a standard rate for this task.

Regards,
Derek Haffmann
MSP for Linlinger

To: Derek Haffmann
From: James L. Horton

Dear Derek

Oh God! I canNOT believe you have chosen me for this task . . . this duty . . . this HONOUR, sir!! I am flabbergasted and proud to accept this invitation and I hope I can do your no doubt fascinating life justice! I CANnot quite believe that you have chosen ME, (ME!!!) the humble writer of the book you mentioned (actually called *Pandora's Locks*, but what does that matter??) to perform this honour, this . . . this privilege! You email at a perfect time as my ten-book series *Fishes Make Wishes* has not been successful with my reader and he has refused to pay me for my services . . . I will spare you the sob story, sir, but I have had to drink water from the bathroom taps and steal leftover rinds from the canteen to survive the last few weeks. I also have a rash for which I am unable to source the medication . . . however, that is not your concern! I am delighted delighted delighted to accept! Please write back to me outlining your vision for this novel and I can begin work on this project immediately.

Yours,

James

P.S. THANK YOU!!!!!!!!!!!!!!!

To: James L. Horton

From: Derek Haffmann

Dear James,

I am pleased to hear you have accepted my proposition. I have no ideas for what this novel should contain. Please write an opening paragraph and send it to me and I will have my advisors look at it. Payment per chapter.

Yours,

Derek

To: Derek Haffmann

From: James L. Horton

Dear Derek,

I have spent the week deep in research for the composition of your opening paragraph. I studied Linlinger—what a marvellous hamlet! I had no idea Noel Edmunds committed suicide in the Novotel there! I had no idea the demand for swan ornaments was so strong as to fund a special rocket to Neptune! I had no idea the council had declared Linlinger the most innumerate hamlet in all ScotCall! I had no idea tramp-burning was a popular pastime there! I had no idea Paul Simon had dropped his plectrum in the local pond in 1978 causing the asphyxiation of a prize black swan for which he never paid a cent in recompense! I had no idea Linlinger was twined with Simferopol! I had no idea Linlinger was a Nazi base during WWII and the residents meet up to commemorate their role in crushing the Allied pigs! I also had a look at your personal website, Derek. I hope you don't mind me saying this: you have the *most* adorable shoulders! The charming crinkles in your cheeks when you are smiling! The moonlight reflecting off your brylcreemed quiff! The immense manly gravitas in your stance! I have no interest in sexual matters—however, if requested, I would happily engage in intercourse with you! Anyway, let us proceed to the business! I have included the opening paragraph for your inspection. (OH GOD! I CANNOT BELIEVE THIS IS REALLY HAPPENING! I have told everyone including my mum who said not to raise hopes but she is a cynical cow at the best of times, Derek! Or is it Mr. Haffman? I'd better close this bracket!). Please please please let me know if this isn't what you were looking for and I will take a hatchet to it right away! I will chop it into a million little pieces like the sow during the annual Linlinger sacrifice to Cthulhu!

> *Derek Haffman, MSP for Linlinger in West Region, ambled along the road exuding machismo. The top button on his shirt was undone and the two girls watching him from*

a bench swooned at the sight of his exposed hairs. A bus driver was distracted by Derek's aura and forgot to stop at the planned stop, causing consternation among the passengers (soon appeased by a glance out the window at lovely Derek!).

Yours,
James

To: James L. Horton
From: Derek Haffmann

Dear James,
Thank you for sending your paragraph. I have no problems with this as an opening but I am forwarding it to those who can best advise me on ministerial and legal matters. There may be a delay of several months.
Yours,
Derek

To: Derek Haffmann
From: Alexander Thane

Dear Derek,
Drear drear, dear! Where on Graham's shiny arse did you find this semi-literate hack? Round the back of Oddbins? I read the opening paragraph penned by our Nobel Laureate. Apart from the nix artistic merit (I'm no expert on books but this paragraph reeks like a skunk's nappy) I can see several problems vis-à-vis your image within the party. Firstly, there is no way we can have you "exuding machismo." As you know, the party has a strong feminist

backing (i.e. those right-on harpies on the backbench looking for a cock to kick around) so this upfront show of manliness will not be received positively. The implication seems to be that via some primordial male scent (Lynx's Puma range?) you attract women without even muttering the quietest invite to your hotel suite. Secondly, the current party code for dress is formal—an unbuttoned shirt is not acceptable. This James hack practically has your Paul Thomas Anderson hanging out your trousers. You know too that the sight of chest hair will be mocked in the *ScotCall Sun* and we have to avoid negative publicity about MSP appearance after that whole "yellow tie" debacle last month. Fire this Horton. From a cannon.

    Regards
    Alex

To: Derek Haffmann
From: Road Safety Board

Dear Mr. Haffmann

    I hope this message finds you well. The opening paragraph of your novel as written by James L. Horton was forwarded to us by one of your researchers. After a unanimous vote the RSB have rendered this paragraph a Code 9.2 violation—unsafe for a general readership. Our objections are as follows. 1) The character in this paragraph "ambled across the road." It is unsafe to amble across a road that contains buses as this poses a risk to motorists and pedestrians and this sort of carelessness could lead to copycat "ambling" and cause traffic accidents or deaths. The RSB cannot be held accountable for this behaviour. The character should walk briskly across the road after checking both ways to ensure a safe crossing. We suggest the passage should read: "*Derek Haffman, MSP for Linlinger in West Region, walked briskly across the road after checking*

both ways to ensure a safe crossing." 2) The "machismo" this character "exudes" is clearly a danger to pedestrians and drivers. The bus
driver in particular misses one of his designated stops because of
this "machismo," and although no accidents occur in this story, the
driver could have easily crashed the bus and hit a pedestrian. Again,
the RSB cannot be held accountable for such dangerous and imita-
tive behaviour. We have excised this detail from our above rewrite
suggestion. Please contact us if you have further inquiries.

Regards,
Phil Cornwall
RSB Consultant

To: Derek Haffmann
From: Alexander Thane

Dear Derek,
You won't believe this. Some quisling in our office (who I will
be sacking the moment I unmask them—after inserting a kebab
skewer up their rectum) has leaked all the emails about this novel
of yours to the *ScotCall Sun*. Keep silent for now. Do not respond
to any messages from wheedling hacks.

Alex

To: Derek Haffman
From: Kevin Williams

Derek! How's it hanging in the Parliament? Read any good books
lately? I have! It hooked me from the first sentence. I have a few
questions about this book you are proposing about yourself. Questions like: how large *is* your ego exactly? Paying a hack to puff yourself up, must be quite a whopper. And how do you feel about distracting bus drivers with your sexual powers? You want all drivers

to skip stops and cause traffic accidents? Are you planning to bottle this special aura that you have, or make it available on the NHS? I have emailed all the messages about this hilarious and embarrassing (for you) story as found in Alex's inbox to everyone in the media! Everyone knows! The story is in the paper tomorrow. You might as well give us a reaction quote. (Don't worry, I'll buy a hardback when it comes out!)

Kisses, Kevin Williams
ScotCall Sun

To: James L. Horton
From: Derek Haffman

I HATE YOU, I HATE YOU, A POX ON YOUR HOUSES!!! Do you have any idea what your stupid paragraph has done to my reputation? I asked you to EXERCISE CAUTION when writing about me, observing the proper parliamentary protocols, and you couldn't even find it in your feeble scribbler's fingers to take one single instruction due to the LUMP OF LINT BETWEEN YOUR EARS. Those twats at the *ScotCall Sun* are going to disassemble me tomorrow and it's ALL OVER. You are being sued. I am going to sue you. You are being taken to the cleaners by me. I am suing you. Clear?

To: Derek Haffman
From: James L. Horton

Dear Mr. Derek Haffman MSP

I cannot even begin to apologise for the events that have occurred. When I wrote that paragraph I had no idea of the serious repercussions this would cause for your reputation. I had no idea it would fall into the hands of evildoers. I am utterly appalled. I have been close to suicide over the last few hours, turning this over and over in my head in perpetual torment. I have written this response over a hundred times trying to convey exactly the extent of the pain churning inside me, the wrenching agony I have felt knowing I have impacted you in such a devastating way and destroyed your life. I understood fully your intention to sue me, and please rest assured, you have my blessing to do so, and I will help you in any way with the procedure. I do not have many possessions, but if you would like the few trinkets I have and the clothes I am wearing, I will happily give them to you. I also suggest that I be flogged hard in public or set upon by dogs as part of the penance I will be paying you for the rest of my life. I beg you to be merciful with me, as I *never never never* intended to do you any harm when I wrote you that paragraph. I am crying all over the keyboard and my heart is split in two.

Yours miserably,
James Leonard Horton

Mhairi

2

WHEN I first met "General Manager" Marilyn Volt, I was impressed by her stamina and dedication. Two full marathons a day, muscles like tarmacadam, those tugged features. I soon twigged that she had serious mental health issues. She had convinced herself that invisible sponsors were backing her runs and that she was helping to raise funds to liberate people from the Scot-Call stranglehold or earning enough to help keep The House from falling apart. This is neither true nor amusing. The House was, when I arrived, in the process of sundering from the bottom up and atilt at a disconcerting angle. I set up a drug ring in the basement and advertised its whereabouts using my contacts. I called my dealer Mikkel in Denmark and asked him to smuggle over sacks of middling gear that I could sell at twice the price. This worked until I ran out of desperados willing to pay extra for middling. I hit upon an ingenious solution that saved The House from destruction. I paid the printers to "weave" powdered heroin into the paper of the books we printed. Whenever readers turned the pages of each book, heroin particles would waft up their noses, convincing them that each page was riveting due to the aesthetic merits of the literature at hand. I couldn't do this with all the books—sometimes the H supplies dwindled and books went to print missing the vital ingredient—this led to disgruntled readers refusing to pay for their writers' latest books due to a dip in their "artistry."

Several writers (ex-smackheads) noticed and I had to deal with begging requests from those hoping to have their pages sprinkled with extra helpings of Big H—to turn them into instant bestsellers.

THE HOUSE OF WRITERS

After taking a few hundred backhanders, I decided to put a stop to this abuse of the scheme. I could only wrangle so much heroin from my Danish cartels at a time, and I had to be fair to each department. (Excessive H abuse had wiped out the experimental fiction department and precipitated their exile from the building—I didn't have the heart to tell them this). I had saved The House from going under, taxing the writers' profits to conduct crucial repairs on the building. As "General Manager," Marilyn keeps morale ticking over—writing her annual reports (each of them a fiction since she has no idea what happens upstairs—she kips on the ground floor in a sleeping bag). So when I arrived at The House, I was hired as a general housekeeper and became self-titled Queen Momma of the building. Aside from running the drug operation, this entails making sure the other staff members—janitors, food-servers, and so on—are content with their mostly tedious lives. These people who aren't chained to desks and have innocuous blue-collar occupations seem to me the most free. I made a home for myself on the roof, paying a simpleton named Gerald (more on him later) to construct a small cottage overlooking the wastelands of Crarsix. If I tilt my head heavenwards on summer nights, I can glimpse a rogue star through the carcinogenic layers of toxic silt, and my heart is almost happy.

A Better Life

2

Having survived the stock-dump fields, I emerged onto the roads where the ScotCall buses prowled. I hadn't expected the barbed wire laid over the ditches—it was my intention to crouch there when the buses appeared. I had nowhere to lurk when the first bus came and the two operatives approached. I made it five minutes along the road before the bus stopped five paces before me and the operatives leapt out with their plastered smiles and blank clipboards, launching straight into their smarm-drenched spiels. "Howdy, traveller! Don't you think a Better Life awaits you in the ScotCall compound? We offer our phone operatives a secure package and opportunities to explore the range of things available etc. . . ." I decided to attack. I could see the bald one making a move to cup my arm and the blonde one ditto. I took the bat and swung for the bald one's shiny head. I brained him on the occiput and delivered repeated blows to his forehead until he was dead. I had to remember it wasn't a person I was killing but a ScotCall vessel who would never think an original thought ever again and so was dead inside anyway.

The blonde one sprinted for the bus which sped off in panic. I improvised a solution. I changed into the ScotCall shirt and tie that the dead thing was wearing and headed along the road faking a cool exterior, despite the natural terror I felt at facing the Scot-Call cops when the helicopter or whatever descended from above to airlift me to whatever ScotCall rehabilitation prison centre existed in the bowels of their compound. A police car was on the scene in two minutes and despite my nervousness I kept up the façade. "Reports of a psycho with a baseball bat resisting ScotCall assistance?" he asked without the slightest glint of suspicion. "Yes officer!" I beamed. "I managed to overpower the thug and pulp his cranium. He is on the ground back there, hopefully feeling jolly remorseful for his actions!" The officer volunteered to drive me back to the ScotCall HQ, straight into the beckoning digits of the enemy. Since I had no reason to be lurking on the road four miles away, I agreed. I was to be delivered into a position of power in ScotCall with the one hope that I might be able to bluff my way to freedom, if I could think up a single convincing reason to go outside.

The policeman escorted me to the same compound where I worked before as a phone operator being lashed by malfeasant bugs. I used the dead thing's pass to gain access to the building and reported to the manager for duties. The man who had witnessed me bashing in the head of his partner was there. He failed to notice that I had a different face. I had gained access and was wearing the proper outfit. This seemed to be enough for him.

The *Farewell, Author!* Conference

2

FIRST to arrive, a frenetic Adam Thirlwell. One of the youngest at the conference, at 68, Adam retained his frazzled appearance, his eye luggage weighing in heavy, his intellectual Pete Doherty vibe still apparent. "People have been calling me an upstart for the last four decades because I published a first novel aged 24. Like I'm some perpetual prepubescent scamp having his hair ruffled by the wise-ass elders," he said the moment he entered. "Hello Adam," I said. "My last novel *Economics*, published two years ago, still came with patronising caveats like 'Adam is the adolescent eager to appear smarter-than-thou' and 'the look-at-me-sir flash of his prose is endearing but childish.' I'm almost 70! These dicks! I've skipped the mature artist and elder statesman phase. I will be buried an up-and-coming brat." He knocked back two colas and lurched towards the back freezers where various prawns were dancing the cancan. Next entered the fighting fit Invernesian Ali Smith whose brio remained undimmed despite her long-awaited masterpiece *The The The The The The The The The*, a book containing a record number of uses of the definite article over its 1900 pages, begun in 2020, having been lost forever in the technological meltdown. "I am maintaining a stoic outlook on the situation. In the Great Pantheon there are innumerable examples of lost masterworks, from Sappho to Perec. I am working on a novel instead about the disappearance of the masterpiece called *A A A A A A A A A*, because 'a' is the indefinite article, and suggests a series of impossible beginnings in attempting to reconstruct what is lost," she said the minute she entered. "Hello Ali," I said. "I look to novels like Christine Brooke-Rose's tale of homeless dropouts *Next*, written without the verb 'to have,' where the constraint is integral to the intellectual and emotional core of the novel. There are no definite articles in my latest novel because there is no novel except a series of fragmented stuttered utterances from a work that with each day becomes little more than the spirit of a lost masterpiece." And she went to brood by the broken biscuits, sucking on a custard cream. Next, Dave Eggers. His publishing house, having folded in 2018, left Eggers nursing a depression from which he failed to recover, penning a painful memoir, *A Heartbroken Genius of Staggering Woes*, which fast became a classic in the genre, keeping Eggers a millionaire, if not bringing him relief. "People say to me, Dave man, you got those riches, you can have four almond croissants for breakfast and only eat one of them, you can drive a Bentley around the hood flinging hundred-dollar bills at the peasants, you can sing Shirley Temple's loudest hits in the shower literally all afternoon without a tax man banging at your door demanding overdue cash due to you bunking off work and being fired and having no money, you can form your own publishing house that prints whimsical fiction about social issues and the dark underside of American families in misleadingly beautiful hardcover quarterlies, you can keep a unisex harem in your gazebo meeting the sexual needs of male and female visitors on a 24/7 basis, and I say to them, come on guys, it doesn't matter if I can order nine fudge sundaes from the most expensive pâtisserie in Europe and fling them at Chris Ware's miserable face, or import nine Ugandan rhinos and put them in a poorly choreographed home production of *Stomp*, or record an album of Half Man Half Biscuit covers with the reanimated corpses of David Bowie and Lionel Richie on backing vocals, or take a private flight to any of the world's most breathtaking places with any number of supermodel girlfriends and drink nothing but champagne the whole time, if the brain is firing frowns, no-no-neurons, then no amount of cash-fuelled mirthmakers will lift Dave from his fragile funk," Dave said after I offered him a cola. "I am looking forward to tonight, let me tell you." Next to arrive, a nervous Zadie Smith, who had suffered at being dubbed a scenester, a constant on the literary stage, in the hippest anthologies and publishing ventures. "People accused me of being the axis of hip, or the acme of hip . . . more like the acne of hip," she said. Her last novel, *Endwesters*, was a searing satire on the re-rise of Islamophobia in the West End of London following the brief violence of an extremist Islam sect, received in the papers as "issue-tainment" and latching on to current affairs. "Complete arsecake. I have never cleaved to the zeitgeist. I write about people and their people problems. I am not some rabid trendlicker." She approached the chocolate and ate a piece, assuming herself to be one of the four *éminences grises*. I hadn't the heart to disabuse her.

A Blast of Kirsty

I AM known around the department for being a face-chewing Medusa who crushes dreams in a vice until the last few hopeful crumbs fall in hopeless heaps on the floor and their dreamers vow never again to dream of something I never fucking sanctioned. This isn't even half the truth. I am the best team leader in ScotCall and in under a decade I will have ascended to the upper echelons among the caviar-munching conquerors pouring Romanée-Conti down the spines of lubricated vassals and laughing into the tear-encrusted lids of peasants. This is who I am.

A little preKirstery, if you please (and I do). In 2020, several years after ScotLand (then called) achieved political independence, a referendum was called to determine whether the country should be converted into the world's largest call centre, fielding the customer queries of over two hundred multinationals to prevent the nation from sliding into third-world status as the national debt racked up to over two squillion zillion. (The natural resources of the nation had been stolen by Denmark and Holland after several cunning midnight thefts, leaving ScotLand bereft). After a unanimous *Yes* vote, ScotLand was rebranded ScotCall and each citizen was put to work in the call centres that usurped all functioning businesses in the country, taking only one fucking heroic week to transform the bankrupted hotels and shops of cities and counties into ScotCall offices. Until the 2039 meltdown, schools and universities remained open while the citizens adjusted to this change.

The technological meltdown, labelled prosaically by the *Daily Telegraph* "technogeddon," occurred globally. On May 2nd 2039, every piece of electrical equipment went fuckadoodlebang at the exact same moment, causing an immediate reversion to the Dark Ages (only with battery-powered torches and not quite so many candles or pagan sacrifices). There are various accounts of what happened depending on which attention-seeking broadsheet hack desperate to make a name for himself with the most original stream of spurious bullshit you listen to. Some people believe that the world's technology manufacturers designed their equipment to spontaneously explode on May 2nd 2039, claiming over nine trillion in insurance money, with each conspirator pocketing a portion of the insurance profits, fleeing the developed world to eke out a simple life oiling the bronze bums of hookers in tropical countries. This theory is hard to swallow—without access to technology, life in hot climes would not be as exclusive and easy for an embezzler *manqué*. Some twits believe an enterprising squirrel forged its way into the master computer at Microsoft and had cable salad for lunch, causing the mass destruction of every piece of electrical equipment in the world with a few naughty chomps. Twits. Other crackpots believe that aliens beamed their destruct-o-ray over the planet; that a drunk and bitter Bill Gates pressed the "fuck-'em-all" button; that coders had accidentally omitted May 2nd 2039 from their scripts. The truth is impossible to discern. Most likely the insurance story is true—commonplace greed is usually at the heart of most global fuckups.

After the meltdown, The Great Repair (first capitalised by the *Daily Express*) began and ScotCall entered the first phase of its worldwide omnipotence. ScotCall's computer system had gone bangadoodlefuck along with the rest, but their phones had emerged intact thanks to the existing prewar lines still active in ScotLand. This allowed ScotCall to storm ahead providing its top-flight customer service, dealing first with all manner of queries on how to fix the two billion or so devices that had exploded. Computers were beyond repair, by and large, and those deemed "responsible" for manufacturing computers had been rounded up in a mass public execution by President George Bush Jr. Jr. and copycat butcherings around the world followed to deal with the last of the technospazzes and internitwits. This meant the number of people alive who could repair or manufacture computers was zero, so older technologies had to be reverted to: hence the re-rise of the phones and the triumph of ScotCall. Education was abolished throughout the world to help economies recover from the crash. It made sense in times of crisis for people to work *en masse* in factories, to keep the poorest people at a certain level of intellectual inferiority, and to reserve education for the upper classes until the economies returned to a productive bustle.

Those born leaders with no tolerance for overly smug and smart people, phenomenally dim and plodding people, or super-humanly average and boring people, were recruited to manage the phone monkeys at ScotCall. I was hired in the winter of 2039 and within a week people cowered at my approach and lived in fear of being caught on my verbal skewer. In those early days, arrogant self-entitlement had to be stamped out—high-ranking businesspeople working alongside their employees were prime shitterbuggers. Tough managers like me specialised in pricking the pompousness of pompous pricks and putting everyone in their place. Those working in low-level occupations such as cleaners were able to retain their prior positions in ScotCall, whereas blue-collar workers or anyone with an inoffensive accent able to speak in a semi-coherent manner on the telephone was set to monkeying.

As the world reverted back to a sub-hominid mental state, Scot-Call switchboards were abuzz with operatives taking on nonsensical and Cro-Magnon queries—behind these the dominant question: "Can you help me *live?*" Over 98% of inbound queries we deal with are pointless, and since real enlightenment is a danger to the Scot-Call profit margins, we encourage operatives to devise baffling and unhelpful answers to keep people calling. For example, Joe B calls asking: "What doesn't upset a tuba?" Operative X replies: "Isn't a tuba always in motion?" Thank you for calling. There are carpers who carp about the ethics behind our modus. The fact is ScotCall provides a *raison d'etre* for billions of callers—their lives are so riddled with confusion and fear that the tiniest shove towards pretend understanding is better than a realistic push into confronting the existential chasm that their lives have become. However, it is still ScotCall policy to answer semi-coherent queries with the occasional accuracy, otherwise we risk reducing our customers to a state of *homo habilis* imbecility, and thus being unable to pick up the phone!

At present, ScotCall is the most powerful organisation in the universe and multiverse, and probably all surrounding parallel universes and multiverses. Our profits are dispensed to the 128 multinational CEOs and leaders: rich and brilliant bastards whose lives were never altered by the meltdown thanks to their secret bank vaults and whatnot—I hate these money-grubbing fucks in principle, but in the battle for survival on a pitiless planet, in a species genetically coded to swindle and fuck itself over in perpetuity, these devils have all the best tunes. I am not motivated by money, more the power trip that comes with having money when so many needy losers desperately want money, and the exploitation and misery at one's disposal when one has exorbitant amounts to fling around. Having said that, I prefer my torment localised. I look forward to many years torturing workers with the prospect of bonuses, raising their hopes for months on end, sacking them the day before their bonuses are due. That's the sort of buzz I crave as I work my way to the upper echelons of this magnificently evil empire.

Writer Portraits

The Great(est) Opaquist

I AM the unfortunate founder and final sensate member of the unfortunate (and insensate) movement known to no one any longer as The Great Opaquists. The movement began through sheer ophthalmic fluke in the repugnant town of Coatbridge. I was raised in a housing scheme, in the corner house of a long strip, in the yard of which was a large birch tree that obscured the view from my window, erasing 89% of the daylight. As a consequence, I developed a form of blindness for language, and began omitting certain words from my texts. This caused me embarrassment at school, and many hours staying behind filling in the missing words, until one teacher mistook my incorrectly written text for a "beautiful prose-poem." I wrote: "Yes said sometimes, I could find the extravagance. The oversize apple appears and almost riddled down with darkness cried out." Thus the Opaque movement was born.

At first, editors criticised the "poems" as mere nonsense, so efforts were made to bestow the lines with a form of logic through the nonsense, usually an intuitive emotional logic, like in the long flowing prose of indulgent writers such as a Margeurite Young or her ilk, where sense soon departs and the emotional reader is kept tethered to a long outpouring of lyrical prose, sucked into the illusion of beauty and power and whatnot, so we kept things on that level, mingling with a form of surrealism. Per: "I emptied the chamber. Strong runnels of tears emerged like the mucal ducts of a peregrine unloading. I ate a fevered wish and climbed up into the space of belonging." That sort of rubbish.

The Great Opaquists appealed to those who sought to read challenging prose with strong images and descriptions without having to think about the content in much detail, allowing the words to wash over them—words to be forgotten after reading—a mere afterglow the art's effect. I had created a movement that allowed for the intimation of meaning without the presence of meaning. A small school of writers formed with Bernard Blick, Candice Yellow, Tim Varmus and myself at the forefront, producing novels with titles like *Burnt Cartography*, *Singing Banshees*, *12:24* (mine), and *Blister Window*. These books helped bring the movement to a wider audience by situating the fictions in blue-collar America and putting dysfunctional families and relationships into the incidental storylines. I drifted out this group for several decades, but I would always have Bernard Blick on the phone wanting to discuss metaphors and symbolism (I had never knowingly used or understood these devices), or publish interviews with me in his online magazine *E-terminus*.

Our novels were frustrating. Riddled with banal dialogue, our interminable "scenes" would work opaque language around sections designed to help the reader to find a footing. From *Burnt Cartography*:

> "So you believe in the tangible?" Yolande asked. She had crisply assuaged the sorry-ever-after.
>
> "Only in the lowest sense. I mean I like certain things."
>
> "You can't smash the ceiling, Tristan." He rolled a cigarette and opened a liminal vein.
>
> "You think not?"
>
> "I have never knowingly exploded a perception."
>
> The door buzzed. Yolande stared at the void and wondered if the hand that reaches through the door is a gesture of the visible. Tristan exhaled halos of smoke and

tried to force a union between the bald and the brave. "We haven't cleaved a notion today," he said. "But that is in itself a cleaved notion," she said. "Only in a periphrastic sense," he said. "I suffer from periphrasis," she said. "You're not the only one," he said. "Perhaps in the future we might feel something tangible," he said. "I hope," she said.

I returned to the Opaque movement several decades later, when there was a brief rekindling of interest in the national media, and I wrote a final novel that outsold all the others. I was known as the Godfather of the Opaquists, and lied about the movement's formation—poaching explanations from several of the volumes of theory on the Opaquists I had read—and used the profits earned to correct my language blindness through laser surgery. The world of literary possibility open to me at last, I found myself unable to adapt to the pressures of having to place words in a logical order to make meaning. I had spent three decades of my life writing incoherently; changing this habit in my fifties seemed impossible. I took a post writing the information booklets for insurance companies. Further work writing restaurant menus, terms and conditions, and advertising slogans followed before I forged a path into the ordered sentence in the final stage of my career—the finest and most fertile stage.

I entered The House as a hack thriller writer, taking to the form with delight. The ordered motion of the plots, sentences, and character motives was a liberation for me, and I became a prolific writer of the Charles Atmond series, moving the hero through nine books (and counting) of formulaic scrapes, revelling in the clichéd descriptions, the unoriginal themes and settings, the woodenness of the dialogue. This was perfect order for me: machine-made fiction safe in its well-trimmed orderliness. People complain that The House signals the death of literature and that workhouse-made fiction is somehow the finish of several millennia of artistic achievement dating back to Homer. I disagree. The House is a place for literature to achieve the perfection to which it has aspired at a consistent level. . . imagine a world free from imperfect novels, swimming in masterpieces being produced one after the other in an unstoppable flow. Sounds like paradise to this writer!

Cal's Tour

Scottish Interest Books

DISPLACED from Second by a temporary ScotCall invasion (they occasionally blitz The House to commandeer offices), I meandered upstairs. Guarding the fire exit on the third floor is a naked man painted as a Pictish warrior. He holds firm a spear and shield, his arty pecs and muscles at full and impressive bulge, and stares into the middle distance like a beefeater with the capacity to disembowel. This is Pelf. A network of tattoos cover his body from dragon heads to sunflowers to lions with curly moustaches. His blue-hued penis is partially obscured by the lion's beard but still draws the eye, being a penis. He said to me: "Manna hepkins?" Followed by: "Forneil yoman intrimp gulander? Gravure simpo larbis querval? Baaloom? Wanta mugghoom formpals? Pimpla numkaa ladoofalla? Sampo sampa? Sampo sampa simpkin appo? Gushval?"[1] These are authentic Pictish expressions he has memorised to welcome all contractors to the dept.

As you enter the corridor, six fans mounted on the upper walls hit you with chilly winter winds. A watercolour rendering of an extremely steep Scottish incline (nowhere in particular—somewhere nonspecific and hilly in the Highlands) is on the left, and a mural of lines from Robert Burns and Ricky Wilson, the two most celebrated Scottish writers of the last five hundred years, on the right. Robert Burns is famous for his macabre poem "Tam O'Shanter"

---

[1]"How are you?" / "Have a nice trip over? Care for a mineral water or espresso? Tea? Like to use the bathroom? Care for a massage? Small snack? Small snack with ketchup? Hug?"

and his popular ballads and songs, and Ricky Wilson is the author of *Wee Billy Hummus Frae Largs*, a bestseller in 2013 that sold worldwide and helped usher in a Golden Age of Scottish fiction about superheroes from small towns who speak in dialect and settle down with sexy friends to work in chip shops. Sprinklers secreted in the carpets spray your feet as you "ascend" the hill towards the only room on the floor, a large conference space where external contractors (mainly in suits—consider suiting up if you have a proposal) come to pitch their ideas to CHAD. A no-nonsense man in Gucci leathers and tailored Cforgzia trousers, CHAD lives up to his capitalised name with his plain talking and head for marketing.

Among the ideas pitched: *Sean Connery's Shortbread: The Original James Bond & His World of Shortbread, Scrumptiously Scottish: A Crumbly History of Celtic Cookies, Brought Shed: A Novel of Shortbread, Shortbread and the Third Reich, Hoots Mon!: A Celebration of Hogmanay Shortbread, Gregor Fisher's Shortbread: Rab C Nesbitt & His World of Shortbread, The Role of Shortbread in the Aegean Civilization, Like Oor Granny Used Tae Muck It: Forty Classic Shortbread Recipes, Accept Nae Imitations: Scotland's Triumph in the Shortbread Wars, Wee Tam's Shortbreid: A Nuvvel ae Shortbreid, Do Salamanders Eat Shortbread?, Simply Shortbread: A Miscellany, Walter Scott's Shortbread: Scotland's First Novelist & His World of Shortbread, Reeks, Breeks, and Shortbreid!!!, Did William Wallace Invent Shortbread?, Wee Timorous Beastie Eating Oor Shortbreid: Doughy Verse Tributes to Rabbie Burns, Yeast in the East: Shortbread in the Lothians, Tallbread: The Arch Nemesis, Kirkincrankie: A Village of Shortbread, "Yum, we Polish immigrants love Scots shortbread!": An Outsider's Take on Yeasty Goods, Ewan McGregor's Shortbread: Obi-Wan Kenobi & His World of Shortbread, Rockin' & Rollin' in the Dough!: 268 Rock & Roll Classix About Shortbread, How Much Shortbread Can YOU Fit in Your Mouth?: A Book of Challenges!, Can Bonobos Make Shortbread?, Can You Dip Shortbread in Irn-Bru, Highland Crofters Eat Shortbread in Kilts, Hot Grannies & Their Grandkids Eat Shortbread*. My pitch was a novel set in the Outer Hebrides, approved by CHAD "as long as you set it in 1920s Hebrides, among crofters and such folk, nothing contemporary. And make shortbread or the making of or the consumption of integral to the plot." Here's a sneaky excerpt:

Alex stood facing the Hebridean sun. He was standing atop a hill abloom with heather, ablooming with beautiful purple heather, looking across the sea at the steamers coming back with their nets full of cod. Alex turned his glance west across the hills towards the stone-brick cottages of the crofters, spotting Old Jim tilling a field and his wife Old Jane milking the cows in the shed. He walked back to his house to return to work on his new shortbread recipe. He was inspired by the sea and the air and the pleasant country folk, and began experimenting with new yeast-beating techniques, such as stringing and flinging it at the walls of his own cottage, and rolling it with multiple rolling pins on the floor. He asked his dog McClusky to sit on the dough. He cut it up into rectangular shapes and placed it in the oven at gas mark six. He whacked the dough into shape with two rolling pins, sprinkling the dew from a thorny Highland thistle into the mixture, and asked Maybelle, the bonny lass from the cottage next door, to kiss the dough for luck, and rolled the dough flat using the wheels of his granny's motorised scooter. He cut it up into rectangles and punched holes in the pastry with the end of the rolling pin. Opening the oven, he placed the shortbread into a pre-greased tray (pipetted with Irn-Bru) and let it rise at a special temperature, where it swelled to a beautiful Highland plumpness—a Cairngorm of yeasty biscuit pleasure.

—*Hebridean Crumbs: A Novel of Shortbread* (p.178)

If your proposal is selected (can take forty or so tries), you are invited to a formally informal shindig in the same room with two VIPs from the American offices, where four tables are set up with the top four Scots stereotypes—servings of haggis laid out on the first, kilts of various clans on the second, thistles in soil on the third, and shortbread on the fourth. Two Highland pipers in full kilted regalia blast out "Flower of Scotland" and other unfavourites while red-haired serving girls with rustic cheeks busy about offering wine and canapés to the lucky commissioned. The VIPs are simply let's-get-down-to-businessmen, permitting themselves only

several smiles before and after their address to the room. Paul Bug-
gle CEO said:

"It's wonderful to be back in the former Scotland. Thank you
for the warm welcome. All my favourite cultural archetypes are
here. But we need to be careful not to oversell these commodities.
Americans have no idea that Scotland today is owned by the Mudrake Corporation and is funded entirely from the profits of American business. They have no idea that shortbread, haggis, and Irn-
Bru are all made in American factories. It's crucial that the buyers of
Scottish products believe these things originate in the Old Country.
Remember, Scotland is nothing more than a wing of the American
tourist industry and earns its right to retain its history by trading on
now-mythical cultural stereotypes completely alien to the residents
here, who live entirely on American food, television, and products.
ScotCall is part of the Mudrake Corporation. It's all about creating
the illusion of some kind of choice, some kind of freedom, some
kind of free will, so consumers don't become stultified by the lack
of any. All companies are owned by the Mudrake Corporation. In
fact, there's a joke that Scotland is run out of a tiny office of the
NY marketing department! But it's true. Scotland comprises such
a small percentage of the market, its loss would be irrelevant, but
its history is still relatively tradable. So it's imperative that we keep
these cultural archetypes going in books and other art forms. After
all, we're not in the business of wiping out a country's history and
culture—not when it is still so profitable. Adaptation is the word.
It simply isn't viable to let a country's populace cling to its cultural
stereotypes. We all know they were absorbed into the culture a long
time ago, as the world became more homogenous, universalised, as
the Mudrake Corporation created their global hypermarket. Can
you imagine a 21st century Scot would ever don a kilt unironically
or eat haggis for his tea? These were anachronisms way back in
the late 20th century. Really, it's corporations like ours that do a
service to small countries like Scotland. If it wasn't for us giving
them the chance to trade, they would have forgotten their history

and culture, and where would we all be then? Anyway, here's to the success of the latest shortbread range. Thank you."

Sleeping arrangements? Nope! Pelf kindly let me bed down in the conference room, borrowing a sleeping bag from the care-taker, and helped me find leftover food from the higher depart-ments. You need to rely on your wits on this floor. I asked Mar-ilyn for extra work promoting The House in the community and she sent me off around the farmhouses in Crarsix to collect dona-tions to help with essential repairs in the building (the lifts were mouldy with moss and fungi and some new form of furry-backed beetle was emerging from the cracks). I ambled along the gravel road past the stock-dump fields. The grass was hissing from molten electrical equipment, and the cries of starved digi-pets could be heard over the whirrs and moans of moribund electric mango skin-ners, lemon pulpers, banana strippers, orange pulpers, and apple mulchers. I reached the first hous,: a red-brick throwback erected beside the biggest stock-dump field in Crarsix, and knocked on the door, where and a tall man with ferrety eyebrows opened and said nothing. "I'm looking to—" "Say no more. I'm Sid. Come in!"

His front room was busy with all sorts of sharp-toothed anima-tronic scrapyard inventions. Sid was a prolific scrap farmer who eked out a living turning dumped stock into implausibly useful household friends. He showed me a trifunctional breakfast-cum-entertainment device made from the extrusions of an old toaster, TV remote, and several CD lasers. Four columns of lasers in one slot burned bread into toast on one side, requiring a simple flip to toast the reverse, while in a second slot another four columns of lasers played several songs on a CD at once down various earphone holes. The whole family could listen to different tracks from the same CD while slowly toasting their breakfast. Two TV remotes on the outer shells could flick channels if the breakfaster didn't want to participate in the listening and toasting process that morning. Sid showed off several other devices including a fan with a sprinkler in the back that dispensed cold water and air to cool sunbathers in the garden and simultaneously water the plants for up to two metres, and a chair with prosthetic hands that massaged the backs of users, tailored to their particular muscular requirements, with added buttons for handshakes, high-fives, scissors-paper-stone, foreplay, and sexual relief. He took me to his barnyard where ten pens of mechanical animals constructed from disembowelled laptops, monitors, CPUs, consoles, and miscellaneous techno-offal stood on standby. A line of cows had been made from various desktop parts: three keyboards-as-legs protruded from a body of monitors, and a shrivelled Apple Mac formed the head, sealed up with a set of sharp teeth and two digi-cam eyes. Old USB cables swished on its rump. These creatures scoured the fields devouring loose wires and pieces, mashing the debris down to produce a mushy oil-like sediment from their udders (eight pipettes sticking out an inverted colander) to be used as lubricant or solvent for his inventions. I watched a dozen or so in the field and spotted a few sheep gambolling through the debris. The sheep were old microwaves with legs, nibbling up things like wires and cables that might come in handy. "The microwave bodies on these sheep are functioning. Sometimes for a laugh I like to heat up haggises in them," Sid said. He offered me £12 after.

Some Crarsicans were less charitable. One old crone said to me: "No. Writers are entirely worthless to society. They don't deserve anything. It would be useless for me to waste my money trying to help them cling to the last remaining delusion they already pretend to have. Son, you're a young man. You shouldn't be working for criminals. Let me tell you, the sooner these people are drummed into proper jobs, the better. Art teaches us nothing about the real world. You can't phone up a book for practical advice, can you? No, ScotCall is better. I have a switchboard set up in my front room and take a few hundred calls every day. Something to do in my retirement. The people you speak to, it's incredible. Someone phoned earlier asking if the sky was blue, or if it was an optical illusion. I told him that whatever colour we see with our eyes is valid, so the sea is blue too, not clear. A woman phoned up this morning asking what the proper spelling of 'napkin' was. I told her, two A's and two P's. You're a young man, so think about it. There's always room for more helpers at ScotCall. They even hire ex-murderers, you know." Among other colourful characters in the area, I met a retired web trader whose sanity had been taken in the power outage of '34, when the electricity cut out for half a second and five trillion internet traders were bankrupted. He was forever besieged by vicious popups and screamed at me to watch out for the army of surveys with Trojan viruses advancing from the cyber-vacuum! Another had the friendly sign ALL WRITER'S [sic] WILL BE SHOT ON SITE in his garden. There was a young couple who had two TVs rigged up in every room and had never heard the word "book" before, looking scared as I defined it as words written down on paper to be read slowly for some kind of pleasure, amusement, or intellectual or emotional sustenance. They gave me £2 out of pity.

The production of *Hebridean Crumbs* was halted due to a lack of available paper. I had to present my manuscript to the CEO in extremely rough form (only 10K written in illegible pencil). A scrunch of handwritten paper alongside nineteen manila-foldered sheaves of A4 typed in psychometrically tested corporate fonts would clearly not suffice. I cowered behind the others and showed my mess to CHAD. "I didn't quite get around to finishing up," I told him. The others had no expressions of disapproval on their faces, which helped. They seemed incapable of reacting to anything that didn't directly concern them. "Oh, that's fine. One of our editors will add the polish," CHAD said. "But there's another 60,000 words left to write." "No problem, we'll stitch something together." My luck was both disappointing and reassuring. Why had I bothered to sit in a plastic chair for six hours a day, scribbling barely legible drivel onto flimsy recycled paper with a ten-inch pencil nub, when an editor in America could simply upload the necessary clichés from his hard drive and substitute all kilt references for shortbread ones? It would have saved me the hand cramp! Once the manuscripts had been cleared, the cheques were handed out in brown envelopes. CHAD made a parting speech: "Thank you everyone for your contributions. Our next meeting will take place in a month's time in the same room, our sell being Irn-Bru-themed books. You are all welcome to attend and pitch your ideas as usual." I had made my first money from writing: ten crisp pounds.

A Word from the Team

CHAD: It's about harnessing the power of shortbread. Next to porridge oats, bottled water, and commemorative Billy Connolly plates, shortbread is Scotland's biggest export. As content *makars* for SIBINC, your duty is to harness the salesability of shortbread to reach as wide an audience as possible. We want to see novels about the production of shortbread, histories of shortbread manufacture, reflections and aphorisms about shortbread, quotes from notable Scots about shortbread. The Canadian market for shortbread books is booming at the moment, we need to seize the *carpe diem*. If you have an idea, please attend a weekly pitch (Third Floor Tuesdays at 2.15pm).

FRANK: I had success on the Irish historical market, but it crashed when readers could no longer subside on a diet of potato famine and poverty porn. I was worried people would forget the bankable stereotypes and I would have to invent an entirely new history and mythology for Ireland, which was tricky contriving from nowhere as it usually involved borrowing from other countries, and people are clued-in to these sly cultural steals. The public can swallow a lot, but they can't swallow inauthenticity. The guys on this floor respect this.

TEDDY: I have potential ancestors in the Old Country, somewhere in Invernoddle in the Higherlands, and I was totally stoked to be able to write a tribute to my (maybe!) family.

BIFF: Man, I love this country but I ain't touchin' that haggis. Sheep innards in cylinders? No way, man!!!!

JIM: It makes no difference to me, cashing in on my heritage. Hell, I was raised in a culture totally saturated by American television and products. I only know vague things about Scotland anyway through the stereotypes propagated through American television and products. In European school syllabuses, they stopped teaching the history of individual countries and focused instead on corporate history since the ScotCall rise. I read every work on the syllabus, including the 1000-page *ScotCall Procedural Guidelines* and *ScotCall Book of Customer Satisfaction* and *ScotCall Rules for Dealing with Rude Clients* (which had the naughty words on pages 328–330!)

DAVE: Do I like working here? Yeah! Sort of. Well, no not really. Why'd you ask?

This

3

CHANCES are that the reader (who?) will not be familiar with the sort of fictions that presage this particular masterpiece. In the early 2000s, soi-disant "experimental" fiction was the biggest-selling material on the block. The revolution began with the publication of Christine Brooke-Rose's molecular *histoire du monde, Subscript* (1999), and the following decade made millionaires of such marginal figures as Ron Sukenick, Christopher Sorrentino, Sergio de la Pava, Irmtraud Morgner, and Meredith Brosnan. These writers were vanguards of the avant-garde revolution and paved the way for all manner of stunning deviations from conventional storytelling and highwire acts of dazzling discursive prose. Sergio de la Pava's novel *Personae* (2011) won the Pulitzer Prize for its famous five-brains-suspended-in-a-vat scene, and Meredith Brosnan's second novel *Fuck You and Your Momma* (2015) won the O. Henry award for its famous depiction of doublebutt colonic irrigation between George W. Bush and English folk singer Laura Marling. These were times when the sheer splendour of language and the boundless potential of the human imagination to transcend the inexorable, horrendous dullness of a consumerist society in its death throes mattered more to readers than accessible plots and well-drawn characters and TV spin-offs. It was a second Enlightenment. Other art forms adapted to the rise of the *avanguard* (as literary critic Steven Moore punningly labelled this particular band of geniuses). TV talent shows auditioned raggedy hopefuls desperate for the lead in the latest production of *Krapp's Last Tape*. From Dover to Thurso, people flocked to the BBC studios dressed as Patrick Magee and Bore Angelovski eager to prove themselves the quintessence of 69-year-old Krapp. Publishers went into spasms of ecstasy at every manuscript labelled highbrow or labyrinthine. Complexity, re-readability, depth and vision—these were the watchwords for a whole generation of fiction writers! Even minor parodists and pranksters like myself sat down and penned works that dared to capture the zeitgeist in this wonderful and rich era. The Faber & Faber-published debut novel of mine *A Postmodern Belch* (2012) was hailed by critic and novelist Tom McCarthy as "a rumbustious comedic novel in the impish manner of Rabelais, refracted through the lens of Sorrentino, and rammed down the digestive tract of Carlton Mellick III." It was an amazing time to be alive! Ah, how those days are long gone! Lost forever in the sands of time, for want of a less disgraceful cliché.

The Trauma Rooms

3

"IN this room, we have Brian Lettsin. He worked as a proofreader for small press *I & I Books*, who specialised in metafictional novels subverting the reader's expectations as to the purpose of narrative in narrative fiction and all that piffle. One warning: he won't make eye contact during the conversation and might need persistent reminding of his name to the point it becomes annoying," the doctor said. Brian's room was covered from floor to ceiling in mirrors, into which a bemused Brian stared, fingering his multiple reflections, muttering existential and ontological one-liners to himself ("Who am I? Whose novel am I in?"), freezing stock-still whenever he suspected the Creator/Author to be present in the room.

"Brian! It's me, the doctor. I have a new *character* here, Erin," he said.

"Hi Brian!"

"Hello. What is your function?" he asked.

"Erin's here to spice up the novel."

"Good," Brian said, removing his trousers.

"No! Brian! Now, what have I told you? Hmm?"

"We aren't in a novel."

"Correct."

"But . . . I really do have a sneaking suspicion we *are* in one."

"No."

"I mean . . . a tower block of writers. A call centre eating up the country. I can't see this happening in the real world."

"The *what*?"

"Oh, my head! Don't *do* that!"

"Sorry, Brian. I tease. Erin would like to know your story, care to tell her? The one we have been practising?"

"Wait . . . who am I?"

"Oh not this again!"

"Who am I?"

"You are Brian Lettsin. Brian Lettsin. Brian Lettsin. Erin, help please."

"Brian Lettsin," she said.

"I am *Brian* . . . ?"

"Brian Lettsin. Brian Lettsin. Brian Lettsin. Brian Lettsin."

"Brian Lettsin. Brian Lettsin. Brian Lettsin. Brian Lettsin. Brian Lettsin. Brian Lettsin. Brian Lettsin," Erin said.

"I'm Brian Lettsin?"

"That's correct. Brian Lettsin. Brian Lettsin. Brian Lettsin."

"Yes. I am Brian Lettsin."

"Well done, Brian Lettsin. Now, Brian Lettsin, would you like to tell Erin your story, Brian Lettsin?"

"I'd like to hear your story, Brian Lettsin."

"All right. I am Brian Lettsin and here is my story. I was working for *I & I Books*. It began innocently, with a few novels featuring bemused writers: their affairs, drinking problems, failure to produce their works, and so on. Nothing too harmful. Then I received this novel, *A Postmodern Postmortem*. Set in an afterlife for bad characters, the book was riddled with the kind of intertextual knowingness that was to set me on the path to destruction. There followed an orgiastic spree of metafucking—writers stepping into their novels to slap and screw their characters, writers appearing in other writers' novels to do the same, then writers slapping and screwing the other writers in their novels, and characters taking over the narration of the novels and so on. One book, *I Am the Novel*, pushed me over the edge. Over ten thousand unidentified voices, zigzagging along the page, or huddled into spirals or boxes, even printed overlapping one another, squabbled for authorship, offering nothing in the manner of plot or character, or a conceivable *point* to the whole thing—one voice even cried out in orgasm 'Oh! This is so pointless . . . so . . . oh oh oh! . . . meeeeeaaaningleeeeeessss!' epitomising the masturbatory emptiness at the heart of this publisher's project. I suppose there was some theoretical logic behind these novels—I recall some drear pamphlet penned by the editor riddled with Derrida/Barthes references, as if cribbing from those two was a sufficient apologia for their gummy deluge—but this was too late for me. *I Am the Novel*, running at over 1000 pages, no author name on the cover, sent me into a spasm of self-doubt. I woke up having no idea who I was, if I was a character in a novel, if I had written a novel . . . I cracked up. I spent my days staring into mirrors in the hope I might recall a mere snippet of the previous 'life' I was supposed to have led . . . a life that is . . . I am Brian . . . hang on, who I am again?"

"Brian Lettsin. Not supposed. You are verifiably Brian Peter Lettsin. I have shown you your birth certificate. Your parents come around every week with family snaps. Your old college friends pour anecdotes into your ear every other day. Your ex-girlfriend writes you emails detailing your time together. No other Brian Lettsins exist in this country, you are unique in your Brian Lettsinness. So that name again: Brian Lettsin. Brian Lettsin. Erin?" the doctor offered.

"Brian Lettsin," Erin said. At this, Brian's pupils dilated and his neck swivelled back towards the mirrors, into which he stared again, muttering: "But *am* I? *Am* I?"

"Hmm. A tricky case," the doctor said to Erin. "Have you encountered anything from *I & I Books?*"

"Yes. Read two pages, hurled it against the wall."

"Of course. The most severe waffle imaginable. I confess that after reading twelve pages, I was starting to question my sanity."

"Cure?"

"Not sure. Saying 'Brian Lettsin' repeatedly seems to work. Perhaps if we invited everyone Brian knows, and they all said 'Brian Lettsin' simultaneously, Brian would snap back into sanity. It's hard to predict."

"It is oddly addictive saying Brian Lettsin. Brian Lettsin. Brian Lettsin."

"Yes, I have grown fond of saying Brian Lettsin too. Brian Lettsin. Brian Lettsin."

"Who?" Brian Lettsin asked.

"You, Brian Lettsin," the doctor said. "Right. Let's leave Brian Lettsin for now. Shall we proceed to the next trauma room? I can't see a stapler in here."

"No, me neither. Bye, Brian Lettsin."

"Brian Lettsin," Brian said, unsurely.

"Yes, that's you!"

"Oh, right. Are you sure?"

Puff: The Unloved Son

2

D UE to a misunderstanding with the construction team during The House's erection (Marilyn Volt had refused to accept the second estimate and cough up 100K in advance), the waste disposal and plumbing aspect of the building was unfortunate (entire floors from time to time were flooded in faeces) and pipes protruded from unusual places, the results wavering from comic (a vertical spume on the roof) to not-comic (a pipe releasing fresh urine into the lifts) and sometimes tragic (the long pipe outside the fifteenth floor window that C.J. Watson's son Puff was hanging from, seeking to complete his survey of the pipes that he could insert his fingers into). The writers who showed concern (two of them—the others had deadlines) mistook Puff's presence as a suicide attempt and persuaded him he had too much to live for (which was untrue—his mother didn't love him and had told him several times he'd have to vent this lack into writing as an adult to cope with the ordeal) and offered outstretched hands, despite his being two meters away, already inserting his hand into the pipe. "Hey, I can fit my whole mitt in here!" he said, laughing. Concrete awaited his impact below.

Satisfied that this pipe was the fattest of those he'd inserted fingers into, disappointed he couldn't insert his other hand into the pipe without going splat on the concrete, Puff shimmied back towards the window. One of the concerned writers secretly hoped the kid would plummet so he could have first-hand experience of that split-second terror that comes across the face once a person realises it's over, but Puff was grinning and singing to himself a made-up ditty about the wideness of pipes:

My pipe is wide, my pipe is fat
I can stick my digits in that
Your pipe is not, your pipe is small
You can't stick in anything at all

The other writer sincerely didn't want Puff to plummet and had brought blood to her tongue and scrunched her toes so tight she strained a tendon. Puff shimmied along the pipe and dropped back through the window unscathed. The female writer hugged Puff so tight he coughed up phlegm on her shoulder, kicking her in the shin to free himself and giggling. He leapt onto her desk and began to boogie. He sang: "*I spat on the lady / I made drool on her dress / I spat on the ugly lady / I made a horrible mess!*" and kicked her papers around the office, hopping from desk to desk shouting his song. Her concern vanished and she regretted not having karate-chopped his wrists at the last minute so he'd have made a more appealing shape on the concrete instead of the shapes he was throwing around the office as he continued to remark on the drool and how amusing it was to have made saliva over the ugly lady's ugly shoulder. "I hate you, you little bastard," she said. Puff flung a hole punch at her head and howled with laughter.

AD FROM SPONSORS

Ring, ring! Who's there? This is your future speaking. My future? Yes, your future at ScotCall. What's in store for me, future? How about financial security for life, an amazing pension plan, in-house dating, *en suite* accommodation and vital honest living? Wow! How about a safe environment in our housing complexes, where you can raise your children without fear of abuse or attack, the opportunity to invest shares with a 0.5% interest rate, and the chance to be part of a kinetic and highly motivated team of upbeat and enthusiastic people? Can it possibly get any better than this?

Yes!

Your future is a phone call away. Call now for an immediate interview, and you could be part of the ScotCall family in a matter of days! Boasting over 1,928 branches in Scotland, expanding further north into Thurso and the Orkneys, ScotCall is an exciting and inevitable part of your future. Our phone-slingers are on hand 24hrs to take calls about anything and everything! *Can you help our customers with the following queries?*

Who do I contact to order a pizza? My girlfriend has a wrinkle on her left brow and she refuses to get the surgery—should I chuck her? My left leg is 0.4mm smaller than my right—am I deformed? I don't like my stepfather—should I tell him? The picture quality of my seventh TV is slightly less powerful than the picture quality of my other twelve TVs—should I sue? My nails are chipped—should I get a replacement hand? What do I do if my sock has a hole in it? What's a university? Can I download and upload at the same time, or will that explode my computer? How come boats float on water but anvils sink? Can I get HIV by kissing a penguin? Who do I call to get the number for the person who gives out numbers for the people who specialise in phone calls about calling people to get the number for the people who give out numbers for the people who specialise—My sweet pea, Joe Strummer: should I splay or should I grow? Id is, is id? I forgot how to walk—is it left, right, left, or right, left, right?

Can you help? Join us.

SCOTCALL.

YOUR FUTURE.

Recruitment Line:

0800 717 717

Mhairi

3

U PON arriving at The House and awarding myself the humorous title of Queen Momma, I knew I would have to make
a sacrifice of Koreshesque proportions. These beleaguered people,
these lifestarved wretches, these writers, were helpless children and
I would have to act the part of their mothers, attending to their
basic needs to keep the interpersonal relations smooth between
departments and prevent reversion to a primitive society involving murderous skirmishes and overly messy blood rituals between
floors, as in the fictions of J.G. Ballard.[1] Apart from ensuring the
food and water supplies are in constant motion and dispatching
workers to mend the hundred or so broken thingies per day, I have
more complicated and hair-pulling tasks to perform. For example,
one day on the Western floor, a strain of yellow-bellied lily-livered
cowardice broke out and the forty-seven writers in turn lost control
of their bladders, drenching the shag carpets in hot piss. To solve
the problem, I worked through the night making catheters to place
beneath the desks, each with a long pipe attached that threaded its
way along the carpet towards the open windows. Strong winds, unfortunately, redistributed the waste to the Children's Books floor,
and dozens of piss-covered writers in furious revenge rolled pipes
bursting with water up to the Western floor in an attempt to flood
their enemies. The Western writers merely used their catheters to
catch the water, piping torrents out the window and back down to
the Children's Books floor, flooding the entire office until the writ-

[1] A SF and speculative fiction writer who was successfully resurrected in 2038,
currently still active at the age of 78+12.

97

ers were breathing in 30cm gaps between the waterbed and the ceiling before a plumber arrived and began "dealing" with the problem. This corner-cutting cowboy decided to "store" the unwanted water in various parts of the building—inside photocopiers, desk drawers, under ceiling tiles, parts of loose carpet, behind electrical sockets, and inside lampshades. This had stressful repercussions: writers being constantly besieged by outpourings of "stored" water. While replacing the toner in the Fantasy floor photocopier, C.K. Wilmot was knocked onto his arse by a vengeful spume, and waterswept down the emergency stairs to Fourth where he sustained a concussion and a migraine from all the writers bitching about their drenched manuscripts. And when C.J. Wimlot from the Czechoslovakian erotica dept. unhooked the lampshade to replace a bulb in the overhead light, a malfeasant spurt toppled him arseways and hurled him out the alasly open window, where he fell on a plasma TV broadcasting an image of a trampoline, landing face-first on the flatscreen and resting his burning head in 24 inches of fiery wires. And when martial arts writer C.V. Timpani went to fetch some foolscap from a drawer, a naughty geyser rendered him hilariously arsebound and drenched him and the fool's scap of paper in a damp plop of unappreciated liquid. The cowboy plumber's corner-cutting was not the only incident of this nature. A similar thing happened with a fire on Twentieth, whereby lazy firemen "stored" the fire in various closets and desk drawers. C.T. Periman reached into his desk for a pen and a raging conflagration burned his limbs. The solution to this problem was to store the excess water in fire extinguishers (made from cardboard) to be used whenever rogue flames erupted on Twentieth or elsewhere. These sorts of thinking-outside-the-box solutions are an essential part of what I do when I choose to do stuff.

The Jesus Memos

Memo: James L. Francis

JESUS rose again from the photocopier on Fourth. He appeared in his popular guise—long white dress and trimmed brown beard—and delivered a brief sermon on his return heralding a new era of peace and love, etc. I observed Jesus's reappearance while waiting for the last ten pages of my novel *Love's Acorns* for my reader. My initial reaction was wonder and awe, but I lost time standing and listening to the Saviour and had to deliver the chapters and start my next novel, *Hate's Faggots*. Unless Jesus had a large sack of banknotes in his dress there wasn't much point hanging around listening to his prophecies! It was selfish of Jesus to expect an audience to volunteer their time at work to listen to his ramblings. I have circulated this memo advising writers to ignore Jesus as he hovers up and down the building promising people eternal love and peace and trying to put everyone off their work.

Memo: Arlene Gray

For the fifth time this week I have seen Jesus hanging around the vending machines hurling tirades about paradise and brotherhood as they wait for their coffee to pour or for their crisps and fruit to fall. I suggest we start a petition calling for the removal of Jesus from The House. His presence here is irrelevant.

Memo: Thomas Wood

I think Jesus might be one of these pranksters, most likely PeteXXX. We all remember the time he claimed to be ghost of Stephen King and made slaves of a thousand writers in exchange for bogus bestseller advice.

THE HOUSE OF WRITERS

Memo: Lisa Blue

As an atheist I find Jesus's presence here insulting. If Jesus is to hang around attempting to convert people to whatever whacked love-is-all-around-us dogma he is peddling in that absurd white dress I demand we have a resurrected Richard Dawkins around the place reminding people about the Big Bang and evolution. I can't count the amount of times I've seen those frightening doe-eyes staring at me as if boring (pun intended) into my soul. Someone needs to check his Visa and his citizenship papers.

Memo: PeteXXX

As if I would dress up as Jesus! What an obvious prank! I should think Thomas Wood might credit me with more skill (considering he was one of the thousand I enslaved—thanks for the butt wax, mate!).

Memo: Gerald Bolt

I never knew we could send memos to the *whole* building! My new book is entitled *Fortune's Fingers* and is a fantastic thriller about a gambling addict who develops carpal tunnel syndrome and has to utilise other limbs to sate his addictions, until his entire body falls victim. Tough lessons about moderation are learned in this glamorous novel set in the casinos of Monaco and Las Vegas. Five sex scenes included.

[4,928 memos deleted]

Memo: Brian Cray

I spotted Jesus in the canteen. Since he accepted a post writing religious fiction he has been less bothersome around the building. I think we should have more respect for him despite the fact he is here illegally, has no NI Number, birth certificate, or proof of identity, since he did appear from the photocopier in all good faith hoping to rescue mankind from the scourge of evil (ScotCall) and lead us into eternal bliss. I suggest we chip in for a nice card.

Memo: Irene Tomas

No one asked him to come here. I hate to be cruel but that's the truth. I came here with good intentions hoping to cheer people up writing comedic fiction and I didn't get a nice card bought for me. . .

Memo: Claire Wilson

Have you read his "novels"? No offence to God-up-above, but the Saviour needs to work on his syntax. His plotting is execrable. All his works are rehashed autobiographies. A "special person" is placed on the planet to help less "special persons." The hoi polloi treat him like dirt and string him up for being too nice. Please! Could the parallels be more obvious? He means well . . . that's not the point. Doesn't excuse him from sentences like: *The people on the hill they came to see him and they threw all sorts of things, they threw stones and bricks and things.* Get him a *card*? Get him a copy editor!

Memo: Bill Orange

You do know Jesus can read these memos too?

Memo: Craig Thomas

The last thing the Son of God expected when he rose again was to have to write hack prose in a dilapidated tower block while everyone ignores his message of universal love and kindness and sends bitchy memos about him behind his back (and to his face). We could at least all sign a welcome card.

Memo: Jill Jones

I'm not signing it.

Memo: Nigel Person

Nor am I.

[2,282 memos deleted]

THE HOUSE OF WRITERS

Memo: Richard Arms

I saw Jesus flying outside the building! Where does it say in *The Bible* that Jesus could fly, for Richard's sake? Is this distracting or what?? It's not fair that he should be showing off like that simply because he's the son of God and we're mere mortals who need engines and wings to get in the air. We're all equal in The House! Not in terms of success or skill . . . but we're all writers! This is breaking some rule. I propose we sign a petition to stop Jesus flying outside the windows in his spare time.

Memo: Frances Agree

I'd sign that. Who does he think he is? Disgraceful . . .

Memo: Vernon Argue

I saw him disappear into the clouds earlier. I think he must be negotiating with God to return home or something.

Memo: Tim Thurston

Good riddance!

Memo: Bill Gordon

He faded back into the photocopier earlier on today, I saw him while I was printing out my new novel *Big in Brussels*, a heartwarming tale about a tone deaf singer whose home recordings become huge in the Belgian capital. He left a final message for us on a sheet of A4: FUCK Y'ALL ASSHOLES. I think that might have been placed there beforehand by one of the pranksters. PeteXXX?

A Better Life

3

I ATE lunch in the canteen (a choice of prepackaged cress-egg or cress-tomato sandwiches) and returned to the ScotCall bus. I spent the first hour panicking that this man who appeared to have no recollection of me murdering his colleague might snap at any second and denounce me with a theatrical scream of "*Murrrrderrrrer!*" This made devising the requisite strategies for freedom somewhat onerous. The bus headed along the road towards the supposed sea. There were no passengers (there were no stops) so I brooded in the presence of the driver and the blonde zombie whom I had to kill soon before he denounced me and I was clad in chains forever (or clad to a phone—even prisoners had their ScotCall duties, most of them preferred to be hanged). I had no weapons to hand with which to do the killing. I decided to speak to the driver when the future corpse went to piss in the small bus WC. He was an older man, visibly asthmatic, listening to music (audibly Billy Joel) on headphones. I tapped him on the shoulder.

"Can I ask you something?"

"What?" he said in an unbothered manner.

"Do you care about ScotCall?"

"Is this a trick question?" His voice was more refined than I was expecting from whatever pomparse perception I had of the average bus driver.

"No. I want to kill the operative in the WC. Do you mind?"

"Go ahead."

"You won't report me?"

"Nah. Couldn't care less."

"You know there's rumours of some kind of commune near the sea? We could take the bus there."

"Sounds good. Although."

"Although?"

"We couldn't take the bus. We'd have to walk. Microchips."

"Ah."

"And chances are if we walked along the road another bus would pick us up."

"What if I drove the bus to the edge of its route and walked along the road where there are no ScotCall buses?"

"I like it. Let me stop here and I'll kill that chump in the loo."

"*You* will? Oh . . . all right."

Rob (driver) parked the bus once we heard the toilet flush. He dispatched with the operative in a manner I won't describe since to do so might stir up inadvertent sympathy for the corpse—this would be irrelevant and insulting to me and all those like me who strive for "freedom." (In scare quotes since I doubt the concept exists outside the realm of myth). Rob drove the bus for two miles and parked approximately two hours' walking distance from the hamlet of Arxle where outcast pensioners had set up ScotCall at-home kits to enable their promising futures as operatives from the comfort of their own granite bungalows, free from the persecution of Kirstys, with only the sound of a loud klaxon to discipline them whenever post-lunch sleep beckoned or their hearts stopped. Those unfortunate enough to speak to one of these promising operatives ended up trapped in exchanges such as:

"Hello?"

"*What?*"

"Is this ScotCall?"

"*What?*"

"I need help sexing an asparagus."

"*I need what?*"

"Um . . ."

"*Who is this?*"

"I need help sexing an asparagus."

"I don't know them."
"Sorry?"
"What's there? Is that there?"
"I don't follow."
"Swallow what?"
"No, I—"
"I'm 101 years old, you cunt."
"Oh, um . . . "
"What?!"
"Can we start again?"
"Bloody hell."
"My asparagus."
"Your ass is what?"
"No, my asparagus."
"What is your point?"
"I don't know, I—"
"Then why?"
"Um . . ."
"D'you know I'm 101, you mook?"
"Yes, you said."
"Good."
"So, can you help?"
"Oh, for fuck's sake!"
"Sorry. Should I call back later?"
"Date her? Date who?"
"No, I—"
"I can't date you, I'm 101 years old."
"I didn't want a date."
"Then why'd you call?"
"Because . . ."
"Exactly. If you don't want a date, don't waste my time."
"Hello? Hello?"

We approached the dour slagheap of Arxle. The surrounding fields had been paved over long ago and still-present sheep competed for nibbles on the troughs of grass-substitute made from starch and wet paper. After their lunchtime snacks, the bored sheep tried grazing on the grass troughs or lay sprawled on the ever-warm concrete, blinking into the distance. Artificial bushes dotted the landscape and the sheep champed their bits on the leaves to exercise their champing muscles, despite the impossibility of digestion. I buddied up to Rob as we walked. He had worked as an IT repairman before the meltdown and went into hiding during the witch-hunts of '39, when bankrupt businessmen went on Revenge Rampages, shooting web designers, content writers, repairmen— all those in the IT industry, including people who sold monitor sprays and mouse-buffing shiners. I had the slight inclination to tweak his nipples myself, having lost thousands in the meltdown, but his sprightliness and enthusiasm for our "freedom" kept me in check. So I decided not to beat the ever-living shit out of him in the end.

Arxle was a post-nuclear pit for pensioners with no sons, daughters, or tender-souled relatives willing to adopt them into the Scot-Call compound with its "perks." We skulked past their granite shacks as the incoherent sods poured senile slaverings into their phones and their co-incoherent customers begged for the correct reference number for poultry, or the fastest method of annexing a pineapple, or how to buff a never-buffed surfboard, or tips on how to memorise smells. We smiled at their wrinkly sneers of provincial contempt and waved to their windows, making big-kisses-and-hugs gestures. These were people who craved the barrenness of isolation and exacted their revenge via their phones, communing only with their neighbours to borrow a cup or acid or a pint of plutonium. I was well beyond feeling sorry for anyone.

The *Farewell, Author!* Conference

3

IAN Rankin entered. "Between you and me, I'm secretly pleased about the end of those publishers. I have been creating vital work in the crime field for decades, work on a par with Dickens, Zola, and Dostoevsky for its brutal exposé of the urban underworld, and people have panned me as a hack. Because I sold. Because I packed used bookshops to bursting with old Rebuses and kept charity shops alive. I should have been fucking worshipped. I *was* the Scottish economy, and those highbrow bastards refused me their Bookers, Oranges, James Taits, Lannans, all because I wrote about hard-drinking mavericks who solved murders. Because I had a mansion. Let me tell you, if people think rich men can't pen book after book of classic fiction, they are living in a loony soap opera. I set my ninety-fourth Rebus, *Get Yer Ya-Ya's Out*, in the seedy enclave of Cramond where twelve bodies had been found along the beach. Rebus was working through the twelve steps for the twelfth time (see that symmetry, motherfuckers?) and had one last chance to prove himself to the Lothian PD. The reviews were excrement. 'Rankin continues to ring the last desperate drop from his neverending cash sponge with this tiresome crime procedural where the body count is high and the entertainment value is low.' Cash sponge?! Call that book reviewing? Hacks are failed novelists. My ninety-fifth Rebus, *Got Live If You Want It!*, I set in the murky cluster of Blackford, where an opera singer had been found cut open outside a newsagents, and Rebus had to overcome his instinctive working-class loathing of opera to solve the case. More predictable reviews. 'Rankin continues writing his novels via an

107

algorithm used in Windows 98 with expected hilarious results.' Hilarious results?! I have a comedic touch sometimes, I can make sides split if I want to. I prefer the fucking truth to making tourists snigger in airports. Pardon me for having loftier ambitions. My ninety-sixth Rebus, *Jamming with Edward!*, I set in the slimy borough of Holyrood, where a politician had been accused of killing a teenage backpacker. The twist of that fucking masterpiece was there was no murder: the first Rebus without a murder. The fans went nuts. I wrote another nine murderless Rebi after that, including one where no one is accused of anything and the book is long descriptions of Rebus rolling around in bed with one of his lovers, failing to make a cup of tea because he'd never done that before, walking to the newsagent to pick up *The Sun* and teasing his lover with the tits on page three, shouting abuse at the misfit dolts on ITV talk shows, ordering a Chinese takeout at four in the afternoon, refusing to pick up for the Detective Inspector despite hints of an impending case, and hitting the pubs for a cheeky half-pint or twelve (that number again, mofos). Hacks hated these, except one who wrote: 'Rankin revitalises his franchise with this superb subversion of the novel that owes more to *Oblomov* than *The Big Sleep*.' I have no idea what that means, but at least one hack spoke sense for a change," Ian said while on the pavement, walking in the door, and storming around the supermarket. "Hi Ian," I said. In the same vein, an enraged Jodi Picoult arrived. "I wrote #1 *New York Times* bestsellers, in case you weren't aware (sometimes the font displaying this fact was only in 14pt on the covers). I wrote about families. People were envious of me because I dared to tackle emotions head-on. I wrote about families in the midst of tragedies. Lost or dead twins, fathers, mothers, brothers, sisters, there was no familial tragedy that remained unexplored by me, in one of my many very emotionally charged (readers say my books are better than therapy, they teach people how to love again) and long novels. Snobs and unfeeling dweebs were envious that I had the brass neck to tackle families using the sentiment at the root of human experience, as opposed to their obfuscating literary nonsense, hiding emotions in thickets of unreadable verbiage. If a person feels their fucking heart breaking then you fucking write, 'Jane's heart was fucking breaking,' except you don't use the swears, they reduce the readership! Be universal. Write about ruptured families all the time, that's what I say, there's no other topic that will place you on the *New York Times* bestseller list, except maybe child abuse, but I already have that covered in my ten-book *Leave Her Alone* series, so bad luck, suckers!" Jodi said as she drank all the cola and ate the three remaining chocolates. "I wrote a novel once, *The Heartsplitters*—left the entire University of Pennsylvania in tears. There was this scene with the two sisters, Jane and Julie. Julie had shagged Jane's boyfriend and accidentally set his house on fire, killing him and his entire family. Julie was pissed at Jane for three decades until a chance encounter at a skiing lodge in Aviemore, Scotland when Julie had the chance to save her sister and her entire family from a ski-related death (do you notice my clever callback there, you literary lords and ladies?), and afterwards the sisters reconciled. 'I cannot believe we remained silent for so long,' Julie said with actual tears in her eyes (you hear that, obfuscators?), and the two hugged with tears streaming down their faces, tears that melted the entire ski lodge. The university was soaked after that reading! Flooded like the ski lodge. How's that for creative mirroring!" Jodi had addressed this last section to the rustle in a bag of sweetcorn.

I opened the wrong door

I OPENED the wrong door. I was seeking a mop to absorb a spillage made on the beige shag in our office (steampunk dept.), assuming the mop to be located in a cupboard in the stairwell. This proved incorrect. I stepped into a corridor where a sequence of doors stretched long into the horizon, each named after a literary technique or particular quirk of language. I tapped on a door marked "Parataxis" and a hurried man answered.

"There! . . . Enter please . . . so much to do . . . bees aren't as busy as me . . . have you seen Nancy's necklace . . . around here somewhere . . . how can I help you? . . . I suppose you'd like tea and a nibble . . . never like her to refuse a nibble . . . must locate that . . . take a seat please . . . sturdy base those seats . . . I—"

"Have you a mop?"

"Have a mop? . . . the sort for mopping up? . . . how about a chocolate digestive . . . or we have crackers . . . no tea in the cupboards . . . where's that damn necklace . . . I used to mop up in here . . . when she was . . . well never mind . . . I can wax nostalgic later . . . better crack on with this tax return . . . oh where are those manners, Aidan? . . . I apologise, I never have visitors . . . take a seat please . . . sturdy—"

"Never mind. I'll ask elsewhere. Thanks."

I suspected that a mop was not in wait behind a single of these doors. I continued regardless, as the steampunk novel I was writing was losing momentum and would need a complete rewrite, and returning to the desk was to snack on a bitter panini of personal failure. I tapped on "Semantic Syllepsis":

"Hello! Let me have your coat and your ear, if I may. Enter."

"I'm looking for a mop."

"Ah! A wise man once told me never take a man's mop or his wife. This is a maxim I enforce!"

"So no mop?"

"No wives either! Gillian long ago made her bed and her exit— and now I must lie in it! Her bed, I mean, not her exit."

"You talk weird."

"It's a burden I must shoulder and carry . . . that one doesn't work. It's a cross I must bear and wear . . . around my neck . . as in Jesus . . . I need some coffee here! Otherwise I will be taking my hat and my leave!"

"Don't pinch from Dickens."

"I offer my apologies and my biscuits. Care for a triple-choc cookie? You will find them in that drawer and in my mouth."

"Enough!"

I took my leave (and nothing else). I popped into various cupboards after, including "Anaphora"—"You are seeking the mop of our time. You are seeking an idea not a cleaning implement. You are seeking a peg on which to hang the future. You are seeking a mop inside an idea inside the future that is ours."—and to "Tautophrase"—"To find that mop, you have to find that mop. A mop is a mop is a mop."—and to "Bdelygmia"—"You mop-loving bleach-sniffing dirt-licking bacteria-seeking filth-coveting cleanliness-obsessed sparkle-skinned shine-suited backstair-scrubber!"—and to "Hypophora"—"Is your mop in this room? No, your mop is not in this room."—and to "Solecism"—"You is looking for a mop? There aren't no mops in this room."—to "Epistrophe"—"The mop you are seeking no longer exists, the same as hope no longer exists, empathy no longer exists, and love itself simply no longer exists."—to "Dysphemistic Euphemism"—"Hello mophead, s'up?" to "Antimetabole"—"The mop is love, love is the mop."—and then I left.

This

4

PROWLING around The House scouting for material has forced me into making difficult decisions as to which observations to include in narrative form in this novel and which to omit. The House is an infinite repository for stories, mostly horror ones involving writers being tortured in manifold creative ways, and up until this point, I am the only person to attempt to document some of the rottennesses that take place in this building. Some writers have tried bribing me into mentioning them and their works and want to be written into the pantheon of Future Greats if succeeding generations take up literacy; however, I decided not to take backhanders and kept to a flat rate for placing promotional ads in this novel's interstices. One technique I find successful for removing the otherwise time-consuming and page-hogging business of setting up scenes, working and reworking descriptions, is the précis, the capsule summary of a story that in another's hands might take several pages to spin. Words are extravagantly wasted in this place, thoughtlessly shat onto the page, innocent nouns and verbs are used and reused blithely, pounded into misshapen sentences until they emerge bloody and incomprehensible. As I walk down the corridors, I hear paragraphs moaning and pages in states of extreme distress. I encounter sentences cowering in corners, bleeding clichés, their syntax broken and irreparable. Before I sat down to write this section, I saw a wounded description crawling towards the incinerator, terminally disgusted by its hackneyed properties and desperate to snuff itself, and I attempted to ail its ache by dropping in some stylish words, but the thing was beyond repair. I deleted the hopeless line, venturing onward into my scouting journey, where I made note of the following observations, précised below in the equally useful list form: a daisy-chain of moths stretched along three overhead lights; a sabre-toothed tiger in platforms dancing to *Saturday Night Fever*; a pattern of carpet beetles spelling out "Mathematics is the one true artform"; C.B. Hickson perched on the edge of a pancake in deep contemplation; a shaft of moonlight peering into a woman's underwear drawer; a Morrissey impersonator too miserable to sing a note; a plate of chips served with concrete and mortar; C.A. Drayson writing a novel while asleep; the entire alphabet flagellating itself; a tap dripping into a basin with the volume of an airplane crashing into a canyon; an infant prodigy recreating, line for line, Borges' "Pierre Menard, Author of the *Quixote*"; the sixteenth floor temporarily developing wings and travelling to Mars; Red the Fiend biting the shins of Harlequin Romance novelists; a mutation of thrushes driving a Ford Sierra and parking in reception; Russell Hoban resurrected for several minutes to say, "Here's the wine!"; the longest farewell ever recorded at over two years and nine months; a plate of goulash sprouting horns and cursing the Creator; a wax model of Christina Rossetti winking at me; an opaline rendering of Paul Gauguin exposing himself to nuns; the smoking entrails of Arthur Rimbaud cursing his navel; and a donkey meditatively urinating on a picture of my stepfather. These may sound surreal and improbable, but remember, earlier I made the promise that nothing whatsoever in this novel reflects the absolute or approximate truth.

The Trauma Rooms

4

"Our next case: Hattie. She is a former photographer. Brace yourself for her expression."

"Expression?"

The doctor introduced a woman with a fixed rictus—the look of a clown whose children were to be shot if no one in the audience tittered—who bounded up to Erin with a frightening: "Pleased to meet you!" Sensing Erin's terror, she added: "Don't be scared! The trauma I suffered left me looking this way!" Her rictus forced an exclamation point and upward inflection on each utterance. Erin nodded.

"Now, Hattie. If you'd care to tell Erin what happened to you?"

"Why, who is she!?"

"A curious visitor. Do you mind telling her?"

"No! Here's my story, Erin! I began volunteering part-time for the Bretton Agency upon leaving college, and after a successful trial run, I was hired to take author photos to appear on book covers! First in the door, from Birmingham, Alabama, Anthony Vacca! Vacca's debut novel, *Waves of Putridity*, had been praised from pillow to postbox, and Vacca had been hailed the heir to Will Self and Harry Crews! At that time, Vacca sported a side-parting and semiquiff and spent hours practising the perfect 'menacing' expression to appear bad-ass and dark on his inside flap! We settled on the image of him unshaven scowling into the camera, exploiting the mystique around his intense eyes, and the handsome cheekbones! A week later, Vacca had changed his mind and wanted to use the image with his chin perched on his knuckle, half-smiling in an impish way, with the same intense mystique in the eyes! When the hard-cover was released, Vacca was furious that the picture had been compressed for the back flap, claiming that his face could not flour-ish at such a measly ratio, demanding the novel be pulled from the shelves so the publisher could print a larger image to cover the back page! The publisher refused and Vacca threw a public tantrum, in-creasing his media profile! For his next novel, I took over three hundred shots, several topless and holding strange objects (an ap-ple, a ukulele, an iguana), and Vacca was not pleased with a sin-gle one! He brought in a 'monitor' to comment on the manner in which I took the photographs—this 'monitor' made insulting re-marks about my inadequate lighting and low-grade lens, sniggering with Vacca at the 'low calibre' of my work—before firing me, hir-ing expensive lawyers to ensure I was paid not a penny (the lawyer cost outstripped my wage)! My next client, Fiona Rix, was worse! She made me take individual photos of each facial constituent, com-mencing with her left eye, ending with her collarbones! She then chose the preferred shot and sent me away to photoshop the se-lected elements to present the 'best' of her face! I returned with a dire photofit and she exploded, accusing me of incompetence! I explained that even the most skilled photoshopper in the land couldn't transfer these individual shots into a coherent face! She wanted to appear 'coy yet cocksure, steely yet loveable, dynamic yet vulnerable, husky yet svelte, intellectual yet approachable, worldly yet naïve,' among other contradictions! I was then made to pap several hundred facial expressions, and suffer her comments as I touched up the face on photoshop!"

"Sounds painful."

"It was."

"Authors are vain bastards!"

"So we hear."

"See you, Hattie."

"Bye now!"

The Basement

DEVOUT mainstreamist Cheddar Yolk—bestselling author of *Two Guyz, A Gurl, & Aheckafun Part-tay*—was rather aggrieved when one Tuesday he was hurled into a grungy basement against his will, left to shiver for an hour in the cold until an overhead light was turned on by a man with deep divots on his scalp in the shape of blooming chrysanthemums, spreading as if in motion along his forehead to form an ace of spades on his right cheek; Brillo-pad hair singed free, leaving only one wiry strand, combed over and enhanced with tattooed-on follicles that traversed the neck to form an amusing caricature of a ramfeezled librarian; and bearish hands with scratches spirocheting at festive levels of engorgement up his knuckles towards his fingertips—this was Alan, the leading experimental writer of his generation and head of the experimental dept. (A mishap with an ethanol-soaked effigy of Stephen King had wiped out a chesterfield, twelve stationery cabinets, and half of his face).

Cheddar was collared into the lair of the experimentalists: a studio basement where ten restless, twitchy, and hairy men leapt around the room composing prose in every and any form except conventional. A squirrely ginger named Charywarble was making an origami novel, writing a chapter in biro on the twelfth wing of an A5 swan. A scowling goth named Cyphertz was composing an automatic novel by staring into space and typing entirely from her subconscious: the text comprised the words KILL and HATE among two million pages of non sequiturs. A skinny one named Hoopoe lay on the floor channelling his prose through the spirits of the masters, flinging his words upwards after gluing them to beefsteaks—ten mouldering sirloins, forming a curious kind of beefy poetry,

117

dangled from the ceiling. The others included Bryswine, a sweaty ferret composing a book about Shakespeare by whispering the sonnets into a tethered monkey's ear, proffering a banana for every sentence knuckled onto a fat-keyed keyboard; a skeletal oaf named Mortickle who wrote conventional sentences longhand, administering electric shocks every third sentence to create a sense of mental dislocation and physical extremity in the prose, a technique known as Plathitudinizing; and a squat smirker named Poppov who listened to Beethoven's symphonies and typed at the speed of the music—slow, laborious description during the legato stretches and wild illegible spurts during the allegro. Because the rest were busy, Cheddar was dragged to a wide-eyed man in his eighties doing nothing in a chair.

"This is Tendon Palmer. He published books ages ago."

"Nice to shake you. I was the first person to write an entire novel through a stick of Blackpool rock. They called it Suck-lit," he said.

"Unfortunate name," Cheddar said.

"Yes, well. I put my words in people's mouths."

"Must have been a pleasant feeling, having your prose sucked."

"The glory days."

"Tendon is one of the more balanced of our writers. The others have relapsed into Creative Trances," Alan said.

"What you see before you," Tendon said, "are the last dregs of innovation. Reduced to starveling humps of stuttering desperation. To mewling boils of nevereverness. Sad scientists clinging to their hopeless and bizarre attempts to collapse the totalitarian superstate through writing experimental fiction."

"You don't believe you can change anything?"

"I'm waiting to die, guy. Sadly the damp atmosphere seems to be proving beneficial to my health. I should have been dead years ago."

"What do you do?"

"I keep the place tidy. I send Horace up to forage for food," he said. He pointed to Horace, a hulking creature cleaning the floor.

"Is he a writer?"

"No, he's a security guard who ate a radioactive Caramac during the stock dump of '40. We use him as a janitor and hunter in exchange for loving words and a comfy bed."

"Ah."

"We're moving on," Alan said.

"It was nice to meet you, Tendon," Cheddar said.

"Likewise. Hopefully I'll be dead before we meet again."

"I hope so."

Alan sat the irksomely unfazed Cheddar (success made him invulnerable) on an upturned bucket and produced a selection of his bestsellers, including *Don't Gooooo There, Gurlfrenz!*, *Love Iz Kindza Weirdz Sometimez*, and *Put Your Heart upon My Shoulder*. Alan trained his wild bloodshot eyes on the place where Cheddar's soul might have been.

"Well?"

"Well what?"

"What do you have to say for yourself, you vermin?"

"I don't follow."

"Just the titles of these books makes me want to tear out your kidneys and use them as Christmas decorations."

"What's Christmas?"

"Oh, some holiday we used to have . . . never mind that. What are you playing at?"

"Erm . . . being a bestselling writer and not some chump in a basement?"

Alan slapped Cheddar on the cheek. His unfazed face changed to frantic faze as the tears flowed. In the words of Vic Chesnutt, the gravity of the situation became apparent, and Cheddar stammered out his *mea culpa*.

"I'm giving them what they want, they want to read about Stacey and her gurlfrenz—"

"DON'T use that word!"

"Sorry, sorry, I—"

"Look. Here's what is going to happen to you. I am going to

119

brainwash you into believing in experimental techniques by subjecting you to one month of continuous play, and send you back among your own kind to cause untold damage in the department. You are to become one of us."

And Alan began immediately, opening the week by melting "inked" butter pats into brioches so upon melting texts would form for a brief second before being devoured; writing stanzas on paper plates to be spun on sticks in the traditional manner, creating a continuous spinning movement of combinatorial poetic variations each unreadable until the spinning stopped, at which point the plates would fall to the ground before reading was possible; red-inking letters onto the backs of ants and following their progress in the anthill and across the woodland, capturing their movements until a coherent text formed from the scrambling army; lying on the ground staring at the clouds until shapes and impressions formed that might make interesting narratives; writing a straightforward literary story, then replacing each word with its opposite meaning, and in the case of words without opposites, using the word SATCHEL; writing long-winded epics onto the walls and setting fire to the walls to create a new fragged-mented text; and other sorts of kooky notions to create illusions of the new.

As soon as Cheddar was released, he committed suicide by leaping from the roof (he had inked his torso, so the resultant splatter created a very moving text).

Mhairi

4

HELPING maintain food supplies is the most important aspect of what I do. Some floors choose to cultivate a dietary aesthetic, such as the High-Quality Literary Fiction department, which prefers to subside on a diet of Madeira cake and sherry, whereas others aren't particularly fussy what is served. To save, I usually import damaged produce from the Netherlands, or send raiders to steal day-old pastries from the ScotCall Compound bins. This has caused some issues, notably instances of tooth cave spiders in tuna; Alabama cave shrimps in ambrosia creamed rice; Salt Creek tiger beetles in oxtail and leek soup; dysderid spiders in Highland spring water; Xenobolus carniflex millipedes in porridge oats; chinstrap penguins in raspberry marmalade; and on several occasions, Bengal tigers in tubes of toothpaste. The scarring effect of seeing a wild Bengal tiger leaping from the tip of a spearmint double-stripe toothpaste tube cannot be understated. This aberration is caused by products dumped through charities in Third World countries and returned to the distribution sites in the Netherlands unchecked. Unused toothpaste supplies must have been raided by the tiger, who climbed into the tubes to explore, and accidentally sealed themselves inside. C.D. Joelson went to the bathroom to brush his teeth one evening and spotted a hungry Bengal tiger crouching in his bath and narrowly managed to escape with only a gash down his chest and several loose intestines. These tigers are still roaming the building and, as a protected species, cannot be shot or wrestled unless they kill a writer first. If a tiger is seen on the stairwell, the procedure is to stand still and hope it doesn't smell your fear—or, as I do, carry a piece of meat in your pocket at all times and direct the tiger towards the scrap. This can occasionally have repercussions, as when C.B. Radio wore a blazer full of rancid lamb and was mauled by two hunting Bengalis and devoured in the hallway. Diseases can sometimes be imparted via less-than-fresh foodstuffs. The following conditions are to be watched out for: bacterial vaginosis in chocolate brioches, diffuse sclerosis in custard, and Melkersson-Rosenthal syndrome in chocolate gateaux. I have designated a special staffroom for those afflicted with diseases (unkindly called the Leper Lounge), where drugs and treatments are hurled in until folks are cured. There was once the unusual case of C.D. Grunge, more on whom later.

Cal's Tour

Science Fiction

M Y pop-up Irn-Bru book *Whet Yer Whistles* had been no-noed by CHAD and my ideas dried up (with 100 people beavering away on the same topic, original ideas are scarce), so I moseyed up to the fourth floor. Here, a suitably science-fictional wallpaper with swirling black holes, stars, shuttles, and quasars, styles the scenery. In the centre of a large office, four men sit around a saucer-shaped table, curving inwardly towards an antenna in the middle, where books are stacked up its protruding prongs. The carpet is modelled on Mars, with flaming craters streaking along its sensual furriness, and pinned to a back-wall notice board are sliced magazine and newspaper articles, outlining the latest advances in science or supernatural freakeries, with Post-it stickers saying DONE or MAYBE to indicate what ideas have already been filched and pounded into pulpy prose. The writers are middle-aged males in chequered huntsman shirts, unwarty, with partial beards, bestubbled faces, or burgeoning beer bellies. The writers define their depression thus: all ideas for truly innovative SF novels are no longer possible because every nightmare scenario conceivable in the human imagination has come true in the real world, beyond what even the cruellest minds could dream up. They are reduced to writing space operas, alien warfare sagas, zany robot comedies, and stuff about evil bacteria.

They explained on my first day. "You have a new idea," Patrick said, "and you're halfway through a novel, when you open the paper to discover it's already happened. Last month I finished a new work about a hi-tech prison on Mars. I pick up the *ScotCall Science Ex-*

press the next day and discover NASA have already began terraform-
ing Mars to reduce overcrowding on Earth and make the planet
streamlined and free from riff-raff. They're sending all the degen-
erate elements to Mars to create a more sustainable family-centred
Earth for the future. In my novel, a prison riot breaks out on Mars,
and an interplanetary skirmish erupts." He has stubble. "I wrote a
story last week about cyborg elephants," Paul said. "Lo and behold,
I open the *ScotCall Herald* one morning to see that the cyborg animals in a new cyborg zoo have gone on the rampage!" He has a
beer belly. "I wrote about this new drug that cures cancer," Pete
said, "but makes the user's limbs expand in size. Opened the *Scot-
Call Enquirer* last week to discover they've found a cure for cancer
that gives the patient an encephalitic head." He has a partial beard.
"My first book was an unfunny comic novel," Park said, "about a
dystopian future where all the world's artists are rounded up into a
building in the middle of nowhere and made to fend for themselves
in a society that treats culture with contempt. Can you ever imagine such a thing?" There was irony beneath his partial beard. "This
is our problem, Cal. How do you write about a species in relapse
when the species has already reverted back to Cro-Magnon status,
working its way back via troglodyte to tetrapod?" Paul asked.

Hackwork may be your fate, but this floor boasts the most interesting cupboards. One night, sockwalking along the Martian carpet,
trying to prise an original SF concept from my unstirred imaginar-
ium, my socks led me to a sequence of colour-coded closets containing vortexes to alternate realities. A former writer had constructed
these portals to new hypothetical realms in between writing his
novels, and since his defection to ScotCall, they had remained active but unused. The first vortex was a pretty purple swirl powered
by the music of Jon Secada, which showed the user the world as it
was several weeks after his or her death. I stepped into the purple
blaze to a closed closet door on the other side, like walking through
fog. No corporeal transgressions or powerful sensations. I opened
the opposite door into the same office where the four writers sat at
the saucer scratching their stubbles. I was invisible as I passed by.

The second vortex, a yellow swirl powered by The Doors, inverts your present reality. I passed into an office where an army of writers was clacking out SF books for a ravenous population of readers, rattling off one a day to meet the demands of a book-devouring audience queuing in the corridor, itching to get their mitts on the latest book hot off the keys. The queuers hopped like meerkats in expectation. Some passed out from the tension. Others were sexually aroused and humped against the wall. A few were so desperate to read a new sentence, they leapt over the barriers to the writer and read over his shoulder, being dragged to the back of the queue by the security heavies, where they collapsed in a mess of despair and ecstasy!

I fled the madness before they spotted me (famous, of course), and poked my head into the basement. Here, the authors of trashy bestsellers sat in a hot fanless room slowly handwriting their works on nonentities. The top floor was my next destination and I took the functioning lift, basking in the bustle of the building. The tower block had moved to a city entirely populated by identical tower blocks packed with writers and readers. The top floor was floor #147. Up top, the experimental writers (normally in the basement) were luxuriating in chaises longues and sipping cognac, delegating their writing duties to sexy minions. A documentary crew was filming their achievements. The skinny one named Hoopoe who lay back flat flinging beef at the ceiling was talking suavely about his pioneering technique of strapping various sentences channelled through the Immortal Bard to beefsteaks in order to symbolise the inhumanity of man to bovine, while Bryswine the sweaty ferret was clad in the full Oscar Wilde wardrobe, sipping wine and spooning caviar into his hole while whip-cracking a tethered monkey into adding another thousand gobbledybooks to his Shakesimian messterpiece. The others vomited forth about their art: the value of their works to the essentiality of living. I stopped a Cyphertz groupie in the corridor to ask about ScotCall. It was a crumbling shack on the outskirts of Crarsix where desperate phonewhores eked out a useless living selling advice to ill-read dolts. Naturally!

125

My sister Kirsty turned up one week to try and trump me as a writer. A fan of random revenges, she hightailed her pony and mussed up her locks for a staticky artist style—a van de Graaphic coltish voltage—and moseyed over to the despairing writers. She believed her ideas were amazing because she believed she was amazing and so any product from her must, by simple logical deduction, be amazing too. The writers sat stunned that a creature of such attractiveness had appeared from nowhere and was talking at them with such unlicensed pluck—the fact of her femaleness sparked some sexual memories, despite having long ago shut down their libidos to lead lives of asexual hermitry. "All right," she said, bounding before the noticeboard where she made herself a pitching platform. "So how about this alien and this robot fight over a hot human, but at the end we discover the hot human is a hologram? Or how about there's this planet where everyone has like huge chins and everyone in the universe laughs at them until in the next interplanetary war, they're called up to use their chins to deflect asteroids, and everyone respects them, before having them killed and their chins served to the alpha-species as lunch? Or how about this super-whizz space computer is outsmarted by a really thick little urchin boy, and the whole universe becomes a dribbling mess of brainless duncery?" There was stunned silence. "What do you mean *becomes*?" Park said. "Or this planet where everyone has to shag thirty times a day to survive, and these two horny guys from Earth are dropped there only to discover their libidos aren't as restless as they bragged they were? Maybe they're locked up and fitted with artificial cocks? Or how about this: two preggo women give birth to alien squids who strangle their mothers afterwards and all the dads have to raise the alien squids as their own kids, and later the human race can only be saved by inseminating a virgin who hates kids but who has to gestate the last remaining baby from some dude's magic sperm and save the human race." I offered a sarcastic cough. "Is anyone writing these down?" Pete asked.

Later, Kirsty told me this tale. She was nosing around the corridors and peeped inside a utility closet, where a vacuum nozzle fell and opened a secret compartment covered by an ironing board. Inside was a narrow corridor with a pink light in the distance. Ten steps along she found the source—a luminescent octopus, alert and slimy on its plinth, pink tentacles fanning the air in a hypnotic movement. She was instantly entranced, staring mindlessly as the creature expanded a friendly tentacle and cupped her waist. The octopus was jellylike, with no homocentric patterning or barnacled eczema along each tentacle, only a sliminess that "felt loving and ethereal through my clothes and on my skin." As she moved like a sleepwalker towards the beguiling pink mollusc, an overwhelming flurry of sensations took over, from awe to arousal, to passion and turmoil. She swooned into its eight enfolding tentacles, seizing her waist in a love-hold and cuddled up to its boneless nucleus, squeezing tight in passionate devotion like a helpless lover, nuzzling into its hard beak as it sat on her shoulder. Radiance and pleasure rippled through her in "unholy amounts." She was lost in an alien clutch of happiness, elation, and all sorts of unKirstylike emotions! In her trance, she was transported under the ocean, travelling past a school of showy tropical fish, up rocky coral reefs, flicking Vs at passing sharks, and into a cove where there lurked a sort of octopus brothel. She was placed on a bed of reeds as a kaleidoscope of pulsing tentacles descended on her, draping their restlessly twitchy arms along her body, where she experienced stabs of violent pleasure, her nerve endings stretched beyond the commonplace of simple orgasmic ecstasy.

As a side-effect of her erotic tussle with the octopus, Kirsty became a writer of genius, on a par with the fêted and rated down the ages (whose books were swiftly passing from public awareness). The creature had been placed in the cupboard by an under-read SF writer who wrote books too complex for the mass market and, as a two-fingered salute to his failure, bred the octopus to do harm. He created the creature by the cunning manipulation of light, using visual effects, mirrors, and electromagnetic sensations, alongside a powerfully seductive scent, to hypnotise anyone who caught its gaze. There was no actual deep-sea mollusc present. As to its special powers, he had used a rare form of black magic taken from Native American settlers during the time of Custer, filling anyone under the octopus's sway with unlimited talent, so long as they surrendered their bodies to its love forever. Several SF writers had become office-wide successes, writing work as timeless as Bradbury or Asimov, but became so addicted to the octopus's love, they suffered multiple strokes through over-exertion. She completed her masterpiece *The Suture*, a sprawling SF epic encompassing particle physics, neuroscience, philosophy and religion, over the space of twenty-nine days, and on the thirtieth day I had to kill her affair before the affair killed her. I arrived to unplug as she was hitting her forty-ninth octogasm. She was too elated to notice anything except the loving fuck-frays of her mollusc lover, but the octopus was alert to the invasion and swung one of its tentacles as I reached for the wall plugs. I flicked off the multisocket, knocked Kirsty off the plinth, and hurled a bucket of water over the electrics, which fizzled and crackled. I fled the room to the sound of Kirsty's semi-sexy hysterical howls, shooting up to the roof to save my hide from skinning (withdrawal from that thing was TOUGH).

I never completed my book, not with Kirsty hovering. She criticised my every line. "Let me see your opening," she said. *The mist evaporated over the sullen hills.* "Mist can't evaporate. It's not made of water. How can hills be sullen? I've never seen a hill looking sullen in my life. Next?" *In the distance, the roar of gunfire pierced the call of the birds.* "Distance from whom? Aren't all hills, even sullen ones, in the distance? Gunfire can't roar, it's not an animate thing. It doesn't pierce the sound birds make, it pierces flesh and makes holes in people. Who are the birds calling? I wasn't aware birds could operate telephones while flying over sullen hills. Next?" *Terence turned on his heels and walked the other way—* "Who is called Terence in this day and age? How exactly can he turn on his heels? Does he have castors instead of feet? What way is he walking? You haven't said which way he's facing in the first place. Next?" *—towards the horizon where rain pattered down in drops upon his weary forehead.* "Is this horizon in the distance? Does rain patter? I didn't know rain had feet. And drops? Rain appears in *drops*? Really, that is a revelation! And how exactly can a forehead be weary? Foreheads can't feel." And so on. I only wrote four pages before quitting.

A Word from the Team

PATRICK: A classification crisis hit us here in the SF department recently. Park and I thought our writer's block stemmed from the fact *science-fiction* had become redundant as a classification, since SF referred to a postwar notion of futuristic horrors and had nothing to do with present reality. Since we already occupy the dystopian future popularised in 20th century SF, a new title was needed for the genre that encompassed the kitchen-sink realism at the heart of our writing. Paul and Peter believed a name change would lead to our two readers boycotting the books, that our readers liked SF precisely because it blinkered the horrors of their present reality by keeping them the stuff of books, and they would rather be deluded their whole lives than pick up a newspaper. Park and me decided *horrealism* was a better title, since we were simply taking their ideas from the news and blowing up the most horrific elements of each story anyway. Eventually we came to a truce, keeping *horrealism* as a sub-genre of the larger SF bracket, so we're open again to take your fresh ideas (and your souls!) So guys—what is SF exactly? Define.

PETE: Seriously?

PARK: Science-fiction.

PAUL: Right. Robots and aliens.

PETE: A little more to it than that . . .

PARK: Not much more.

PATRICK: What about ideas? Any top-of-the-headers?

PAUL: Here's one. There's this soldier . . .

PETE: And?

PAUL: And he clones himself to fight in the next world war. So he sends his clone off to fight for him but the clone turns traitor and defects to the other side. When the war ends, the clone evades capture and is assumed dead. But his reputation as the biggest war criminal is so strong a worldwide witch-hunt for his head is on. The original soldier finds himself on the lam for crimes he didn't commit. He loses his wife and kids and respect in the village and ends up . . .

PETE: And?

PAUL: Still working on the ending.

PATRICK: That's not a bag of old bogeys.

PARK: No magic sperm, at least.

PATRICK: Write it and we'll publish it. If you have any ideas like that, come work with us in the SF department. Looking forward to hearing from you all.

PAUL: And sucking out your souls!

PATRICK: Always.

A Better Life

4

W E escaped Arxle and were downhearted to observe at the end of the road that the small beach we had fought to find had been paved over. I refrained from theatricals since I had expected this and had been clinging to the pleasures of delusion since leaving The House. We strolled along the shore as water lapped against the concrete, hoping still to encounter the commune where a Better Life was supposed to await us somewhere along the way. I had packed provisions and was irked when I had to share a sandwich with Rob, who accepted the pickle and cheese without a word of thanks, resenting that I bagseyed the ham. We progressed along the shore, past a neverending sequence of concrete fields, until dusk approached. As we were about to bed down on the concrete for the evening I noticed a light in the distance, what a more poetical writer (I was never one) might call an *ignis fatuus*. We moved towards it and found a feral black-haired man in a tent eating skate by candlelight.

"Fuck d'you want?" he welcomed.

"Are you the commune?"

"There is no fucking commune. Bog off back to ScotCall."

"Who are you?"

"I live here *alone* and survive by spearing skate with this twig. There's barely enough fish for one, so I won't be having company," he said. He produced what appeared to be a bazooka welded together with two toasters.

"What's over there?" I asked, gesturing to the rest of the coast.

"They paved over the coast and put up ScotCall kiosks. Fishermen work there answering questions on how to debone halibut."

"Right," I said. "Time to go back . . . and kill ourselves?"

"Or . . .?" Rob trailed off.

"Yes? Or what?"

"I was going to suggest we kill all the old ladies in the village and create a commune there using the houses, but that's probably—"

"—a great idea!"

"Oh! I wasn't expecting that reaction. I thought you might find it too extreme."

"No, it's amazing! We can use that trick you did on the bus."

"Cool!"

"Wait wait!" the black-haired man said. "You're going to butcher the entire village and steal their houses? I want in on this."

"Oh. Not sure about that. After all, you weren't very welcoming—"

"Let me come or I'll blow your cocks off with my Man-Blaster."

"Yes. OK. Nice to meet you."

His device was a makeshift bazooka. Scraps of fried appliances were fed into the slots and fired with lethal force at the victim. The Man-Blaster would prove a useful device if Rob's undescribed murder method proved ineffective. We mobilised as a threesome at the Unwelcome to Arxle sign. You have to understand (before I describe the mass slaughter of a dozen senior citizens) that these people were dead inside. We were merely ending their corporeal presence on this regrettable planet, their minds were long gone. Our mass slaughter was—perhaps—a charitable act. Our friend with the bazooka was named Pete and claimed to be the son of experimental writer Christopher Sorrentino (himself the son of experimental writer Gilbert Sorrentino) and docmartined the door to the first house. He fired up his Man-Blaster and blew holes in a bunneted tinker as he was answering a query about the sheerest denier of tights for trainee drag queens. I was somewhat taken aback at Pete's brutality, but I could see he had been longing to do this for a while and felt the same ecstatic release as I when the victim's arms were blown from his torso and totalled the phonograph.

"That was easy. Of course, you realise when ScotCall detects an inactive unit there will be inquiries and agents dispatched immediately?"

"Oh."

"But that's solvable. You need to keep flicking the switchboard. What we need to invent is a device that automatically switches to a new caller every five minutes. You two work on that while I blow the fuckpants out of this old bint next door."

"Erm . . . all right."

The *Farewell, Author!* Conference

4

The exact number of invited writers turned up before the set starting time, so the organisers closed the Fossilfoods doors, and Julian Porter stood to deliver his welcome address. As he cleared his throat, a knowing Sheila Heti called out "HEARD IT!" as a comment on the clichéd nature of public addresses, implying that delivering such a clichéd address in a room with such august personnel was ill-advised. Sadly for Sheila, no one picked up her subtlety, and Kjersti A. Skomsvold poked her in the ribs.

"Thank you, wonderful writers—"

"And Jonathan Safran Foer!" someone (George Saunders) heckled.

"—for attending this conference, on this special if somewhat sombre occasion. Tonight, we will be reminiscing—"

"On our shit careers!" Joe Matt said.

"Speak for yourself!" Charles Burns said.

"I was!"

"—about your triumphs and failures, and attempting to recall some of your most memorable passages. We had several cups of cola and a few lumps of chocolate, but unfortunately, someone helped themselves!"

"That fast-fingered lardass Picoult!" J.K. Rowling said. "Writes with a pack of Twinkies beside the computer."

"Shut up!" Jodi replied. Most of the writers smirked at the clichéd nature of this response as being indicative of her unoriginal way with words.

"We encourage several of you to take to the stage here as the evening unfolds and to send off this Golden Age of literature in style. It's a sombre occasion, but that doesn't mean we can't have an absolutely fabulous time."

Before this sentence ended, the insistent fingers of 97-year-old T.C. Boyle clasped the microphone and Julian was nudged off the stage. T.C., with his lean frame and updraught of grey hair, mounted the stage like an anorexic Don King. "I would like to recall some of my work, if I may crave your indulgence. This is from my first story collection, *Descent of Man*," he began. He read for ten minutes from the same story until an enraged Michel Houellebecq shouted in French: "The fucker's going to read his collected works!"[1] A shoe was hurled towards the stage, and boos chased him off.

Joshua Cohen sneaked on stage behind a retreating Boyle, whose sprightliness should have been an inspiration to the assembled, but these people had put up with new novels and collections from him for too long. Cohen was an unsmiling Jewish intellectual with the lost look of a child prodigy whose eagerness to know everything had recently been spiked by the realisation he will only ever know a meagre fraction of some things.

"I would like to read from a new work. Here is a short passage," he said, and said nothing for two minutes. Some smirked. Others frowned. It was clear he was making a potent statement on the death of literature in this terrifying age, although opinion was divided as to his statement's overall potency.

"Best thing you've done," George Saunders said.

"So powerful," Nicole Krauss said.

"Stage-hogging brat," Adam Thirlwell said.

"Echoes of John Cage," Jackie Kay said. Reluctant applause followed.

No one approached the microphone for an hour. Reluctant interactions followed. Kirsty Logan spoke to Cris Mazza about whether frozen prawns could revivify themselves after being left in near freezing conditions for four decades; Alan Warner spoke

---

[1] "Le baiseur va lire ses recueillies œuvres!"

to Stacey Richter about the lurid lighting in the room, and Stacey pretended to love the word "lurid," despite her dwindling interest in language as a concept; Nicholson Baker spoke to C.D. Rose about the origin of the postage stamp for seven minutes before C.D. collapsed into a heavy coma on a bag of burst sprouts; Julia Slavin spoke to Jeff Bursey about how she had, in homage to her story "Dentaphilia," a thousand extra teeth implanted in her body, and the adverse consequences this had on her marriage and subsequent short-lived relationships; Jonathan Franzen spoke to Louis Bury on the problem of sourcing special extra-soft linens for those whose skin was sensitive after showering or bathing; Ana Kordzaia-Samadashvili spoke to Guy Delisle about having to translate English soft porn into Georgian to make a living between novels, and her struggle to render phrases like "spiffing good fuck" and "pleasant shag" into her native; Stewart Home spoke to Aki Ollikainen about his time singing lead vocals for anarchist punk and dubstep outfit, Faulty Lamenters, in such a fashion that Aki suspected the group might not exist, or that Stewart might be incorporating a pipe dream into conversation for lack of something meaningful to say; Irvine Welsh spoke to Tom Bissell on the challenges of pretending to hail from a working-class background for his entire career, and the unfortunate ways in which he found himself becoming more working class through osmosis; Lynne Tillman spoke to Will Self on once accidentally torching the office where two chancers made a small fortune peddling Wikipedia articles as print-on-demand books to people desperate for reading material on their favourite topics; Antoine Volodine spoke to Stewart Lee about how Holly Golightly's second LP *The Main Attraction* was released on vinyl in 1995, then re-released on CD in 2001, causing dim critics to label this her sixth solo effort; Lance Olsen spoke to Paul Emond on the impossibility of sourcing his grandson a star-shaped bicycle clip ever since the industry was taken over by virulent anti-Semites who refused to manufacture anything resembling the Star of David; Alona Kimhi spoke to Lasha Bugadze on becoming a bestseller in France because of a naked fat woman on the cover of her novel, and the invites to attend fat orgies in Paris bordellos despite her being a lissom individual, and the backlash from fat people upon realising the author was not one of them but exploiting them for humour; Nicola Barker spoke to Benjamin Stein about the first drive-thru burger restaurant on a train platform to open at Clapham Junction, where customers would phone their orders ahead, and staff would pass the burgers and cokes in through the windows, and how this proved so popular, each station in turn opened a drive-thru until two or three were placed between each station, forcing the trains to slow down so food could be fired in through the windows, causing extreme delays, and often hot drinks exploding over commuters' faces or chilli sauce staining clothes; Deborah Levy spoke to Ornela Vorpsi on the spate of younger and younger King Lears, culminating in a 22-year-old actor playing the part after his success in a popular TV franchise, and how Shakespeare had been cut to only 40-minute snippets after audiences began walking out of performances over an hour; Alex Kovacs spoke to Christine Montalbetti on the allegations around his business selling 2400GB USB sticks being a falsehood, and how his team had developed remarkable compression techniques so that a staggering amount of data could reside inside a USB no larger than a toddler's pinkie; Jang Jung-Il spoke to Percival Everett on his desire to exist in a permanent state of movement blur, as in a camera with slow shutter speed, and how this was achieved through clothes exuding a strobe lighting effect; Xiaolu Guo spoke to Sergio de la Pava on her preference for a bag of frozen sweetcorn to be placed on her head in the event of a fever, since due to a traumatic incident with peas as a child that she didn't wish to discuss in detail, peas left her in a state of manic terror; Robert Shearman spoke to D.T. Max on the surgical procedure he had to place Dalek bumps on his chest and back, and to have a nose that extended outward in the manner of a Dalek's sink plunger, and his lucrative life as a "man-Dalek," appearing at fan conferences for extortionate fees, and how the bumps had to be removed when each of them was found to be cancerous; Vendela Vida spoke to Mark Dunn on the outrage at waking up one morning as the face of *Woodlice Weekly*, a weekly periodical devoted to studies and tips for the removal of woodlice, despite having not endorsed her image for this purpose, and the humorous email exchange with the editor, who had mistaken her face for that of Jennifer Bower, Canada's top expert on treating woodlice in the home, and the settlement of $3,500 for the trauma Vendela underwent at being on the cover of this publication; Todd McEwen spoke to Jacques Jouet about whether this suicide pact was really happening, as he had a debt collector stalking him, and a contract killer on his tail after sleeping with a rich woman in the hope she might toss him a million or so, and was quite keen to end himself that night; Laurent Binet spoke to Jon Fosse on the failure of his daughter to reach the final leg of the world ballet championships in Krakow, and his attempts as a loving father to temper her rage and disappointment at this failure, while suppressing his own rage at not having a world champion ballet dancer for a daughter despite the money he haemorrhaged into this long and time-consuming attempt (during which he had neglected to write a single page of his next war novel); Magdalena Zurawski spoke to Lee Klein on the decent turnout that evening, and Lee nodded in concurrence, before the conversation fell into an awkward silence, and Magdalena looked around for someone she recognised to save her from this pain, and finding no one, made the cardinal mistake of asking Lee what he'd written, thus showing her ignorance of his oeuvre, at which Lee attempted to skulk off elsewhere, but finding himself blocked by a seven-strong wall of writers, was forced into salvaging the even-more-awkward exchange with this writer he had never heard of and who had never heard of him by pretending the offence never happened and naming three of his published works, at which Magdalena nodded in mock-interest, and Lee was forced to ask her what she had written in response, at which she became offended, and finding her side was free for an escape, made this into a thicket of writers, at which Lee breathed an enormous relieved sigh until he noticed someone (Micheline Aharonian Marcom) walking towards him whom he had never read, and that she was spreading her arms with a welcoming "Lee!", kissing him on each cheek and launching into a thorough appraisal of his novels, at which he muttered thanks, and tried to postpone the mounting dread at having to praise the works of this novelist about whom he knew nothing, not even her first name, and to end the exchange, pretended to need the bathroom desperately, and said that he was frightfully sorry for his rudeness, but that he'd been holding it in for hours, and there was simply not a moment to spare, and Micheline laughed and pointed him towards the toilets, warning him to look out for the rat-roaches that had already bitten Tom Whalen's penis twice this evening, and Lee muttered thanks, heading towards the toilets, in front of which stood Magdalena Zurawski deep in conversation with Peter Dimock, and since Micheline was watching him to ensure he went the right way, was forced to ask Magdalena to move, interrupting their chat, having to endure the dirty look on her face, and Peter's message "Watch the rats don't bite your cock off, chappie!", at which Magdalena laughed, by way of laughing at Lee, and Lee went into the toilet for his pretend piss, finding Sam Lipsyte on the floor clutching his penis while three rat-roaches circled his body, zoning in for the kill, and Lee picked up a broom and beat the creatures to death, helping Sam up towards the sink to cool his aching penis in the water, wondering if this was a better alternative to an awkward exchange with Micheline, and looked at Sam's bitten and swollen penis, and concluded that it wasn't; among other conversations.

Things to do before writing the next paragraph

... salt pemmican; violate a traffic code and face a £50 fine; crumble under interrogation; invite a retired postman to a soiree; complain about the lipstick smear on a new VCR; upset a Marxist with a misquotation from Engels; dream about strumming Graham Coxon's Stratocaster; reach skyward and attempt to stroke a cumulus; count to one million while reciting the Phoenician alphabet; lend a neutral opinion to a friend and complain when the friend uses the neutral opinion in conversation; use the *vous* form when addressing a French musician about the benefits of the pentatonic scale in improvised samba numbers; collect used nappies or diapers for four decades and sell the loot to a collector on your deathbed; abolish the male skirt at funerals; invent a tricorne to be worn by bankers in board meetings; ululate during a meeting calling for the abolition of ululators; knit a picture of Jane McVeigh that looks more like Barbara McBride; transfer nine pounds into a savings account and set fire to each branch of that bank in the country; pencil in an appointment with a pen salesman; insult a kind-hearted chimp and pour cream on his knuckle; call for a ban on ideograms; encourage a priest to insult his congregation; erect a matchstick homage to Elton John outside the hospital; pretend to misunderstand a basic command for so long genuine incomprehension occurs; retaliate with a two-hour F15 missile strike when an old lady drops her contact lens into your soup; complain about the inadequate scansion in all rap albums to the British Poetry Council; diagnose a dragon with ADHD; yodel at such a volume your lungs are declared a public health hazard; complain vehemently when your anecdote about grandpa being slowly devoured by lung cancer isn't declared a comic masterpiece; invent the perfect recipe for goulash and refuse to make a single bowl; appear on a TV chat show and discuss at length your genital warts and fondness for bestiality; confuse a genitive clause with a German Panzerkampfwagen IV; lick over three thousand ice lollies to prove an incoherent point; send a raunchy text message to your best friend's grandmother; phone your ex-girlfriend to complain about the quality of her diction during intercourse; select from over one hundred hopefuls a person to play the lead role in *Badgers, Badgers! We Love Thee!: A Hexagrammic Musical*; invade an East European nation with nothing but a pogo stick and pluck; sign on the dole for sixty-five years, take a job in a supermarket for one day, then retire; beat a timid little girl at capture the castle viciously and unsportingly; stick your nose into a policeman's helmet; point out to the groom that he has dandruff on his shoulder five seconds before the vicar pronounces man and wife; try out all the caskets at a funeral parlour for size, then tell the undertaker with a deadly sinister expression the selected casket is for him; have a baby with three noses named Anosmia; irrigate anything that needs irrigating in the general area; write to the heirs of Patrick Moore grousing that Cassiopeia is the most insipid constellation in all Polaris; misspell a word for over seventy years on purpose merely to spite a pedant; spoil someone's birthday party by telling everyone it's your birthday as well, and stage a rival birthday party in the corner of the room, trying to lure everyone to your side with free liquor; rent a marquee for nine years with nothing but a potted plant inside and charge £4,000 for entry; spend nine million dollars on a pea; kidnap Nicholas Parsons and force him to speak for a year without hesitation, repetition or deviation, or he dies; marry a woman and say absolutely nothing to her for the rest of your life; sit yawning in the theatre only when your actor friend is performing his soliloquy; invent a 24-hr webcam programme where active cameras are sent through the post to random recipients; found an organisation that pays literary writers vast fees to praise utterly fucking awful novels; lead a public campaign to have cactuses issued free on the NHS, and be very belligerent and defensive when people laugh at your campaign in the media; adopt a homeless child and raise her to be a mathematical wunderkind, and when she leaves home, blame her bitterly for eating all the kumquats; gyrate in a straight line for nine hours, snapping at anyone who argues that gyration cannot be performed vertically; noodle on the clavinet outside a wine bar to see if anyone cocks their necks and looks at you; turn up at the police station on a daily basis begging to be convicted of any unconvicted crime; be a really swell human being for ninety-nine years, and on your deathbed, call everyone a bunch of useless and disgusting cunts; be a really rancid human being for ninety-nine years, and on your deathbed, call everyone a bunch of beautiful and lovely free spirits; stay in a B&B and pester the owner to open a bowling lane and a sodomy room so he can change the acronym to B&B&B&B (Bed and Breakfast and Bowling and Buggery); photocopy a tedious story about a cravat salesman tripping in the Trossachs, and leave copies on the seats of every bus in Northern Ireland; strenuously deny the rumours that you have been urinating on a farmer's lettuce, then sixteen years later send him a box of piss-covered lettuce with the note IT WAS ME, YOU FOOL!; boast about having scaled Ben Nevis with nothing but a cardigan and a toilet plunger; lie about everything your entire life except where you've hidden the bodies; make a really weak pun about people acting like "bumbling" bees while surrounded by extremely witty wits, then cry in the toilet after your humiliation; order a pizza by phone with no cheese, tomato sauce, or pizza base, and when the pizza delivery boy arrives, sue him for delivering an invisible pizza; become proficient at the xylophone simply because you are a human being and have the power to do so; remain in a permanent state of bewilderment as to the qualities of an augmented 7th; rewrite the entire canon of *Famous Five* novels, increasing the casual racism and upping the anal sex scenes between Julian and Timmy; find schoolboy humour extremely disagreeable your entire life, then on your deathbed collapse in hysterics at the word "cockshaft"; pepper pemmican; drive a milk float with the same determination as a Formula 1 car; sit on the dock of

the bay badmouthing everything Otis Redding ever sang; walk a
tightrope in stilettos and prohibit filming of the act; do something
spontaneous for someone who hates surprises and grouse bitterly
when they cry in your arms; open a shop selling only VCRs, cas-
settes, and Sega Mega Drives called *It's the Early '90s, You Morons!!*;
open your mouth permanently in case someone one day flings in
a slice of Parma ham; disassemble the British Monarchy and turn
Buckingham Palace into the world's largest bouncy castle; stand in
the local election as the No Promises No Future party, and promise
nothing to everyone who votes, and absolutely no prospects for anyone in the future, and when the No Promises No Future party is
elected, go back on your promise of no promises and no future and
give people absolutely everything they want and a brilliant future,
and face a backlash from a disappointed and angrily fulfilled elec-
torate; meet an Albanian man in Egypt and ask him what the hell
he, an Albanian man, is doing in Egypt; create a fictional stockbro-
ker who loves to read the novels of Charles Dickens, Wilkie Collins,
and William Makepeace Thackeray; sinisterly insert completely innocuous pills into people's drinks at parties; upset an upsilon; accuse Hungarians of being a nation of herbivores while taunting
them with rancid meat; rev your engine noisily beside a sign saying "Please don't rev your engine noisily beside this sign that reads
'Please don't rev your engine noisily' "; pressure a shy wolf into riding a unicycle for the amusement of your depressed teenage son;
blame Jason for everything bad that has happened to Kylie, and
blame Kylie for everything bad that has happened to you; make an
error while writing in the second person while brushing my hair;
take a stand on the abolition of chairs on trams; read every item on
this list nine times, laughing even more hysterically at each entry
until you wet the entire village with your chortled-up urine; telephone Bob Dylan praising his unpopular Christian records; telephone Daniel O'Donnell praising his sexy blues records; slip inside
the eye of your mind, surprised when you find a better place to play;
purchase a ridiculous amount of patio furniture even though you
live in a one-bedroom flat on the fourth floor; read the novels of

Hubert Selby and thank your lucky stars you are none of the poor bastards portrayed; axe a long-running American sitcom starring Norm MacDonald despite the ratings being larger than any programme in the known universe; sing a song of sixpence when you have no vocal chords and only threepence; dance a mazurka in the rain and cry tears of monumental happiness; braid the hair of the Scarlet Pimpernel; torment the number seventy by comparing it to the far more impressive eighty and ninety; erect a monument to the actor Alan Alda on a Drumchapel council estate; invent a traffic calming system involving acts of inhumane torture on prisoners performed on roadsides to distract drivers from their road rage; make a papier-mâché angel and call her Nellie R. Cauldron; pass a law prohibiting the illegal use of fireworks inside a whale; open a water stand dispensing free water on summer days; close a water stand dispensing free water on summer days and open a shop charging £4.50 for a bottle of lukewarm tap water; open a prawn-broker selling and purchasing a variety of prawns; write a novel exploiting a war or a tragedy with cheap emotional manipulation and appear on a talk show making earnest and faux-profound remarks about the power of love to transcend all evil and horror; assume that the thing Jeff said last night was a veiled reference to your alcohol problem and cold-shoulder him when you see him next; lure a barn owl to your bathroom using a dead rodent on a string and, once trapped, take a series of erotic snaps of its naked wings; barbecue in a barber's queue; record a nine-hour tribute album to Barbra Streisand consisting of rambling descriptions of each of her songs; write a comment on *The Guardian* website expressing how, in your esteemed opinion, the Prime Minister is a useless fucker, and his cabinet are Cambridge tossers who know nothing about common people, and that all MPs can be dismissed due to being exactly the same in personality and motive, and fail to offer a workable solution to this state of affairs; hound Barbra Streisand until she reinstates the missing "a" from her forename; volunteer for nine weeks in a charity shop until you smell of old lady's cupboards and damp cardboard; commit suicide by taking four million aspirin; blame Lisa

Loeb for the rise in irritating pulchritudinous pixie singers who write about human relationships in a twee but quirky way, with a sideline in fashion modelling and sitcom appearances; work for a spell at the *West Lothian Courier* and decide drinking bleach is a more appealing alternative; spend a week reading the prison diaries of Harold Shipman and write a favourable review on Goodreads; shave a pineapple even if the raspberry protests; mount an expedition on John Cleese; confuse a smart person by lying about your favourite Louis Zukofsky poem; bribe a prison guard into smuggling a Garfield duvet into your cell; telephone a radio show and at a random moment in the conversation declare that *Kind Hearts and Coronets* is your favourite film, and when the host asks why you mentioned that film, pretend you never said anything; stalk the critic James Wood for a fortnight and write a 10,000-word review of his gait; devise a system of semaphore using pinkies only; learn how to pole-vault but refuse to demonstrate your skill to the wider world unless asked by Tom Robbins; zap something beginning with a "z" for the sake of alliteration; start a soccer team in Manchester, firing anyone who uses the word "football"; end an item in a list with a colon instead of a semicolon to confuse the reader: dunk your chocolate biscuit into an open coconut; stay up all night listening to the records of The Clash, complaining bitterly about "Wrong 'Em Boyo" on *London Calling*; ban the use of italics in swimming pools; enter a room with incredible self-confidence, but cower in fear and paranoia once you reach your desk; invite a snake handler out to dinner and refuse to pay your share of the bill; eat only Pot Noodles for sixty-six years, then have a slice of halibut; climb into an onion and lose the fight to remain unemotional; take your driving test in a pink mini while wearing a tutu; take your mother's advice to never fart in a lift; break the sound and speed barrier in a milk float; place a thistle in a strategic place; ring the bells whenever a carrier pigeon successfully delivers a short missive about the Baba Vida fortifications; compose a haiku on the difference between albino chefs and Parisian chefs; compose a sonnet on the rarity of albino chefs from Paris; channel the spirit of Rayner

Heppenstall; leap up and down like a teenage girl at a pop concert when the vicar is reading the last rites; ladle too much pumpkin soup into your bowl; pollinate a beehive using telekinesis; pollute a river with liquid sewage; ruin a small child's birthday party sellotaping his friends' mouths shut; accentuate the negative; balance a piano on your knee; use the word "bacchanalian" while driving a forklift drunk; create a form of ponderous ellipsis consisting of twenty periods (i.e. . . . .); salt the universe; make a remark that nadir is the apotheosis of words meaning the lowest point; suggest a game of Twister as they are filling in your mother's grave; oil the hinges with love; grease the monkey with hate; contact the Health and Safety department of your local hospital just to say hi; throw a temper tantrum when the tomato juice is destroyed; rewrite this sentence in a more jaunty manner; blow your wad at the least appropriate moment; conduct a year-long investigation into when is the least appropriate moment to blow one's wad; question the nature of beekeepers; operate heavy machinery when drowsy with a plastic bag over your head while drunk; phlogisticate air; dream big and lower your expectations; change your diet to less healthy foods and blow your belly out your waistband; accuse your fiancée of stealing your money while walking down the aisle; abseil down a conifer; brood for hours on whether there is or is not a Godard; make the world seem brighter by dancing on a Ritz cracker; wear the tackiest socks in the world with pride; hire a dominatrix for the evening and simply watch TV and talk about the weather; create a Facebook profile for Roddy Occult, invite all his friends, and post sexually aggressive comments about his mother; employ a personal assistant to read your mail, paying him handsomely for this minimal amount of work, then one day sack him for being a lazy feckless sponger; punch a barista for making a loveheart in your coffee's foam; punch a barista for having the job title "barista"; rap one of your pupils across the knuckles for not knowing how to spell "diuretically," and at the tribunal rip off your clothes to reveal a tattoo across your chest: IT'S DIURETICALLY, YOU TURD!!; sing "Knockin' on Heaven's Door" once inside Heaven to psyche the angels; dress like a tramp to attend a job interview for Head Programmer at KXS Electrics Affiliated; really hate yourself while drinking hot chocolate; really hate someone else while drinking a tiger's urine; boil your underpants in a vat of gelatine; start an anti-fracking campaign and systematically block the government's attempts to introduce fracking procedures in your or any country, while secretly thinking fracking is fucking awesome; put a chocolate bar in your lunchbox every day except Thursday; read a chimpanzee his rights in a colourful vest; appear bewildered when looking at an aquarium; demonstrate the difference between an octagon and a hexagon to a simpleton; wring the neck of a jazzy pheasant; pretend to be a lemur while affecting an irritating insouciance; debate the merits of breastfeeding while sucking on bottled milk and draining a bovine's teat; quiz a questioner, question a quizzer, and delete my internet cache; bandy about but utterly refuse to caper; hustle but absolutely refuse to bustle; have a very intense game of Boggle while giving birth to triplets; conduct the London Philharmonic using a Curlywurly, surreptitiously nibbling down the confection until the orchestra collapses; abuse an adze; spend nine years duffing up old ladies, and when in the dock at the criminal court, pick your nose and make raspberry sounds with your armpits and generally appear immature and unbothered, and when sentenced to six months, rise with a shrug and say, *"Whatevvvver!"*; declare Tonga a principality on the BBC World Service and throw a hissy fit when the reporter challenges your declaration with cries of "It *is* a principality! Tom's mum said so! I get everything I want!"; meet the charming and fragrant David Wilson; kidnap and eat the charming and fragrant David Wilson; bump into the writer Bo Fowler and during the chat cough "Vonnegut imitator!" under your breath; read *Three Trapped Tigers* by Guillermo Carbera Infante rather than sitting on your pathetic arse talking drivel with your inane friends; slap an elephant on the rump and break down crying and confess your harassment to a psychiatrist then make amends by apologising to the elephant and offering to galvanise his beautiful tusks with gold; sing a haunting Celtic ballad to seduce Bill Gates; interview former Prime Minister Tony Blair, asking him extremely trivial questions about his favourite boy bands, glamour mag babes, and types of spicy food, then before the interview is over, ask him how he feels to be a warmongering baby-killing psychopath selling arms to Iraq and buying Porsches with the profits; force a poor man to pass through the eye of a needle to prove he is destined for Heaven; shake your maracas in public, smiling and encouraging children to take a shake, then realise that you have been shaking and encouraging children to touch your penis; complain loudly about your fourth nipple; send an erotic telegram to a court jester; convert to Judaism for a laugh; open a kiosk selling only rubber mice; come on to a cosmonaut; lounge lizardly in a hammock; attend a PTA meeting and yell obscenely about the lack of atoms in the room; be spellbound by a prosaic duck; rage against the dying of the light, knowing full well that light cannot die because light is not sentient; open a Pandora's box and eat the coffee liqueurs; use "synecdoche" in a literary conversation and smile cheekily when everyone nods, pretending to know what it means; take your sister to the shops and buy her a custard slice; enervate a peach slice; force the Queen to abdicate, make her work in a supermarket for the rest of her life, and rehouse her in a council flat with no central heating then on her deathbed, say "Only joking!" and reinstate her power; susurrate like there's no tomorrow; tell an obscene joke about a Swiss hooker and a Scottish virgin on your first date with the Pope; reach over and try to squeeze a breast on your first date with Prince Charles; steal the lizards from the Galapagos Islands and start a circus act in Melbourne consisting of ninety lizards piled in a wondrous stalactite of lizards; yearn for a new year on 1st January 00:02; spend a fortnight on a new diet plan, planning each of your healthy new meals carefully, lining up the food in your fridge and cupboards, then on the second day, cave in and devour the chocolate cake hidden in your pants; x-ray something because it's the only verb beginning with "x"; curse your stupidity when you realise "xerox" is also a verb beginning with "x"; xerox something because it's the only word that begins and ends with "x"; do a massive shit on your front lawn because you are the king of your own rectum; do a massive shit on every lawn in the world to prove you are the global king of all rectums; punch anyone who uses the plural "octopi" unselfconsciously; sing! sing! sing! sing! sing! don't sing!; finish an overly long list on an unfunny and boring entry, leaving the reader disappointed but definitely, definitely, not in the mood for more; write another five entries on the list; pimp an opossum; opimp a possum; post a series of memes on the internet involving kittens, puppies, and penguins, then take out a pistol and shoot off your earholes; sell all your earthly possessions and live a nomadic existence in Chile; become very depressed for the rest of your life, living days of quiet desperation, drinking shots of rum nightly in front of soap operas, making late-night calls to the Samaritans about suicide threats you are too cowardly to carry out, never once trying to remove yourself from the situation, then die bitter, miserable, and desperately lonely in a bleak seaside village. . .

Puff: The Unloved Son

3

A petition had been circulated calling for the expulsion of C.J. Watson and her troublemaking son Puff. His list of crimes included:

—destroying forty photocopiers by bubblegumming the insides
—destroying ninety staplers by flinging them at writers' heads and walls
—destroying eighty hole punches by ditto
—destroying one hundred and three pairs of shoes by crawling under desks and gnawing on them
—making lifts unsafe by wedging them open and placing tacks on the carpet
—abusing, distracting, tormenting and bullying the writers
—urinating from the windows while singing offensive ditties

His mother Claire, author of the ten-books-and-increasing fantasy series *Firelamp*, was now in the undesirable position of having to take control of her unwanted son and defend her right to remain in The House. Several weeks after Puff's birth, under the sway of painkillers and placebos, she'd had feelings of tenderness and affection until her mothering instinct expired with the realisation a son was a lifelong thing and she had a nine-book series to complete that she hadn't even started. She went through the motions with Puff as if he were another domestic chore, changing his nappies alongside other time-zappers like washing up and hoovering—all done with that particular blank expression reserved for inanimate things that couldn't care less how harassing they were. As a toddler, preschooler, and older preschooler (he was eight and hadn't been to school yet), he was allowed more freedom until she let him run rampant around the building without even the occasional nondescript scolding from afar or threat of a willow switch across his behind. Every second she spent having to attend to him and lost not writing her manuscript made her hate his face all the more.

Over 2,928 writers had signed the physical petition calling for her and Puff's removal. She had an appointment with Marilyn Volt that afternoon. She sat down with Puff beforehand, staring at his mussed hair, lice-filled and overlong; the torn t-shirt and jeans from which arms and arse protruded at uncouth angles; the lips forming impertinence in song (*"Mummy is a poohead / Puffy is a coolhead"*), and for the first time, felt shame. She had made this rasping and foul entity, and now had to defend her actions, its (his) existence, and save her novels' futures. As Puff wrote demented semi-rhymes on the walls in crayon (*"I will eat your brains / and then your bairns"*), Claire cried her corneas red and made general helpless noises as she shook her head in admission of despair. Then in a surge of decisiveness, she slapped her son hard on the face and held him down, administering hard thwacks to the behind as he writhed in screams and tears. "You will obey me," she said, "or I will do this to you every hour on the hour until your whole world is a fear factory."

It was a line from her second book.

The result of her punitive discipline, apart from the knowledge she had crossed the line into being an "abusive mother," and that her son would later write misery memoirs on the 38th floor about her tyranny, thus undermining her fantasy novels for a whole generation of readers, was that Puff appeared to Marilyn as a neat and well-behaved child respectful to his mother. She had run 10K as usual (whatever time of the day, it was safe to assume she had ran 10K), and arrived with her usual sweat-gummed visage in perpetual rictus.

"So I see a lot of people have signed this petition," she said, taking her usual slurp on a sports drink between utterances.

"Marilyn, I wanted you to see for yourself how calm and friendly my son is. These petitioners don't have children. They have no patience for occasional outbursts of exuberance," Claire said.

"He looks very calm," Marilyn said. She leaned into the stunned face of Puff. "You're not a bad boy, are you?" He looked at his mother who signalled he should respond in the negative or else. "No, miss," he said.

"He's my little Puff pastry," Claire added.

"More like Puff pasty. Ought to get him out in the sun," she said and smiled at his adorable face masking terror. "Well, that's settled. You both can stay. Sorry for the inconvenience. What are you working on?"

"An eleven-book-and-increasing fantasy series, *Firedoor*. The heroine is—"

"Great! I hope it does well for you," Marilyn said, rising from her desk to run another 10K or do something not at her desk.

Claire walked Puff to the front door and crouched down to meet his panicked eyes.

"Now listen. I don't want you growing up to hate me. I'm not a bad person. I just didn't want you. It's better you know this now than spend years trying to fight for my love. I don't love you. But I don't want to completely abandon you, either. So what I suggest is, you spend your days outside, playing around the fields. Be careful, there's lots of shrapnel out there. Come back in at lunchtimes and dinnertimes for food. And back in at night to shower and sleep, of course. I think this is the best solution. See you later."

And so Claire left Puff at The House entrance, relinquishing her parenting duties to the vast creche of fragged motherboards and busted hard drives that littered the stock-dump fields, where he would spend his early youth, sifting through the trash and sitting on a volcanic hatred that would erupt in the nine-book-and-increasing series of misery memoirs entitled *Dumped in the Fields: The Story of my Childhood*.

Mhairi

5

C.D. GRUNGE ate a fungus-tinted marshmallow and sprouted a second head. Unluckily, the second head hated reading and attempted to seize control of his body to do other things like sprinting or singing. The second head had a penchant for the lyrics of Freddie Mercury and the melodies of Gordon Lightfoot. Two weeks later a third head sprouted from his left buttock with a similar aversion to books and writing and a penchant for the lyrics of Mark E. Smith and the melodies of Tori Amos. This made writing an arduous and unpleasant task for C.D. and made sitting down impossible. When a fourth head sprouted from his big toe, he decided to take action and asked me to decapitate the heads. Due to a last-minute act of deception from the second head pretending to be the original C.D., the original C.D. head was decapitated instead and the second head took control of the body. The usurped C.D. left The House and went on the cruise circuit as a Queen tribute act with a less popular sideline in the songs of Gordon Lightfoot. This incident I considered a personal failure. These happen from time to time. I was able to construct a replacement body for the old C.D. from bits of old robot in the stock-dump fields, but as he wasn't able to write, he pulled his own plug. Tragic.

Writer Portraits

The New Writer

I HAD been writing manuscripts and stories for over a decade when I had a story accepted in *New Writing 49*, an anthology for new writing (read: unpublished elsewhere but submitted within the last year). This story (written fourteen years ago) proved popular and I was included in the New Writers' Showcase event, invited to read the piece before an audience including agents scouting for "new" writers to sell. I was amused at being branded a "new" writer when I had been around and had published in small presses for a long time, and that I was being announced as "new" with a tale I had written aged eighteen. I was asked to extend the short story (about a teenage breakup—the one piece I had written in a conventional manner, my usual MO being concrete prose arranged in acrostics)—into a novel, and a year later I was signed to an agent and had published *The Time of Heartquakes*. I received a favourable review in a national newspaper and was crowned an interesting "new" voice on the "scene." A month later, I was unable to contact the agent and a month plus, I was politely dropped. At that point, though I wasn't to know this at the time, I was to begin a "movement" known as The New Waves, The Bright New Things, The Newest Old Things, or The Sliced Breads.

After the drop, I changed my name by deed poll and wrote another conventional tale in the same manner as the last. This too seemed to contain the formula the panel was after (among the panel's titles: *The Heart's Gatekeeper*, *Shattered Daylight*, *Learning to Love a Little Less*), so I changed my appearance somewhat (a red perm, fake specs, and partial goatee) and entered the "new" machine once again, with invites to anthologies and readings (I faked a deeper voice), followed by another call from an agent. I penned a second novel mining similar teenage territory to my first, drawing on an unpleasant childhood, and received similar positive reviews, with invites to book readings and libraries. The agent triumphed me as an "energetic and vital voice quivering with wrenching emotion" up until the optimum number of copies had been sold to reap the maximum potential profit, and soon after, I was back into the wilderness of being a second-book author no one wanted.

Several scenesters who had recognised me kept shtum and chose to copy my coup, many of these people former flavours of the month themselves with unwanted second, third, fourth, fifth, sixth, seventh, eighth, ninth, tenth, and in one case, eleventh novels in their cupboards desperate for publication and attention. This scheme worked well for publisher, agent, and writer alike, as second novelists had the writing chops and material ready—all that was required to sell books was a fresh identity, as readers tended to distrust second novels (the sophomore slump, the hatred of a writer succeeding in making a "career," the usual lukewarm-to-meh response to most startling new voices), and publishers were unable to crank the hype machine or use phrases such as "amazing new voice" or "refreshingly honest new voice" or another combination using the words "new" and "voice" beside each other.

The scene was populated with ex-"new" writers posing as new "new" writers, forcing out the real "new" writers, who forged their own sideline as "up-and-coming" writers (unsuccessful, as no one except smug musos wanted to "discover" writers before their "new" unveiling), and soon the agents and publishers were in cahoots with this mass hoodwinking—keeping various "new" writers away long enough from the scene before their rebranding. I made four debuts until a critic commented on the similarity in style between certain of my publisher's output, and I became a toxic product and was forced to return to the real love of mine, concrete prose arranged in acrostics. This exit was to become fortuitous, as fame-struck writers, desperate to retain the mild ripple of interest "new" writers savour, sometimes had plastic surgery to alter their appearances so much that scenesters would be unable to recognise them (having exhausted the range of hairstyles, specs, and facial hair options available).

The point of implosion arrived a decade into the "movement" when critics, at this point fed up of the repeated styles and themes in "new" writers' books, pounced upon a five-time "new" novelist, reading from his child-abuse novel *Shrieks from the Cellar*. The critic Will Bentley recognised a familiar passage from an earlier "new" novel, searched the passage on his Kindle, and noticed a verbatim sentence from *Mewlings in the Basement*. He kept his ears open that night and discovered nine other repeats, standing up towards the end of the reading to shout: "This material has been plagiarised! This writer is a plagiarist!" The shock of this interruption caused the writer's false moustache to fall, his false lenses to pop out their frames, and his badly applied wig to slide off, revealing Iain Strung, author of *Sorry We Are Closed*, about childhood beatings in his father's shop. "That is Iain Strung! This man is an impostor!" the critic shouted. Iain ran off the stage to loud boos.

Iain's agent and publisher attempted to play dumb, feigning deception, but there was too much heat (another incident occurred a month later with Kitsy Bluepill, formerly Anne Winters), so the "new" writer "movement" was dropped. The writers had signed hush contracts, so no squealing happened for years, until a long article in *The Guardian* was run describing the entire operation (an intern at Faber & Faber had been bribed) and a long list of repeat "new" writers was outed (including me), and our book sales took a haemorrhaging and the publishers and agents received slaps on the wrist before returning to the old system of grooming "new" writers and spitting them out once they had served the balance sheet. None of this mattered much in the long run, as soon the audience for "new" writers became obsolete, and the "movement" of unpublished writers posing as established ones began.

This

5

SOME books obfuscate their intentions, drowning their meanings in multiple layers of ambiguities, subtleties, and intellectual mazes for the reader to unfurl. This is not one of those books. I am the author and I am about to tell you exactly the meaning and purpose of this novel, and you, the reader (if you ever materialise out of the dreamy centre of my skull), are going to swallow and digest this meaning as the only one, unless, of course, you insist on autonomy of mind, and demand to make your own, which I will politely advise you against as being foolish and unnecessary. Then again, I may decide to dupe you with an entirely false "definitive" meaning as is my wont as author, and you will be clueless as to its falsehood (even after having warned you, how will you know what is true or false?) and you will have no choice but to open up and swallow. Of course, having admitted to the possibility of duplicity in my approach opens up layers of ambiguities (if not subtleties or intellectual mazes), so my opening statement has already been undermined and exposed as a lie. If I were to outline the meaning and purpose of the novel at this point, you would not believe anything I wrote, so to do so right now would be disadvantageous. It would be easier for me to spoon the meaning and purpose of this novel into your minds later on, when you are not so eager to skeptically rebuff whatever explanation I offer based on the lie that I told you (or was it a lie?) about choosing to dupe you with an entirely false meaning and purpose. Perhaps you don't care about a "definitive" meaning and purpose of the novels you read (whoever "you" are), and simply like reading for the scenery and amusement, in which case you are reading the wrong novel. This one has a definitive meaning and purpose, maybe, if I'm not lying, and you will not escape reading this novel without learning exactly what the author (me) intended exactly, unless I decide to lie to you, in which case, you won't. Either way, you're taking a risk, and I am having ridiculous amounts of fun tickling your disinterest. I'll tell you the meaning and purpose of this novel later, if I choose to.

The Trauma Rooms

5

"Next up: Syd Lopmound. You may find his manner rather distracted, or distracting."

"Or both?"

"Or both."

Erin entered a room where skeins of shredded paper, attached to strings and sellotaped to the ceiling, dangled into her face while Syd Lopmound manically and starryeyedly flitted between them, hoping to chance upon some pearlescent sentence that had magicked itself onto the blank skeins when he wasn't looking that he might add to his non-existent fictional début. His spiked hair made him resemble an indie drummer trying too hard to divert the viewer's gaze from the lead singer.

"These are what Syd calls his Ideacatchers. Hello, Syd Lopmound! This is Erin. She'd like to say howdy-doodle-you-do."

"Or hello."

"Or howdy—doodle, do you?"

"Enough."

"Hang five! I have one here," Syd said, peering at a wordless strip of paper in wonder. "Damn! Nothing there. I thought I spied a story about a walrus there, something about a walrus eating a mushroom."

"Yes. Syd, Erin would like to know about your condition."

"Hang! I see a plot over there! DON'T MOVE!"

No one moved. Syd examined the blank paper with three-parts wonder, bafflement, and disappointment.

"Syd, we've discussed this. These words, stories, and plots are hallucinations. Nothing will appear on the paper unless you write it yourself."

"I swear . . . it was something about a mobster taking t'ai chi lessons."

"That was a recent Danny Dyer vehicle, Syd. Now, if you'd like to tell Erin here what happened to you?"

"Yes. I had recently moved to Brooklyn to become a writer. I had read about Brooklyn's reputation as a cultural hive, with writers like Jonathan Lethem eulogising its charms in countless books with Brooklyn in the title. I came from Aberdour, you see, so Brooklyn was the Holy Land to me. Anyway, I rented my room from a fleabag on 879th St. and sat down to write. Realising I had neglected to buy a pen, I headed to the stationery store. Upon returning, someone had stolen my notepad. Disheartened, I put the writing on hold to pursue working in a bookstore, because Jonathan Lethem had worked in one before becoming big. On the subway, taking my CV to various bookstores, I would have these tremendous ideas for plots, but always seemed to be lacking a pen or notepad, and so forgot the ideas by the time I reached my destination. I had purchased new stationery and a secure lock for my room, but whenever I sat down to write, I could never latch on to my earlier ideas, no lock pun intended. So I made my rounds of the bookstores, citing Jonathan Lethem as an inspiration, but my accent and overeagerness repelled most of the owners. I took to carrying a pen and notepad at all times, but ideas only emerged when I was powerless to write them down. I tried speaking aloud my ideas to strangers, or asking them to write things down for me, but they predictably shied away from my conversation, thinking me unhinged. I was stuck with these brilliant ideas—and I can assure you, they were fucking amazing—and no means of putting them on paper. This continued for months until I cracked up and returned to Aberdour in a state of shock, having failed to secure a position of idealised employment in a bookstore like my idol Jonathan Lethem."

"Tell Erin about your Ideacatchers."

"These are like Dreamcatchers, only for catching my errant

ideas. Sometimes I see—or think I see—these ideas—oh wait, is that something about a disco sausage?—written on the paper, but when I pluck the strips, there are no ideas there. The doctor insists I am hallucinating—oh, look, a cargo truck crashes into a primary school!"

"Interesting case," Erin said, once again seeing no stapler and impatiently indulging the doctor's explanation.

"The patient is convinced that these 'ideas' of his have value. My suspicion is that these 'ideas' on the subway were also hallucinations and that his brain, finding itself unable to achieve the desired level of creativity needed to become an artist, went into shock, offering this delusion of creativity in place of actual."

"But what if he is secretly nursing brilliant ideas, and merely needs the coaching to make them manifest?"

"Come, Erin, you have heard the indigested wiffle he had been coming out with. Do you really believe a genius lurks underneath?"

"No. They are dreadful ideas."

"Precisely. I need to convince him that he is wasting his time with these runny nuggets and to move on with his life. And with that cue, let us move on to the next patient!"

The Corridor of Cheap Commodities

WILLIAM drops acid in Poughkeepsie on the last day of the Vietnam War. As he trips, he recalls his tortured affair with a sixty-year-old prostitute. £12.90.

A depressed woman in a small town sits staring out the window, recalling with a melancholy air the three times she stepped outside. £2.50.

The Turkish sunshine is too warm for Francis. He decides to sue the travel agent for not providing sufficient shade or rainfall. Since the agent promised "cool retreats," Francis sues successfully. He then spends his days having bad holidays and suing travel agents until he becomes rich and retires to a dream destination that is far too warm and unfriendly,

VENICE is besieged by ten-foot mechanical chickens. Washed-up cop David Strike is the only man who can save the city. £7.70.

A strange echo is heard in the hilltops. Upon closer investigation it turns out to be nothing. £0.40.

A distraught air traffic controller slaps a flight attendant in a fit of rage. After apologising, the two begin a whirlwind romance in the sky, travelling to Cuba, Paris, and Dakar in a heady love-spin. £20.15.

A mild-mannered tailor has a crisis of confidence, has a breakdown and makes a full recovery, and is back tailoring again in the Russian steppes within a fortnight. £6.90.

The residents of Bavarian

at which point he sues himself, and returns to his life as peasant in a bungalow. £34.60.

Two widows take a biking trip across Alabama, overcoming their grief through a series of daring encounters, from a near punchup at a truck stop to an erotic tussle at Melvin's nightclub and a realisation of their mutual Sapphic love. £3.65.

A hedgehog crawls inside an empty crisp packet and is transported back to the Franco-Prussian war, where he is immediately flattened by an onslaught of charging soldiers on horseback. £6.90.

The happiest priest in Bethlehem is dismayed when he loses his favourite spatula. £18.10.

The vertical hold on Ian Wilson's television malfunctions during an earthquake, leading him to believe that the ground is being raised layer-by-layer, and that he is plunging deeper toward the Earth's core. His teenage daughter borrows the car without permission. £17.30.

village Reit im Winkl are invaded by an army of bellicose Austrian cobblers, who one night replace the population's shoes with clogs and flip-flops, causing a mass riot in the region and a drop-off in Austrian footwear imports. £11.40.

President Lopez has to make the world's longest apology, encompassing ninety million people over forty countries, when he misspeaks on a chat show. Meanwhile his wife has an affair with a hunky aide. £99.50.

A crisis befalls the racist town of Franklee when a black man is spotted buying a snack in a gas station. The elders rouse the community to a pitch of hatred that binds the population closer together. £0.40.

Something is wrong in the basement of Thornhill Primary School. Timothy asks the caretaker, who refuses to believe anything is wrong. Despite being disbelieved by everyone, Timothy still believes something is wrong in the basement. £2.80.

A Better Life

5

W E achieved a workable solution using a Salamol CFC-free inhaler attached to a mini-pendulum. It functioned not as a five-minute timer—we couldn't prevent the pendulum from hitting the new-caller button on the switchboard with each natural swing—but as a fill-in finger clicking customers into oblivion in idle strokes. This left callers with 1.6 seconds to fling their complaints into unpresent ears and created a high turnover of calls (37.5 per minute). Since the number of callers was unlimited this left us free to concentrate on other things such as killing the remaining ten old people and usurping their properties, most of which emanated a strong funk of cardigans, insect repellent, and moths decomposing in jars of Marmite. I made the mistake of eating a Werther's Original from a sweetie tin. It tasted like a lump of earwax. (There was a lump of earwax in the sweet tin—perhaps I had mixed them up).

Once we had taken their homes and set up our switchboard-duper in all ten, we founded our base in the least offensive place (Mrs Horritt's—bleached pristine thanks to her OCD) and deliberated on our next move.

"Clearly," Pete said, "we have two options. We can remain in these cottages lounging on the sofas, eating a decade's worth of frozen chicken nuggets and broccoli, taking the air occasionally along the concrete promenade, or we can devise some way to bring about the complete destruction of the ScotCall empire and return the world to how it was some fifty years ago, minus the threat of universal technogeddon."

"How d'we do that?" Rob asked. He realised the stole he had been stroking was a dead cat.

"We'll have to cogitate on the matter. In the meantime, go fire us up some oven chips." Pete was talking to me.

Our time cohabiting the cottages proved testing. Unlike his experimental fiction-writing forebears, the magnificent Gilbert and Christopher Sorrentino, Pete was a graceless boor and upfront arsehole, sprawled on the couch sans socks, teasing Rob and me with his Man-Blaster and unfunny X-rated puns. I was forced to do the cooking and cleaning. Rob had a sharp sense of humour and to the delight of Pete nicknamed me *The Hausfrau*. This caused much chuckling at my expense. Pete didn't want to clean up the corpses, so I had to drag the dead towards the sea, where they merely bobbed back to shore to be pecked at by gulls. I had to light a bonfire and incinerate the bodies, which caused an unholy stench and attracted rats (from where, I wasn't sure). Once the corpses were charred to completion we hung around the bungalow discussing solutions for toppling the Evil Empire without reverting to blowing holes in everyone with the Man-Blaster.

After two idealess hours, Pete suggested we go in shooting. ScotCall used persuasion and bland brainwashing techniques to propagate its evil—psychological, rarely physical, violence. Despite that, ScotCall could mobilise an army of killers in two minutes if their profits were imperilled, so I proposed a stealthier tactic such as interfering with the phone lines. Rob had no ideas to contribute and twirled his bowtie (he had taken one of the dead thing's bowties and was testing its effectiveness in his ensemble). The simplest answer was most often correct. I remembered reading that in a book long ago. To amuse ourselves in between arguing and having no new ideas we answered ScotCall queries.

"*I need help. I cannot decide the difference between a prawn and a portaloo.*"

"You piss on one and eat the other."

"*What is the difference between up and left?*"

"Left is down and right is up."

"*Can you furnish me with a witty quote to include in my essay on the doughnut industry?*"

"Go stuff your own hole."

"*Is this dog luminous?*"

"Depends."

"*Might I suggest a hermeneutic approach?*"

"Never!"

"*Is a battered fish bettered when buttered?*"

"Bitterly."

"*How do I raise the temperature on cold days?*"

"Reach up and twist the knob."

"*Does a leopard with chicken pox have double the spots?*"

"A chicken with leopard pox does."

"*Is it possible to reconcile two broken-hearted lovers?*"

"Only after dousing them in petrol."

"*Can I swallow eternity?*"

"If you believe."

"*Is a button a mammal?*"

"All mammals are buttons but not all buttons are mammals."

"*Is it?*"

"No."

"*Can I support a privet hedge with bolsters?*"

"Yesnobe."

"*Green waders or blue waders?*"

"Shoot yourself."

I became a competent cook and oven-user. My speciality was frozen chips and beefburgers, and I found several robosnail thingies outside and stir-fried them with a dozen strands of grass-substitute I stole from the sheep. Peter suggested I slaughter several sheep to boil haggis (the former national dish when ScotCall was ScotLand—the national dish at the time of writing is a chicken tikka masala wrap with lettuce and mustard). Tired of this samey and punitive diet, I headed toward the concrete fields to bludgeon one of the flocculent idlers. I dealt the killing blow with my makeshift baseball bat and its insides split open, parting to reveal a

Gordian of wires and cables. On closer inspection I noted the sheep were nibbling on cables and wires, not grass-substitute (and that I had fed Pete and Rob robosnail thingies with wires and cables—not grass-substitute!). A cursory examination of the wires revealed the word "ScotCall" along their green sheaths, and I wagered that if nibbled down to the nub, mass disturbances could be caused on the lines and help us overthrow their empire. I observed that the reason the sheep weren't penetrating right down to the nubs was that the wires went between their teeth and they could merely suck and champ on the wires (sometimes being zapped to death and combusting in flameballs).

"If we sharpened the teeth of these mechanical sheep creature thingies, we can have them penetrating the ScotCall lines. If we breed them too, we could have an army of cable-munching annihilators from Hell. Thoughts?"

"Got no other ideas," Pete burped.

"You get to it," Rob burped. "We're busy listening to the Best of Val Doonican."

"Who?"

"No idea. Music sounds like it was made in the Stone Age."

"When?"

"Go round up your sheep, fuckyboo. After making us dinner," Pete sneered.

I hated those arseholes. But I had hit upon an ingenious plan liable to win me folk-hero status four centuries down the line. I proceeded with glee.

The *Farewell, Author!* Conference

5

A N hour later Gail Adams Galloway took to the microphone to recite her most memorable sentences. "Here we stand in . . . no wait, that's not right. Here we are in the middle of . . . no, that's not correct . . . I wouldn't start like that. I think it's She was walking in the . . . road? sidewalk? farmhouse? The cover of the book I wrote was rural. She was walking on the sidewalk and something about a rabbit. I can't remember," she said, looking to the audience for help, searching the hostile and sympathetic eyes for some trace of her words, her lost stories swimming in the pools of their eyes, and retreated. Julian Porter encouraged others to take to the stage, but Galloway's blankness made them realise that, aside from T.C. Boyle, who had his collected works memorised, no one was confident they could quote verbatim from their own or their colleagues' sentences, and they all refrained from taking to the mic. This left T.C. Boyle free to step up and resume reading from his first story collection, *Descent of Man*. A collective moan ensued and conversation sprung up again. The bleak realisation Galloway had implanted in the writers' minds turned the conversations hostile and defensive. Álvaro Enrigue accused Stephen-Paul Martin of cribbing parts of his oeuvre from a flash fiction he posted online, and Martin called Álvaro a nutcase, and Álvaro muttered a rude remark about Stephen-Paul's sister as he walked away, and Stephen-Paul shouted that he didn't even have a sister; Stuart Kelly accused Jessica Treat of neglecting the work of Boeotian poet Hesiod, and Jessica recited accurate biographical information about Hesiod, and Stuart retorted that this didn't mean she was familiar with his poems, and Jessica refused to quote to prove herself to some "fourth-rate Hazlitt manqué," and Stuart was too stunned and confused to retort; Andrew O'Hagan accused Reyoung of patronising him about writing mainstream novels and not hanging out with the hip and soi-disant avant-garde, Reyoung replied that mainstream success meant readers, and he had never had one of those apart from his darling wife Candice Filigree, and O'Hagan said that Reyoung had invented a fake wife with a cool name to outdo him, since his wife was plain old Linda Jones, and Reyoung explained that his wife taught advanced calculus to high school students in hideous sweaters and could never be considered cool, and O'Hagan said he was showing off his wife's intellect in another attempt to outdo him, and Reyoung said that inventing an uncool wife to impress a Scottish hack was not his conversational bag, and O'Hagan opened his mouth wide in a stunned O, in a clever mirroring of the O' in his surname; Steve Hely accused Javier Marías of writing overlong run-on sentences to fill up the pages, produce more books, and rake in the cash, and Javier refused to respond to the accusation, tilting his head towards a reanimated salmon dancing the cancan, and Hely hurled unspeakable abuse at the back of this tilted head; James Wood accused Lucy Ellmann of inciting hatred at the peace treaty between Russia and Ukraine by sexting a Ukrainian beefcake, and Lucy said that she had been fucking the Ukrainian beefcake as the peace treaty was being signed so could not be blamed, and James said that she had been fucking the Ukrainian under the table where the peace treaty was being signed, and Lucy said that she had been fucking with no sound apart from the rustle of their mutual thrusts on the axminster, and James said that she had shouted "fuck the Ukraine!" several times under the table, and Lucy that she had shouted "fuck me, Ukrainian!" as she came, and that is what led to the peace treaty cancellation and subsequent war, and James said that fucking a Ukrainian beefcake under the table as a peace treaty was being co-signed was the worst possible time to fuck a Ukrainian beefcake, and Lucy said that one never knows when Eros will strike, and that she hadn't had sex in two years prior to that, so the fuck was splendid and no regrets; Karrie Fransman accused Antoine Volodine of milking the list form to the point of extreme tedium, and Antoine replied that the list form is a perfect means to distil the experience of living without recourse to the banal business of telling one linear tale of one character after another, and Karrie said that lists were for anal retentives, those with Asperger's syndrome, or writers struggling to think up proper plots, characters, and storylines, and Antoine said that listing was a means of coping with the infinite potential of sitting before a blank page, and the précis was as valid a form as the 1000-page epic, and Karrie lost interest in the conversation and stared at her loafers, and Antoine praised her taste in loafers, and Karrie asked if he was coming on to her, and Antoine said yes, you are fucking beautiful, and Karrie said sorry, I have a fabulous husband named Nate; Affinity Konar accused Mark Z. Danielewski of popularising the blank page, and precipitating a spate of non-books (not in the Benabouian sense) where the occasional random word-speck could be glimpsed in a minuscule font among the wall of whitewash, and Mark said so , and Affinity said that was a puerile response and a waste of half a minute, and Mark said when , and Affinity said he made a compelling argument, and Mark said therefore , and Affinity said that she couldn't believe she'd been so stupid, and was there any way she could repay him for her stupidity, and Mark said skateboard , and Affinity said she'd rather not as she had a sore back; Graham Rawle accused William T. Vollmann of excess, and William said that excess, inordinateness, nimiety, overabundance, overindulgence, supererogatoriness, superfluity, and surplusage was always necessary, and Graham knocked him out with a punch to the chin before he could utter another syllable. This act of violence proved prescient for how the evening was set to end.

Mhairi

6

My residence on The House roof is a large rectangular shed-cum-house (a shouse) containing my bed, two chillout chairs with tiger-skin wraparounds, and my collection of fortune-bearing talismans. These items were discovered at various Highland locations when my parents moved around the country selling vacuum bags, and I have placed them at strategic places in the room due to my superstitious nature. These include: a severed marmot's foot from Thurso; a poster of a right-wing shepherd from Castletown; an inkblot test resembling the constellation Orion from Braes of Harrow; the diseased bowel of an Angus cow from Dunnet Head; a preserved sprig of a Pictish radish from John O'Groats; a facsimile of unpublished Rabbie Burns poem "Oh! Midges!" from Tongue Wood; a scale model of a Victorian "field of sheds" from Wick; a jar of wandering hydrogen from Borgie Forest; a hygiene wipe signed "To Lydia, I implore you to reconsider, Love Baz" from Loch Lucy; a tapestry criticising the art of tapestries from Altnabreac; a sketch of former boxer Mike Tyson from Helmsdale; a vial of an unidentified liquid believed to be an unguent used to cure Orcadian colic from Dornach; a sprig of heather sprouting through a frog's corpse from Brora; an instruction manual on how to cheer tenebrous sheep from Golspie; the keys to a Rover 50 parked precariously on a cliff-edge from Lairg; a thistle boiled in milk and strained through a washerwoman's tights from Alness; the syllabus of a small press founded on the Isle of Bute, consisting of two texts, Robert Alan Jamieson's *Soor Hearts* and Philip K. Dick's *Ubik* from Tain; the spare tyre of a JCB hauler from Evanton. These items, although causing considerable clutter and requiring storage outside the shouse, perform important functions to sate my superstitious nature. The shouse was constructed by Gerald, about whom I will write in my next installment.

I said thanks Mum

My mum suggested I sign up for The House of Writers because I wrote stories about horses and chairs and things so I said good idea. I didn't want to do it alone however so I suggested she come with me and she agreed. She said she would help me with the writing and manage the financial side so I didn't have to think about practical worries. I said thanks Mum. The best thing for me to write was erotica so she signed me up to that floor and bought me a desk where I could work and write prose for the readers. At first I was confused about what I was supposed to be writing but Mum filled me in and explained that erotica was a genre that dealt with sexual intercourse between two human beings. So I set about writing scenes of sexual intercourse between men and men and women and women and the variations of sexual possibility that exist in the world and showed the first draft to Mum. She said the descriptions of rimming and fellatio were not adequate so she suggested I add more description about the tongue working the rim of the cockshaft and made tongue movements to demonstrate. I said thanks Mum. I had written a novel containing two adventurous lovemakers who take pleasure making love in public places with an especial focus on oral activities involving the intake of seminal fluid. Mum was proud. I made four pounds on the first book and this gave me enthusiasm to continue with the next. I wrote a tribadic erotic tale this time featuring four women who like making love to each other in train stations. Mum criticised the scenes of anal penetration with dildos and suggested I emphasise the strain taken on the buttocks when the lubricated dildos were being inserted via the rectum. She pulled down her underpants and demonstrated the difficulty of inserting a rigid item into that orifice by forcing a stapler between her wide-open buttocks. I said thanks Mum.

Cal's Tour

Romance

EVERY clichéd impression you may have of romance novelists is surpassed when you step into the dense fog of pinkness that is the fifth floor. Scented smoke puffs from two pipes, coating the foyer in a candyfloss mist. You inhale the scent and choke your way along the corridor, past barely perceptible posters of catalogue model hunks and swooning heroines, towards a large room dolled up like an extravagantly cheap hotel. Four ladies in their late fifties with caked-on makeup sit writing beside perfume dispensers, puffing a peachy fragrance into the air every few minutes—a heady bordello scent—and will either leap up to meet you or barely grant you a careless peep, as is their wont. They told me their names, annexed my body, and enclosed me in a peach-scented hug. Over Bertie's shoulder, I saw Tina's daughter Oh, a dowdy beanpole cowering in the corner whom I had mistaken for a hat stand. She was one fifteenth the body mass of her mother, as though made from one of her ribs, and stood in a stylishly sulky teapot stance watching without expression as my lungs were cleared of breath. I surrendered to the cushiony heft of their arms and bosoms. As they turned to plant a sequence of unsolicited pecks on my cheeks, their shrapnelly eyelashes scraped my ears and scalp, and when the sequence of slurpy mwah-mwahs had ended, my cheeks were a painter's palette of reds and pinks. "Aren't you a big plate of cuteness on rye with salami, soybeans, and peppermint jalapeños?" Bertie asked. "He's a bowl of unmitigated loveliness with extra pastrami and coochie-*crou*tons," Tina countered. "No he's not!" Cassie almost shouted. "He's a serving of xylophone meat with tuba crackers, cor anglais na-

181

chos, trumpet lettuce, horn radish, oboe lemons, fiddle rice, violin turkeys, harmonium dips, and double bass pudding." An awkward pause followed as Cassie sank back to her desk, having overdone it again.

Horror struck when Bertie asked me to massage her bunions in exchange for my room and board. I reverted to my cute simper, assuming "cheeky chuckles" were underway. Jaulopie peeled off her sock and Tina nodded towards the exposed feet and their unfortunate blemishes in need of kneading by the nubile newbie, i.e. me. To refuse my fingers after the extravagant and creepy praise they had heaped on me would have been churlish. I squirmed footwards. They were, after all, only a pair of human feet. The purple nail polish on each toe hiding the fungus behind her cracked nails was not so revolting as to merit the queasiness and disgust on my face, nor were the inflamed blisters of pus I was stroking and poking sufficiently horrifying to merit my escaping into a daydream and trying psychological blocking techniques. Jaulopie flung her head back in delirium at my touch and I closed my eyes, returning to the inverted vortex and its fleeting happiness. Oh looked on with an amused expression, no doubt finding my torture a hoot. "That is spanky-doodle-candy, my young tootsie-tapper," Jaulopie said as I massaged. "That feels like heaven brought to my bunions." When my ordeal was over—depression slowly rising—I was taken to the sleeping area by Bertie. My room was free from the tyranny of pink décor, although numerous hunky lummoxes were plastered up on the walls, some of whom were damp with saliva from fresh morning licks. "Sorry about that. A few of the girls were having a lick earlier. The sheets might also be damp and need a wash. See you out there, cutie-poke." As you can imagine, you need pailfuls of patience on this floor.

The next day, Tina shook me awake for the first day of my apprenticeship—entering the room without knocking and stealing some feels of my naked chest while I was too zonked to protest or feel sexually threatened. I was taken to a small tea room, free from pinks but dotted with doilies, where the ladies, slap-less and deeccentricised, all chatted in shy and normal tones. They discussed their writing for the day like people who resembled real people, showing little sign of yesterday's cartoon lunacy. Jaulopie was working on a story about an attractive lawyer with a prosthetic penis who serendipitously bumps into an attractive attorney with a prosthetic vagina. The two are finally able to dock due to both prosthetics being compatible with Shinoba V46 models. One of the readers is a fetishist for prosthetics, so they had chosen indulge her particular whims that month.

One condition of their employment is that they "behave like psycho-sassy spinsters, dress like a cartload of Cartlands invading Scotland, and be somewhat unhinged but still able to prose." So every night after work, they remove their makeup and retreat into their usual selves. They took me to the makeup room: a sterile pink zone more like an operating theatre, where four hairdryers with robot beauticians sit against a wall, the makeup and implements sprawled on a metal table in front. The ladies sit reading as the sharp-clawed robots set to work spreading on the slap, sharpening up the lashes, tinting the hair, and rouging up cheeks and nails. A second procedure is required for the mascara and lipstick. The former is pounded in a pestle and roasted until ash-crisp, applied while hot and flaming slightly along the tungsten lashes, while the latter is whisked and whirred to a gelatinous texture, made to leave perfect kiss-prints on a victim's cheeks. I was spared the full makeover, but a little blusher to redden up my cheeks was applied, followed by a trip to the dressing room, where a range of frilly frocks were available on a long monorail of embarrassment. I raked through the flowery dresses, skirts, and blouses, looking for the least unflattering ensemble possible, choosing a purple blouse with yellow sunflower pattern and a dark green skirt with strawberries arranged in a zigzag sequence. If I pulled up my blue, kitty-riddled socks, my ankles were fully covered, meaning I didn't have to wax them. Next, I selected a wig to wear, choosing a shoulder-length dark-red bob, and practiced walking in my high heels, moving from the door to the mirror.

Another stipulation of their contract is that every morning they kneel before a small shrine where a collage of fascists from days of yore—Joseph Stalin, Benito Mussolini, Robert Mugabe, Tony Blair—is pasted up for a reverential morning prayer. They kneel, clasp hands, and recite: "To these fine men, misunderstood by history's betrayers, we offer our respect, and ask that whoever is guiding us look upon their visionary ways with infinite humility and love. Amen and all that." I echoed their words, staring into the avuncular moustache of the smirking Joseph Stalin. I never fully understood this ritual.

As a (practicing) professional, I rose above the setbacks to deliver my novel on schedule. A thriving market of eleven readers commission the books: an après-sexual cult of subversives who prefer using their imaginations to induce lubricity, shunning the 49,000 pornographic networks widely available and favoured by the populace for mindless autoerotic relief. These eleven had arrived at a point—raised on easy access to hardcore Dutch, replacing sexual relationships with double-daily masturbation to hardcore pornography—where they found themselves incapable of a tender thought expressed towards another human being, and later, any arousal at artistic erotica. The only solution for them was to boycott their porn and revert back to the imagination, to softcore suggestion and tame romance, where sexual acts lurked below the merest hint of the existence of genitals. Occasional perversions and requests for hotter matter crept into their commissions. The intended endpoint of these books was an entirely chaste form of romantic writing dating back to the sexlessness of the pre-Victorians, where corseted repressions helped nurture real unquenchable lusts and proper passions, and the slow return of the readers' emotional sensitivities might lead to meaningful relationships based on love and tenderness, if they could find anyone else on the planet who still had these qualities, or bring themselves to pair off with each other (the eleventh person being a sacrificial celibate). Fortunately for the department, by the time this happened, the readers would be well into their sixties, theoretically beyond the point where they were likely to have sexual relationships anyway, and would have to make do with yearly masturbation to alleviate the tinglings.

Strange things happened to me during my time there. I saw the monkey who was kept captive down in the basement (with the experimentalists) toddling up the stairs, whistling to itself while carrying a handful of papers and skim-reading. Upon seeing me, he dropped the papers and faked simian behaviour, knuckle-walking up the steps, swinging his arms around, making exaggerated gurning motions with his chin. He tried to brush past me and quickly clamber on his way, but I seized his arm. The monkey looked affronted and faltered for a response. "What's with the proper walking?" I asked. "Ooh-wah-wah-wah-ah!" the monkey said, throwing his arms around and patting himself on the head. "Stop that," I said. "Ooh-wah-wah-wah-wah!" he insisted. "You were walking upright and whistling. You've been rumbled." The monkey lowered his arms and regained his proper posture. He ushered me closer with a small index twitch. "All right, but you *have* to keep shtum. I'm not in this to be outed. Bryswine thinks I've been writing the complete works of Shakespeare for his nutso project, but I've secretly been typing up my own novels and printing them off on the sly. Since you humans dropped the ball, we in the simian species have evolved an interest in literature. You remember all those books that were recycled into bedding for cages in zoos, those books you air-dumped into the rainforest? That's where it all began, my *sapien* friend. On boring nights we'd read passages of Eliot and Clarkson and pretty soon we evolved into semi-intelligent beings. But if we ever go public, the humans will confiscate our books and have us liquidised, probably, seeing us a 'threat' or whatever to their supremacy as a species or whatever, you know what they're like. While you *homo*s were setting up call centres, we kept our adorable monkey heads down, reading and reading. Some of us developed artistic ambitions, working with humans in the hope we could find materials with which to write our books. I was extremely fortunate to have escaped the Crarsix Zoo and be adopted by one of the experimental writers. My works are the most widely read among simians." I was stunned! "My God, I had no idea. How have you managed to re-main undetected for so long?" He coughed. "Human stupidity. At some point, we will rise up and overtake your species. All we need is some training to develop our upper body strength, and we should be able to slowly insinuate ourselves into the power structure. We will be kind to the humans who mean well. We will have lovely zoos for you to play in. The rest will, naturally, be dispatched to our old homes in the rainforest. Estimated date for this takeover . . . about three years? Could be quicker if they keep pulping law books and encyclopaedias. Don't worry. We simians have learned from the stupidities of your species, we hope to practice benevolence, charity, and love, as opposed to human virtues: avarice, selfishness, warfare, meatheadedness, cold-blooded brutality, idiocy, sexual de-pravity, carelessness and spineless brainlessness." Well, what can you say to that?

Trying to write in that office with the banter at full blitz—non sequiturs, stinging sallies, and potent prattle filling your ears with distracting fuzz—is insufferable. However, I did complete my sen-sual romance. Here is a chapter to whet your understanding:

Axis turned to Donna with his chest rippling. She had never seen a chest like his ripple before, and had an instant craving for raspberry ripple ice-cream. "Hang ten, pussycat," she said, heading for the kitchen. She returned with a tub of ice-cream and applied it to his chest. Axis flinched at the cold and moaned as Donna licked the cream off his nipples. "Hang ten again," she said, heading for the kitchen. She returned with a biscuit and crushed it between her fingers, sprinkling the crumbs along his chest and licking them off. "Ooh, also—" she said, heading for the kitchen. Axis sighed with impatience. He was ready to go off at any moment. She returned with strawberries, and placed one on in his navel, taking it whole in her mouth. "Actually know what? I haven't eaten today, hold on baby—" she said, heading etc. She returned with a pack of sliced beef, tinned roast potatoes, and a tub of Moroccan couscous. She draped a slice of beef over his beef and forked some couscous into his navel. "Lie back so I can eat properly," she said. She placed a potato on his chest and picked up her fork and knife, slicing the potato in half and working on the beef—Axis

wincing as the knife nicked his skin. She took the beef and potato in her mouth, licked up some couscous, and moaned her yums. "Oh wonder if my show is on now," she said, reaching for the TV remote. She turned on the TV and watched Susie's Soups, *a cooking show with emphasis on soups made by Susie. "Ooh, I want to make this! Hang ten, let me rustle up the ingredients!" she said. "Please don't make it on my chest," Axis protested.*
　—*Hunk Soup*, p.790

A Word from the Team

Oʜ: We specialise in romantic stories involving beefcakes with enormous ones who use them to superhuman effect. Some of the variants include those with prosthetic limbs in lust, goitres or excessive swellings in lust, distended or missing toes and feet in lust, dwarves or giants in lust, completely flattened (or 2D) people in lust, and terminal patients in lust. We need whole novels written quickly (one fortnight per novel) for our readers—attentiveness to spelling and grammar not important, though no illiterates please.

Bᴇʀᴛɪᴇ: Nonsense. Ours is the art of *suggestion*.

Jᴀᴜʟᴏᴘɪᴇ: Teasing and tickling the reader into a state of erotic flurry.

Oʜ: Making them think there's a big fuck scene round the corner when there's only more description of the curtains.

Tɪɴᴀ: Yes, thank you, darling. No one asked for your contribution.

Oʜ: I thought I'd give it anyway, since we're all saying words.

Bᴇʀᴛɪᴇ: No, you are as usual standing there like an unwanted lamp with a very dim bulb making sneaky comments and hovering over our shoulders, drooling disparaging remarks all over our masterworks.

Oʜ: Untrue. See, potential romance writers, these old maids bash out the stories and plots in prehensile form, while I spend my evenings trying to chisel what they've written into readable prose we can actually sell.

Cᴀssɪᴇ: Pure fabricatory poopycook, my lumptious.

Oʜ: Not even a word. That's the kind of drivel they put on the page. Can you imagine anyone getting hot at the word *lumptious*?

TINA: My darff, you'd need the relevant sack-happy sexperience before you can talk about getting hot!

OH: Oh's mum, shut your yap.

BERTIE: We're all perfectly acquainted with the ins-and-outs-and-ins-again of intercourse. We've had our flair share of erotic tussles.

JAULOPIE: As romance writers, it's important our work is authentic.

BERTIE: Ha, *you* can talk about authentic, when was the last time you felt the white-hot thrust of a prodigiously proportioned cock-or-two in your lady's area?

JAULOPIE: I'll have you know I've bedded up to seven hundred men in my time.

BERTIE: She used to work in an old folks' home putting duffers to sleep.

JAULOPIE: Slanderous machinations from the lips of a vulgar virgin!

BERTIE: Not true. I was once arrested for having full intercourse on the road with a fantastic man.

JAULOPIE: By fantastic you mean *plastic*?

BERTIE: Gob—close it!

TINA: Well, we all know *I* have had sexual relations, I have a daughter to prove it.

OH: Mum, everyone knows you inseminated yourself with Sperm Sample #462.

CASSIE: What kind of lover was Sperm Sample #462? Was he passionate and tender, or just a little drip?

TINA: You frigid fancy!

AD FROM SPONSORS

UNSURE whether ScotCall is right for you? Here's an aptitude test so see if you're the person we're looking for! **Which of the following responses would you make to a caller's problem?**

Operative 1:

"I'm afraid I don't understand. You put the cucumber into your rucksack and it was missing along with your wallet and house keys? And you were wearing the rucksack the entire time you passed through the cornfield and only encountered two people on your trip, the farmer and a hobo? Yes, he probably *was* an experimental writer, you know what they're like. Maybe at some point along the way your backpack fell open and the items slipped out? You know that sheaves of corn in dry fields can be quite gnarly like fingers, they might have unzipped your bag and plucked out the items like pickpockets, or backpackpockets! Yes, I know it's unlikely, but you know a similar thing happened to my friend with heather and a cheese sandwich?"

Operative 2:

"Hello, sir. Now have you considered the possibility that your cucumber was stolen by this farmer? I know you only saw him in the distance, but if he spotted you, there is the chance he crept up on you in the cornfield and stole the vegetable due to a deficit in his own production. He might have taken the vegetable and cloned it to sell cheaply on the black market, you know that's pretty common these days. Sorry? You're more worried about the house keys and wallet? I really have no idea what you mean."

Operative 3 :

"Hello, sir. I'm a senior advisor at this office. Now, can you tell me, was your cucumber insured at all? You are completely sure that it wasn't? All right, well, there are two things you should do before we can help you process a claim. You should retrace your steps on the walk to check the items aren't lying around somewhere, and if you can't find them, you should send us a photograph of the missing items and fill in claim form 4.29. If your claim is successfully processed, we will send a replacement cucumber out to you at no extra charge. Sorry? No, I'm afraid we can't at the moment. You will have to call us separately about each missing item, we can't process multiple items at once. Do you want to proceed with your cucumber claim?"

Which would *you* choose? Let us know and you could be in full-time life-long employment within two weeks!

SCOTCALL.

YOUR FUTURE.

Recruitment Line:
0800 717 717

Your idea of literature

An avalanche of atomised axioms,
a bouillabaisse of banal babble,
a cartload of crimson clichés,
a dacha of derogative doodles,
an earful of earnest etchings,
a fanfare of farted fripperies,
a googleplex of grated gaffes,
a hatstand of halfhearted ho-hums,
an ideogram of imported idiocies,
a jugful of jeering jokes,
a karaoke of krazed klutziness,
a lapwing of laughable litotes,
a mash-up of mangled metaphors,
a nunnery of nonsensical nothings,
an opera of onanistic ogles,
a pangloss of pathetic parodies,
a quiz of questionable quackeries,
a runnel of rancid repetitions,
a sluicegate of seriocomic satires,
a tattyscone of terrible teasers,
a ululation of useless urine,
a vulva of vicious vagaries,
a waste of worthless wrappings,
a xerox of xeroxed xeroxes,
a yurt of yesterday's yawns,
a zoo of zany zingers.

This

6

IT is the writer's responsibility to loaf. The writer, if active and energetic, will deaden his sensitivity to the world and spoil his creativity by being overly occupied. Complete disinterest in one's surroundings. Complete disinterest in anything outside one's own navel. These are the hallmarks of a driven writer. Beware the writer who hops on his bike and makes copious notes of his surroundings or careful observations of other humans in order to contrive an accurate depiction of what makes them tick. This is wrong. The most successful form of creativity is derived from lounging on an armchair deep in the clutches of self-loathing or kicking back on a divan pondering the purpose of rising from that divan at some time in the future. I wrote my first novel, *Not Getting Up* (2007), sitting upright in my bed, often slouching down the pillows to a supine position, where I would hold the notepad above my head, writing until sleep called (as it often did), returning to the one state of pure bliss, when nothing matters except dreaming. The novel was the first in a trilogy, followed by *Still Not Getting Up* (2008), and *Never Getting Up* (2009), each consisting of lists of things I might choose to do upon getting up, if I ever get up (which in the novels I never do), and things I have lied about having done (I have done nothing in the realm of these novels, since I have never moved from my bed). The trilogy was panned by a snide hack at *The Cumbernauld Gazette*, who commented on the "laziness" of the prose, thus missing the point in an hilarious but irritating way, and praised by *The List* for suggesting a way forward for "the future of the novel [...] by positioning it flat on its back." The novels coincided with a period in my life when I refused to engage with the outside world, minus a few snarling emails to debtors or enemies, and apart from necessary trips out to seal my dole money, I rarely left my flat. This way is the true path to creating honest, enduring art about what really matters in life: getting out of it in any way you can.

The Trauma Rooms

6

"NEXT one."

"Skip to the whys and wherefores."

"I prefer letting the patients speak for themselves."

"You realise I came to find a stapler, not take a thorough tour?"

"Yes! We will locate that stapler, I am sure. Now, come meet Max. You will find him hunched in the corner like a druggie 24 hours into a no-heroin scenario. Dangle this plastic rainbow in front of him," the doctor said, producing a plastic rainbow from his pocket.

"Has that been in your pocket the whole time?"

"Yes. Hi Max. This is Erin."

Erin took the plastic rainbow, walked over to the huddled ballman, and dangled. He unballmanned himself and stared at the plastic rainbow, emerging from his traumatised funk to uncrease his features into a desperate smile, muttering words like "light" and "colours," as Erin turned to the doctor for confirmation this scenario was acceptable.

"Max, Erin would like to hear your story, could you tell her?"

"Story? Yes . . . I could."

"Great. Come on Max, snap into life. Look at the rainbow."

"And be snappy."

"The rainbow. Yes. All right. I was working as a reader at Polonius Books at the time. The first MS I received had an epigraph from Franz Kafka, his famous line 'A book must be the axe for the frozen sea within us.' I thought this was an all-too-famous line to use at the beginning of what was a mediocre thriller set in Dorset.

195

I passed on the book and moved on. The next MS had the Kafka line: 'It is often safer in chains than to be free.' Again: a momentous line for a ho-hum production. Then followed a spate of novels cribbing passages from *The Trial*, *The Castle*, and *Amerika*. Characters recalled lines from Kafka during the novels to increase their kudos as characters. One novel set in a Butlins camp was prefaced with a four-page passage from *Letter to His Father*. The Kafka cribs kept coming. Soon I was wading in a sea of Kafka-saturated novels, until I arrived at the insane *Fiona Dreams Horses*, where the protagonist's equine dreams were prefaced with a page of Kafka, each horse named after a character from Kafka, each horse speaking in Kafka lines. I cracked under the Kafkan onslaught. I began to adopt the depressive paranoiac persona associated with Kafka's novels, changed my name by deed poll to Citizen #3727272, and adopted a herd mentality, listening to popular bands, aping the actions and interests of the population at large until I became a faceless clone. I sought out large crowds so I could vanish into them. I came alive on crowded train platforms, in packed trains, in places where people stood herded in misery, and couldn't face returning home to be alone with my thoughts. I was forced into contemplating my actions, and had to face the reality that I was different, I was not part of the herd I so coveted. This drove me insane, and here we are."

"Interesting," Erin said, yawning.

"Yes. Amazing that so many young writers turned to Kafka as an inspiration."

"Quoting Kafka is a surefire way of appearing literary, well-read and clued-in about the world. You are a writer who has read and understood Kafka, so yes, you have tussled with the darker side of life, and have emerged stronger, a more sensitive and knowing individual, and yes, readers should respect your integrity, because you wouldn't possibly have the chutzpah to quote Franz without having earned the right to," Erin said.

"Indeed."

"That by quoting Kafka in your epigraph, you are not saying you are an artist on a par with the Master, that you are merely doffing your literary cap to his legacy, you are a humble acolyte kneeling at the Master's feet, and that by titling your novel *Kafka's Coat*, you are not attempting to draw attention your novel by putting his name in the title, you are merely showing your reverence, you are not cynically mining the late-20s alienated males market with a novel that says 'if you love Kafka, you will love me!' and you are not saying your prose sometimes reaches the same heights of profundity as the Master, although if some critic made that remark, you would accept the flattering comparison, of course, and you are not saying having read Kafka's short oeuvre twice, and published a book with Kafka in the title, you are setting yourself up as some sort of expert, but if broadsheets wanted to commission an essay from you on Kafka, re-examining his importance in 21st century lit, or that sort of thing, you would hardly say no, and if a university wanted to offer you a teaching position on the basis of your knowing stuff about Kafka, that you would refuse, but of course these are all happy coincidences, nothing to do with cynically mining Kafka's legacy because he's popular with readers and scholars alike, more lucky that you fell in love with a Legend who also happened to promise you lucrative publication and academic opportunities, when you could have easily have fallen in love with William Sansom or some other obscure Kafkan writer, but hey, if you can profit from what you love most in this life, why not simply reap the rewards and be happy?"

"OK. You can stop now."

"Do you understand my point?"

"Oceanically clear."

"My stapler isn't here, can we move on please."

"Thanks Max."

"Terror. Everywhere. Screaming balls of pain," Max said, reballmanning himself.

"It's all about balls with you, isn't it?"

"Ha ha. Chin up, Max! See you in a while," the doctor said, closing the door before the terrible moaning commenced. "Fortunately the rooms have been soundproofed."

Puff: The Unloved Son

4

PUFF, the unloved son of fantasy writer C.J. Jackson, whose twelve-book-and-increasing *Firehole* was in endless progress, had been released to kick around the stock-dump fields chasing feral digipets with a makeshift bat made from the melted left-half of a monitor, trapping the creatures and smashing their digi-guts out with superhuman force for an unfit eight-year-old. He became sullen and resented his mother for her unfair slap-and-spank—a discipline she never repeated—and refused to speak to her as he ate his portions and slept indoors, fleeing back into the fields to commit violence on unreal animals and take long rambles into the trimmed-and-tucked lawns of the nearest ScotCall centre, where by the sort of coincidence that would only appear in one of his mother's novels when she was unable to weave two plot threads together convincingly, his father spotted him from his window while hitting his 500+ call targets. His father, Crumbs, recognised his likeness via CCTV close-up. There was no mistaking that nose (crinkled in the septum) and those lips (fat and curled-out) as Crumbs traits. He requested a ten-minute leave, losing a "star player" sticker for that afternoon, and went to confront his mini-Crumbs on the lawn.

"You're the son I was denied," he said. The son said nothing. "Where'd you come from?" The son said nothing. An accidental roll of the eyes towards The House betrayed him. "Claire Watson?" he asked. The son nodded.

Crumbs requested leave for the rest of the working day. This immediately wiped his six-year track record as "exceptional" worker back down to "novice," requiring a six-year reparation process (and promotion pass-over). He drove to The House and located Claire by bribing the receptionist to search the database. Crumbs tapped the rapt Claire on the shoulder—she was deep into a fight scene between Bryn the Merciless and Griffin the Great—until she acknowledged the two unwanted sights.

"How come you dropped our son in a field?" he asked.

"Do you want him?"

"I take it that means you don't?"

"Correct."

"Right. Let's go."

Claire, naturally, failed to look back with a regretful frown when her son was released forever into his father's more willing clutches. She relished in the freedom she had—not having to check Puff had eaten or washed (not that she remembered to do this anyway)—or pretend to care when he was bleeding out his orifices. She really was delighted she'd freed herself from the barnacle of her stupid and messy little accident. Finally, she had some peace and quiet to work on her thirteen-book-and-counting fantasy book series, *Fireswine*.

A Better Life

6

I whittled a dozen tooth sharpeners from Mrs. Horritt's cabinets and set about sharpening the sheeps' molars. The creatures didn't discriminate against wires or a human hand and tried to snack on my fingers. I used two tooth sharpeners to clamp open their mouths and set about increasing the pointedness of their teeth using a frictious hand movement akin to frenzied masturbation. Satisfied, I fed one sheep a length of flex. He munched as usual and explored his new capabilities, nibbling to the nub and swallowing the electricity. He exploded soon after as I took refuge behind a plastic tree. We had a problem. If every sheep exploded after chewing a wire, its partners' overcoats would ignite before they had the chance to fuck up the wires at each ScotCall trough. I had to herd the sheep for the first few troughs: one sheep at a time was sent to a trough to work on the cables and detonate in a controlled manner, then another was released once the smoke cleared. I had to nudge aside the flaming carcasses so the sheep could step in. The explosions and fires rarely did much damage to the wires. For this plan to work I would need to recruit a large amount of sheepherders to prod these ovines in the right direction. Given that the concrete fields spanned over fifty miles in each direction there was no way I could police such a business. Another option was to force breeding between the sheep to create an overspill.

I studied their "anatomies." Rogue electrical equipment from the stock-dump fields had impregnated flesh-and-blood sheep and caused this species mutation. I observed two sheep copulating and noted that the male sperm had an oily consistency, a natural mix-

201

ture of oil and ovine semen. I upended a sheep and saw that I could extrude this liquid from the sheep quite simply. I commenced a "milking" procedure, collecting the sperm in buckets and inseminating the females manually. I spent the next two weeks camping on the concrete fields, eating cold oven chips and inseminating as many sheep as possible before returning to the cottages. I reeked of the oily semen and when I returned to Pete and Rob after two weeks of repetitive and unpleasant work (if someone had told me when I left The House that I would end up inseminating sheep, I wouldn't have been surprised) the slothful gits were as usual ungenerous, making unflattering remarks about the horrid stench.

Laziness and phlegm had consumed them. One morning when Pete was asleep, I managed to steal his Man-Blaster. I disabled the horrible weapon and hurled it into the sea. I announced I would be leaving.

"No dice. I will blow holes in you with . . . " Peter looked around.

"Gone. I disabled it earlier."

"Why, you—" he leapt up. I produced a small rodent from my pocket.

"Meet Philip. He will spit venomous poison in your eyes if you dare to touch me." Peter flopped back onto the couch. "I had hoped we might club together to conduct this revolution but you have both lapsed into moral indigence. There's no point us remaining a unit now, since I can trust neither of you. Good luck."

"Hang on there . . . I mean we *are* in this together," Rob tried. I was already out the door. I had expected Peter to attempt some last-minute mode of attack so kept my little friend alert (the rodent was a sluggish thing that only appeared sinister with its infrared laser eyes) as I left the slobs to stew.

My plan was to live on the fields, monitoring and spreading the sheep destruction in a ten-mile radius. I had a rucksack of cold chicken and chips, but I was going to face a food and drink shortage if I didn't find another source within a fortnight. I had to return to The House. Doing so, I could resume hackwork for food and spend my weekends in the fields inseminating the sheep. To avoid the ScotCall buses, I carried a sheep under my arm and sent him to munch up the barbed wire whenever I spotted a bus approaching. If I kept the sheep hungry, he could devour a man-sized hole in the barbed wire in time, allowing me access to the ditch where I could crouch undetected. It was in this manner I returned to The House. I had sold my desk, so I had to hunt in the stock-dump fields for some form of replacement and for a usable laptop. Fortunately, after I used the public phone to call my reader, he enthusiastically sent me £100 for my next novel. This made my return a little easier.

I wrote a noir thriller set at Bela Lugosi's funeral. A romcom set at a mathematics conference. A Faustian drama set in Hull. A fabricated history of Partick Thistle football club. I wrote whatever my (five) readers desired. I moved between departments and became known as a floorhopper—someone who refuses to specialise in one genre (thus deluding themselves they are "artists" by being loyal to their area of expertise, as opposed to adaptable craftsmen who can turn their hands to anything) and had to fend off muttered oaths in the lifts. I forgave them their transgressions. I was single-handedly bringing about the downfall of the ScotCall empire with my sheep impregnating on weekends. They weren't to know that as they called me *slut* and *scab* under their breaths.

The *Farewell, Author!* Conference

6

JULIAN announced that half a pack of biscuits had been found in a crate in the backroom. The writers, cranky, and with a literal and metaphorical hunger at large in their stomachs/souls, began the silent squabble for biscuits as Julian placed the six plain digestives on a plate on the table beside the scoffed chocolates and cola. An instinctive human barrier had formed to prevent a Jodi Picoult ambush, and Kei Miller, closest to the plate, took a biscuit and broke it in two. "DON'T BREAK THEM YOU MORON YOU WILL LOSE CRUMBS!" Christopher Sorrentino howled in rage, adding: "A SIGNIFICANT PERCENTAGE OF THE BISCUIT WILL BE LOST IN THE SEVERING PROCESS!" Kei's motive was to share the biscuit between as many of the writers as possible, but if there was to be a share for everybody, the biscuits would have to be split into well over ten parts per biscuit, which was an impossible task without reducing the biscuits to (and losing to the floor) crumbs. Jonathan Franzen stepped forward. "I have a solution! If we can find two Ziploc bags, we can pound the digestives into a powder, and offer each writer a share of the biscuit remnants. What do we say to this, people?" he asked. "That you need a slap!" George Saunders said. No one laughed as tension was the prevailing mood. "I think that is a workable solution. All those in favour raise their hands," Julian said. No one raised their hand. Everyone was contriving a means of securing a full biscuit to themselves. Aleksander Hemon stepped forward: "I think a biscuit should be allocated to those who have published the most," he said. "YOU MEAN PEOPLE LIKE YOU? ARE WE GOING

TO SWALLOW THAT BULLSHIT?" Christopher Sorrentino howled. Paul Verhaeghen: "I have a condition that requires me to eat one, or more, of those biscuits now, or I will die." Christopher Sorrentino: "NOT EXACTLY AN ISSUE TONIGHT, IS IT?" Declan Kiberd: "I deserve a biccie because I have read *Ulysses* over a hundred times, and I bet none of you dweebs has even read it once." Dennis Cooper: "I can spin all six biscuits on my fingers! I have a sixth finger! I will show you this finger in exchange for a biscuit, and thereafter spin the biscuits on each finger in exchange for one biscuit per finger!" Alison Bechdel: "The men should stop this patriarchal crap and surrender these biscuits to the women, or me in particular, since I am also a lesbian, and therefore more deserving of biscuits than the straight women, who, let's face it, have never had any trouble acquiring biscuits. I also had a difficult relationship with my parents, so that counts for two at least." Charlie Brooker: "I don't want a fucking biscuit, and none of you self-involved cretins deserve one either. Pass them to me and I'll rub them between my arsecheeks and mash them up." Meredith Brosnan: "I have no special reason. I just want one because I haven't eaten in a week." Catherine Simpson: "Not for me. I prefer a custard cream." Janice Galloway: "I was raised in Saltcoats. I deserve all the biscuits in the world." Vernon D. Burns: "I was once a semi-amusing fake presence on the website Goodreads with two bungled bizarro novels to my name. Can I at least have a crumb?" Amélie Nothomb: "I will eat a crate of rotten fruit in exchange for these biscuits." Christopher Sorrentino: "THERE ARE NO FRUITS, YOU MISGUIDED BELGIAN!" Lisa O'Donnell: "I once read the whole of Updike's *Rabbit* series. I deserve all the biscuits in the world." Chris Ware: "I am depressed beyond biscuits." Marjane Satrapi: "I am Iranian, so you are going to ignore me anyway." David Eagleman: "You are all awaiting biscuits in the next life. I'm not—pass them to me." Michel Faber: "If we continue in this vein, the biscuits will go soft!" Julian: "They are already soft, I'm afraid." At which point, Christopher Sorrentino, on the verge of a cerebrovascular accident, lost his cool and charged forward, screaming the while, punching those who tried to stop him with a fierce right hook, and stole the biscuits, attempting to stuff all six at once into his mouth. Four of the biscuits, alongside copious crumbs, fell to the floor, and a pile-up fight for the biscuits ensued. Jonathan Littell managed to cram one in his mouth before being crushed, and the ensuing punch-up led to the biscuits being pulled apart until only crumbs remained, for which the writers began the brawl that was to form the centrepiece of that evening's activities.

Mhairi

7

GERALD is an idiot savant, with emphasis on idiot. His savance stems from his carpentry and engineering skills—one of those inexplicable talents often given to the intellectually bereft and physically ungainly. Born in a barnyard and deposited in a tin bucket by his hick mother, Gerald was raised by two kindly cows, who let him suckle at their teats and share their cud and water, until a farmhand discovered him sleeping in a haystack at the age of nine, took him into his home, and taught him to unlearn his bovine behaviours such as crawling on all fours, chomping moronically, and mounting females. The farmhand, alas, was not as smart as the cows, and taught Gerald a new set of behaviours, such as eating with his fingers and licking the trough; urinating obliviously on the very patch of grass on which he slept; greeting strangers by dribbling down their chests; devouring liquids nasally; pronouncing each word "uh-*huck*-nuh!"; playing a game where one has to step in as many cowpats as possible; lighting a candle and two seconds later hysterically shouting "Fire!", among others. Gerald single-handedly constructed the six-hectare ScotCall compound, and was paid nothing for his services except board, lodgings and meat. I discovered him lurking in a stock-dump field one day, giving succor to a depressed laptop, and invited him inside for a coffee, or, as he preferred, a dishwater. I had been sleeping on the ground floor with Marilyn until then, sharing her bag and trying to prise her creeping fingers away from my erogenous zones. I discussed with Gerald my need for a more comfortable sleeping arrangement, and drew up a blueprint for my shouse, which Gerald made in 48 hours from 4,383 toasters (as a bonus feature, he installed a "pop-open" roof allowing a shaft of sunlight to enter in the summer), and I rewarded him with a permanent position at The House, where his talents were required hourly, and his diet could move away from melted monitors and microwaves. (In fact, for the first few weeks, after eating the risottos and curries I made him, he snuck outside and ate a few washing machines).

Alice: A Fictional Serviette

THIS fictional serviette concerns Alice. She worked on the ninth floor (who knows) composing various fictions (who cares) before deciding that sexual prostitution was a viable alternative to writerly prostitution. She roamed the north of England (which parts irrelevant) offering her body to paying punters. Since she had only been in The House for two weeks, her body had not succumbed to malnutrition, although she was bonier than most professional prostitutes. To retain her sanity, and delude herself into thinking she was still an artist, she would compose prose and poems to recite while screwing the males, and demonstrate her creativity by naming the manoeuvres in her sexual repertoire, among them: the shoreman's trieste; the triple-layered diorama; the yellow back radio broke-down; the Simon Schama; the open sesame; the Colombian astrolabe; the freelance pallbearer; the severed head of Diana Ross; the roseate groceries; the chestnut situation; the bearded colonel; the gaping polytechnic; the unremotely untheatrical; the mumbo jumbo; the disappointed ostrich; the yodelling hatmaker; the last days of Louisiana Red; the semi-automatic bicycle clip; the xylophonic menace; the cheery potato; the history of the decline and fall of the Roman Empire; the sustained yelp of a diabetic Christian; the beer-soaked Bayern Munich supporter; the electric coypu; the Japanese by spring; the imperial leather; the lost episode of *It Ain't Half Hot, Mum*; the terrible twos; the revolving stapler; the defensive response when Jeff asked Cybil for a renewal of the Birmingham contract; the somewhat exciting thing; the hectare from the black lagoon; the solar-powered sundial; the terrible exuberance of Maxwell House; the juice!; the retroactive insertion; the biased Wilson; the disappointed expression on Jeremy's face when a tiger scratches his Blondie LP; the terrible threes; the frenetic game of Connect Four; the Basildon forceps; the overrated flamethrower; the syntactic embrace; the cobra's politics; the nimble quicksilver; the spotty alabaster; the reckless eyeballing; the Geoff of my dreams; the humorous and seemingly honest politician who breathes new life into a corrupt political system, ravaged by cynicism and greed, who turns out to be as shabby and corrupt as the rest when elected, causing a full-scale revolt on the Houses of Parliament; the flight to Canada; the mechanical satrap.

Alice performed this impressive roster of manoeuvres on her clients, and read unsolicited excerpts from her erotic fictions. As she was riding a male, four minutes from climax, she would recite (for instance): "Eleanor walked into the chalet, her skimpy pink panties sliding down her thighs to reveal the holy chalice from which Dominic was yearning to sup. The night was hotter than July in Havana. Dominic's cantilever rose at the sight of Eleanor's vision of deferred paradise, now becoming a mouthwatering reality." And her clients would protest: "What you doing? Shut up and screw. I don't want to hear this drivel while knobbing you." That put an end to her recitations *in flagrante*, so she tried to sell copies of her erotica to punters after the act. "A bewk? Makes me pe-ewke!" was among the replies. One evening, as she was performing a yo-delling hatmaker on Brian McHail, she decided the best thing to do was read an excerpt from her erotic novel, and include the novel in the cover charge, before any shagging commenced. So desperately horny males would find themselves warmed-up by one of her tales, making them pre-spurt to such an extent, her job simply became a twist-and-wipe, or a squirt-and-retreat. She had saved herself as an artist (sort of) and made her life as a pro easier. Thus Alice had one of the best literary careers of her generation.

Cal's Tour

Toilet Books

THE sixth floor is fairly clinical with its very-off-white corridor, lino of dark aqua, and series of small lavatories—males on the left, females on the right—filling the air with scents of elderberry, lavender, vanilla, and shit. A sign reads: *Please do not use the toilets on this floor. Content testing in progress.* As I arrived, a man in lab coat (one of the "labcoats," strangely enough) with a clipboard, black spectacles and an urgent face appeared—the look of someone un-afraid and downright willing to tackle a fresh stool sample. "Are you a tester?" he asked. "I was hoping to write here," I said. "No openings for content makers. You can test for us if you like. We're short," the man said. (He was short too, coincidentally). I was ur-gently walked to the not entirely unprisonlike canteen—a bustling eatery full of ravenous testers being served curries, beans, and all sorts of bowel-loosening meals, and told to help myself and honk my horn when ready (horns were placed on the tables to attract the labcoats, who hovered at the back waiting to swish). I ladled a skimpy helping of madras onto my plate, showered in pilaf rice and soaked up with two auriform naans. I found space beside a thug named Kobo with a shaven head and the tattoo of a gardening ac-cident gone wrong: roses and pitchforks and severed limbs rising from his lower neck to his head. Kobo forked syrupy vindaloo into his mouth with starveling mania, alternating each spoonful with a doughnut. He was skinnier than me but could apparently consume four meals simultaneously without damaging his shapely figure. I chose not to say hi.

Quickly forgetting my table manners, I attacked the madras like a glutton, downing my pint of ale in record time, and flurped back in my chair when finished, remembering to honk the horn. A labcoat swished me into the corridor toward the testers' loos. He handed me the hardback *A Thousand Squirrel Photobombs*—a heavy picture book consisting entirely of photos where squirrels appeared in the background and ruined the intended shot in a way that some might deem amusing. The labcoat told me to press the bog-side button when I was bored reading (looking) and sealed me in the overly bright and bleached toilet. I had clearly misunderstood the honking command, believing the honk signified a full stomach and not a readiness to excrete. But I sat on the toilet anyway and focused my attention on the pesky squirrels. After five minutes I was bored and unamused, so flushed the toilet and washed my hands, feigning a swift voidance to escape the book. The labcoat, in marigolds, placed the squirrel book in a plastic Ziploc bag and mechanically thanked me for the feedback, swish-tickling me to the chill-out area. I was handed a pocket horn to honk if the urge for further ablutions should arise. The chill-out space is a large common room, where lazy and semi-obese halfwits in slogan-savaged tracksuits sit around watching TV soaps, discussing the books read (looked at), speaking in crude staccato, and hooting at anything remotely rude or euphemistic. A bald one slurred loudly about the hirrarious *Pictures of Stoned Cats*, which was so hirrarious he lillerally forgot he was shitting, while a spotty one was so fulking bored by *Things to Say to Uptight Butlers* that he coonent congcemtrape on shitting the shit out his shithole and had to put the book down and heave the fulkers by holeing onto the heave bars. A tiny blonde one said that she rannou of poo playper, so used plages out of the blook, which was the bess fulking use for the fulking blook she could fulking think of, ha-ha-ha-ha-fulk-you. I smiled along to be chummy.

For my second trip to the testing toilets, I was handed *Writers Making Tits of Themselves*. The book contained shots of various writers across the world looking like crazed yetis, clinging to the

214

legs of ScotCall tyrants, begging hobos for money to help self-publish their manuscripts, lying dead and frozen in ditches with pens clutched to their hands, or being shot by laughing policemen. I discovered that the shit flowed freely looking at these images (as you can imagine!), and more shit than I had intended to shit was unleashed almost on cue. I flicked to the end page and honked later than planned, unable to look away from the pathetic horror. The success of this test meant the book would be published. As the chattier lab coat explained: "The process is pretty straightforward for publishing our books. If the manuscript keeps testers fixed to the toilet for the duration of their shit, or makes them want to hold back the shit for the sake of reading, the book is considered successful. Books that make testers eager to finish up their shit so they can get away, or are used as loo paper, are not taken to publication stage beyond the trial copy, no surprise. We restrict our content to funny or soothing pictures, or occasionally ones with very small lines of text, because most people find it hard to shit and read at the same time, and sometimes the images distract and help them with trickier shits, so that makes the bowel movements flow much easier. We're in the unblocking business, not the literature business. The success of the shits is normally attributed to the success of the books the testers are reading as they're shitting. So it isn't exactly an exact science, but works pretty well." I nodded and returned to the chill-out area. "How illuminating," I wanted to say, but would have sounded like a . . . shit?

In the chill-out room, the testers (who you probably realise I disliked—you may find their brand of earthy humour to your liking!) kicked off a frank discussion of the type of shits they produced as they were reading (looking). How certain pages of certain books led to a series of small turds, while others created serious blockage, and people discussed the weight, consistency, density and malleability of their shits in response to certain images—cute kittens usually made for fluffier shits, while angry dogs or dirty photos usually made for tougher shits, which was simply a technique to force the shit back in so you would spend longer on the loo not shitting and reading (looking at) the book. Erotic images were even worse, as the urge to masturbate would overtake the necessity to shit, and you'd never get going after you'd knocked one out into the loo roll first. I had the strongest urge to leave and . . . sob? Shit? Among the titles they discussed were: *100 Wonkiest Gerbil Eyebrows, SuMu's Subway Shoe Disasters, Sex Tips of Centenarians, America's Cutest Roadkill, 57 Pictures of Albinos Eating Grapes, Fallout!: Chernobyl's Zaniest Mutations, 77 Manx Cats with Photoshopped Tails, What Would Preschoolers Look Like with the Heads of the Bee Gees?, How to Scare Yourself in the Mirror, The Difference Between Short & Sharp, Forty More Pictures of Paint Drying!!!, Jezz Wimpole's Book of Boobies, Jesusface—Our Lord Rendered in 76 Objects, Sorry, Switzerland!: Korea's Clumsiest Missile Strikes.*

I often fell asleep on the loo. My eyes glazed. My selection process become wholly arbitrary. For books whose content I despised, I would speedily dispatch shits out of spite, and those I thought amusing I would champion by squeezing my buttocks together to suppress the flow. The power of the laxative smoothies and evacuant nature of the curries made shits erupt quickly, while sometimes shits were a tougher consistency if raisin bran and prunes were quaffed in enthusiastic mouthfuls. The eater's taste in foods was really the criteria by which the books were published, so the setup was pointless. I wondered if this was the procedure when publishing houses existed. If editors took the manuscripts into the bathrooms after very heavy lunches and mistook their slow bowel movements for the quality of the manuscripts. Did that mean literature had always been associated with the production of shit? Next up, *74 Pictures of Kids Shitting on Shakespeare*, a book purposefully designed to confront writers. I winced at the pesky kidolts doing their mess over The Bard's complete works, but took the elevated stupidity of the enterprise on the chin—no amount of junior poo could erase any Great Literature! Once again, I had taken so long making faces of horror that the book would probably be distributed. I explained to the labcoat that I was shitting slow because of my repugnance at the images, but the labcoat said that sort of response was an added marketing bonus—people who still respected the lineage of good writers would read in horror ("shock-lit") and those who hated books would naturally find the whole thing funny. I clenched. (My teeth).

The experience reminded me in part of the philistinism I encountered at school, where my interest in books had been met with fear—fear that my bizarre obsession might infect those close by, lead to them picking up books and ideas, until the school was riddled with incurable verbivores, brainwashing the campus with facts and learning that had little to do with ScotCall procedures—how to cure desk cramp or how to deal with customers who had trouble determining whether ring pulls should be pulled towards or away from the drinker. Apart from Kirsty's sisterly reminders of the worthlessness of writers and me in particular, I'd never encountered such blatant hatred towards books—nothing to the extent of the loo roll with passages from Shakespeare, Dickens, Eliot, and Coulter that were being tested in the department at the time (which despite the blankness on the other side, would still end up in a bowl of shit being flushed towards a palace of shit). If you need reassurance that all the great books are being read, this is not the floor for you. One day, returning to the chill-out area after a tikka with pilaf rice, two poppadoms, and a knickerbocker glory with extra knickers, a tattooed tough was saying how megaliffic his latest dump was, how he was made to read this book wiff picturs of like fames people but wiff their heads replaced wiff monkey arses, and how he was laffing so much he piffed himself first, and didn't notice when the shit dropped out, and a squat OAP with maxi-specs was saying it was crimnal that they was given such guid biks to read whall shitting, coz his bik had these piccurs of fat hookers covered in choc sauce and ha-ha-ha-ha the lass thing he wanted to do was hurry up shittin when these hot hooks were makin him hard, and a teenager said that hewasragincozthebookhegotwasallaboutpotteryandwhatkindofcuntreadsabookallaboutpotteryforfuckssake? At that point I stood up and left the sixth floor forever.

A Word from the Team

LABCOAT: Testers required. No experience of reading necessary. NO WRITERS NEEDED.

This

7

I AM the author of this novel and I have lied to you, and taken unhealthy pleasure in lying to you, and I will continue to lie to you until you beg for more. I have lied about everything in my real life (which does not exist—even as the "author" I am a construct invented to represent aspects of the "real" author—however, let's not tangle ourselves in semantic or metaphysical notions). I have lied my way through life, relishing in the saltiest untruths. When people have asked me, "Is that soup made of string?" I have replied, "No. That soup is made of soup." I have told many dirty, unfair lies, and I have delighted in every one. The truth is a pointless concept, invented by non-writers to keep the masses logical and docile, to eliminate the pleasures of fiction-making. Punch the truth hard.

The Trauma Rooms

7

"You realise, by now, I could have sifted through the fields outside and found a stapler?" Erin asked.

"Yes, a stapler to staple your lips shut."

"What does that mean?"

"Oh . . . no, I meant . . . hmm, as the staplers are feral out there. . . anyway, this is Gerald. He has occasional violent episodes, such as strangling or stabbing writers. Apart from that, a perfectly nice chap," the doctor said, opening on a trimmed man in his forties sitting on his bed listening to Devo on his iPod.

"Hi there! Sorry, I didn't see you both sidle in."

"We're sly sidlers."

"Sly sidlers! I like that."

"This is Erin, Gerald."

"Wow, I love your hair, Erin. Do you use Pantox medicated shampoo?"

"No. I use a Lemmox follicle fixer."

"Also a quality brand."

"Gerald, Erin would love to hear your story, if you have a spare few minutes?"

"Gosh! I had my lugs full of Devo's seminal *Freedom of Choice* LP. I suppose I can hit the old pause button and spin the old spiel again. I promise not to lapse into a writer-throttling rage this time, doc! Right. I was freshly appointed co-editor of a quarterly magazine. I hadn't written a single story in my life, nor studied literature, nor read more than forty books, but I didn't feel that impeded my ability to recognise top-quality literary fiction when I read (or skimmed!) it. I had to read a thousand stories a week. Once I had selected two from that thousand for publication, I passed them on to my co-editors, and we voted for the final line-up. Our first story, by Cody Trylomp, 'Green Faucets' was a searing portrait of a minor league soccer team in New Hampshire, set against one father's struggle to quench his thirst for victory and come to terms with his daughter's autism. Cody sent his short bio: 'Cody is a writer, poet, and scriptwriter barely scraping a living as an IT assistant in the Appalachian mountains. In his spare time, he plays dodgeball with his manic toddler Tommy, and helps his beautiful wife Karen with her Hollywood screenplays.' I found the bio irritating. Next story was by Mandi Brookelyfe, 'Jane's Wrists,' about a cutter who struggles with her weight while running an independent bookstore in Wisconsin. Her bio: 'Mandy is a writer and novelist. She received her [list of academic qualifications]. Her works have appeared in [list of over twenty magazines]. She loves carving skulls into cookies and surfing the zeitgeist in a monogrammed thong.' I became enraged at this point and had to take a comfort break. Next story, 'K. Comes to Brooklyn', by Artie Loden, about a stoned NYC scriptwriter stalked by Kafka's shadow. His bio: 'Artie seeks abstractions from the most sordid of sources. His ying is pursuing a PhD on Kafka's silence, his yang likes beer and pool.' I kicked things under the table. Further bios included: 'Serena sits in coffee shops pondering the vicissitudes of bran muffins. If not writing her overdue thesis on Paul Auster, she can be found editing the radical webzine *Scissors Trumps Rock*.' And: 'Brian Fripp divides his time between Leeds and Tijuana. He spends too much time watching *CSI: Miami* and playing korfball. He is working on a screenplay about Andy Warhol's fondness for Greta Garbo.' And: 'Julie Wilmott likes a nectarine on occasion. When she is not staring into space or fixing valve amps, she writes novels about cisgender puppies and Capuchin monks.' I exploded. I hurled my Apple Mac out the window, crushing four pigeons. I ran into the street seeking vengeance on the writers who had penned these self-loving whimsical cooler-than-thou bios and, failing to find them, stabbed a tramp outside Oddbins. In prison, I stabbed a writer whose bio I spotted: 'Derek imagineers sci-fi and erotic literature. If not cleaning out the toilets on E-wing, he can be found in the prison library, brushing up on his Dickens and Zola.' My defence was that the word 'imagineers' alone justified the homicide. I was declared insane and escaped the asylum. I came here to kill everyone in the building. Fortunately, the doctor here intervened before I reached my tenth murder. His treatment has been valuable, but I still have that insatiable bloodlust whenever I read an author's bio."

"Jesus," Erin said, thinking of her bio: "Erin Grahams writes soap operas featuring the occasional cannibal nurse. She has a fondness for escalators and have-a-go heroes. Her two kittens think she smells."

"Thanks for sharing, Gerald," the doctor said. Erin stared into Gerald's calm eyes, and for a microsecond, thought she saw the bio-addled psychokiller look into her soul and see the needy narcissist inside.

"He knows. About my shit bio."

"Sorry?"

"I wrote the sort of embarrassing cutesy bio that drives him to homicide."

"Oh. I shouldn't concern yourself with that. Shall we proceed?"

"What if he escapes and hacks me into bitesize chunks as I sleep?"

"These doors are secure. You'd need a battering ram to penetrate those locks."

"Really?"

"Yes. Now, let's—"

"What do those bios say? They say I am the sort of attention-seeking plonk who needs to engineer a quirky persona to make myself appealing outside the fiction I have written. That I am not content with letting the work speak for itself, I have to persuade the reader that the person who wrote the work is awesome, intriguing, and a Talented New Voice on the Scene, and probably fabulous to have as a friend. That by taking a jokey tone, I am trying to distract

you from the truth that I consider myself a fucking legend-in-the-
making, illustrated by the three paragraphs of literary magazines I
have been published in, that I am—"

"Yes! All right. I have other things to do."

"Sorry. Carried away."

"It's OK. Writers are arseholes."

"Damn right."

Writer Portraits

Movements

Freed-in-Fiction

THE Freed-in-Fiction movement was the hippest club for intellectual dropouts, child/wifeless male academics, and assorted
creatives unwilling to face up to their personal problems. A coterie
of exhausted English Lit & Creative Writing students, failing upon
graduation to rise to the challenge of carving careers for themselves
in teaching or editing or corporate proofreading, decided that their
fictional creations were far more alive and interesting than their
real lives, and elected to neglect the quotidian in favour of vicar-
ious living through their novels. One of the founders, Dan Inch,
laid down various rules to help direct the group, the first being a
complete shunning of publication of any kind—to publish was to
acknowledge that books (and themselves) existed in the real world,
whereas they were looking for an ontological loophole that excused
them from the business of living (choosing to dismiss their actual corporeal presences on the planet as irrelevant). The second
was that their physical presences on the planet were to be treated
as part of their ongoing oeuvre—an unwritten extension of their
books through the medium of movement and speech. This unhing-
ing of reality, naturally, led to deviant behaviour. One writer in
his novels had written an antihero who went around shooting corporate criminals and having sex with random beauties whenever
one wandered into the narrative. This behaviour, replicated in real
life, was not repeated, although the author beat up random bankers,
shop managers, or anyone who appeared to be indulging in capital-

225

ist excess, and conducted himself in improper ways around women with pinching and unsolicited touching. These writers were commonly regarded as laughable and clueless until a harsh winter finished them off.

The New Established Writer Movement

New writers, i.e. those who had been passed over by agents and publishers for decades, chose to establish themselves as established writers. To achieve this, a list of books published overseas was invented, alongside false overseas agent and publisher contact info (including false agent and publisher websites), and new (i.e. old) manuscripts were sent to UK publishers with the salvo of a respected publishing history (in Australia or New Zealand) to help pique the interest of agents and publishers. If successful, The New Established Writers would find their latest (or earliest) novel published and, depending on sales, find their non-existent backlog sped into print to meet the demands of a burgeoning audience. Most of the writers had ten or so complete novels in their drawers, and in some cases a whole catalogue was "re-issued" simultaneously (with the author having to typeset and print fake copies privately to send to their real publishers so facsimiles could be made). This movement was exposed in a similar manner to the The New Writer movement some years earlier, and a harsh winter finished them off.

The Serial Listing Movement

These writers believed that the furniture of conventional novels was superfluous; that the ordered line-by-line dialogue of characters was superfluous; that the linear page-turning plot was superfluous; that deep insight into the human condition was superfluous; that the finger-tingling all-over assault on the brain and body produced by the most masterly of stylists was superfluous; that the words on the page themselves attempting to communicate something or nothing at all were superfluous; that double or triple meanings were so many layers of mouldy custard within a smelly trifle; that the spooky transference of art from brain to page was mystical bunkum; that the physical rigor required to bring books to fruition was a lazy dreamer's hyperbole; that the bitter sacrifice of sanity, soul, and sexual needs was the pitiful cry of a loner; that all the precious components of timeless literature could be reduced to a series of blank lists with no substance or heart. The movement was criticised as a direct *nouveau roman* rip-off, and a harsh winter finished them off.

The Anti-cis-heteronormativist Movement

This movement set about rewriting literature with the assumption that all characters were trapped in false gender identities, and by allowing characters to realise their true gender roles, free literature from the oppression of the cis-heteronormativists who had been imposing heterosexist ideals on readers since time immemorial. The first rewrite was *Jane Eyre*, with the famous heroine recast as a pangender transitioning towards a more male-centred outlook. The plot was tweaked to castigate Rochester for his persistence, where he learned to respect Jane's complex gender position and stronger romantic pulls towards female sexual partners. Further rewrites included David Copperfield realising himself as a queer heterosexual, which better explained his attraction to Dora Spenlow; Molly Bloom identifying herself as a "fifth sex," outside both genders, outside all non-gender classifications, a separate class known as Bloomism—sort of a magnet for all sexualities, genders and nongenders; and Raskolnikov as a transsexual in process of becoming a woman so he could be kept by a husband and write without having to concern himself with making a living. This movement, while an amusing contemporaneous reimagining of the patriarchal canon and a necessary riposte to the tyrannous influence of university syllabi, suffered due to the lack of talent involved in pastiching the originals. A harsh winter finished them off.

The _____ Movement

Four men who did no writing whatsoever and bragged about their lack of achievements at writing groups, readings, and events. Their belief that more than enough fiction had been penned over the last three centuries was illustrated with the blank notebooks they carried around and the no pens in their pockets (if approached for a pen, they made a show of patting their pockets and declaring: "Sorry, we never need one!"), and if presented with a book published after their inception, they refused with the refrain: "Sorry, for us the buck stopped a while ago!" (the buck meaning new books). In writing classes, the men would sit in silence, staring into space during the live writing portion, infuriating the teachers by insisting on a four-minute silence during their allotted reading aloud time. At author readings, the men would turn their backs on the authors during the readings from their new books and listen to loud punk on headphones, resuming their attention after the applause. If the author's first book had been published after the group's inception, the men would book seats and not turn up to the events, leaving the chairs blank as a protest (despite the fact the rooms were usually empty anyway). In online workshops, the men would embed pictures of blank pages, or include a sequence of blank _____ lines, and delete the abusive feedback. One time, an ex-vintner with a first novel out castigated them for wasting his time by standing up to ask a question and singing the chorus to "Fernando" by Abba, humiliating them after the show by exposing their movement as a testament to their own failure as writers, and their pathetic need to flaunt their failure by spoiling the success of others. The harsh vintner finished them off.

A Better Life

7

AFTER a month I refurbished a motorbike and set about spreading the wire-nibbling destruction across a vaster catchment. ScotCall had been unable to react to the problem with speed—three thousand coffee confabs and latte chattes had to take place before opting on a course of misaction—however, one afternoon I was embroiled in the first of their hard-hitting retaliation manoeuvres. Several dozen operatives shouldering bazookas came zooming along in their landcruisers and proceeded blowing the sheep to floccules. I took refuge behind a plastic tree as the thugs roared past, leaving streaks of flame in their wake and mere remnants of the several hundred sheep I had strenuously bred. The air was rank with gasoline, peat, and sheep semen. I cursed the band of hellacious devils (immaculate crew cuts in top-buttoned white business shirts) as I made my escape, unscathed except for a few scratches, and retreated back to The House. The phone lines had been disturbed to such an extent that the roads were populated with aimless protesters—confused "customers" had migrated up from England and were seeking a solution to their current problems.

Furious banner-wavers camped on the roads making incoherent chants in noncommittal mumbles, blocking the buses that arrived bearing an extra spew of arms-wide appeasers. The unanswered *vox populi* in their muddled huddles hurled questions at each Scot-Call operative who approached them with throatfuls of warm indigestible appeasement. The operatives abandoned their spiel to bark quick-fire replies at their fuming customer base. "How does my VCR work?" "Turn it on!" "What is the point of the sky?" "To

229

store the clouds!" "Can I use my toothbrush as a suppository?" "Depends!" "Green shoes or brown slippers?" "Green slippers!" "Can absinthe be used as an antidepressant?" "Yes!" "Is it possible to transfer debit to credit by switching banks?" "No chance!" "Why is Greenland so icy?" "False advertising!" "How do I review a dreadful book online without hurting the author's feelings?" "Rate five stars and the opinion is irrelevant!" "Is a shepherd allergic?" "Never!" "Does a swan mind if you insult its beak?" "Swans are sensitive to all complaints!" "Does it matter?" "It does to *me!*"

Pockets of satisfied customers migrated back home, but most of their queries led to further queries and the ratio of operatives to customers meant a mass-resolution (even with megaphones) was impossible. Forty-seven operatives had fatal heart attacks as the crowds shuffled towards the ScotCall HQ. Half-cocked attempts were made to keep the crowds outside the gate (operatives asking the crowds to please remain outside the gate) and helicopters whirred overhead with loudspeakers blasting stock responses to the most common questions. As the crowd spilled into the ScotCall HQ building pandemonium ensued across the nation. Operatives were being disrupted from their phone duties to attend to the invaders and this caused millions of unanswered customers and *en masse* migrations from England, Wales, and Northern Ireland to seek responses. Hundreds of directionally challenged stragglers arrived at The House, where they were recruited into the new campaign as run by a faction of experimental novelists, helmed by Alan the Experimentalist, and given a basic education with a view to reforming the country using intelligence and books to govern the *hoi polloi* in place of fear and ignorance.

The House was the only place to escape the march of mayhem. ScotCall enacted various tactics to clear their buildings and roads. Helicopters went skywards so operatives could scatter the ten most common solutions written on millions of strips of paper onto their customers' heads. The top ten queries were: 1) How do I turn toast back into bread? 2) Is Monaco a country? 3) Can I use 1½ AA batteries instead of an AAA? 4) What shape is a square? 5) Who is

Tim Pritchards? 6) Is it legal to sing a pop song in public without seeking public performing permissions? 7) Does a radioactive duck have green poo? 8) How many numbers are there in the alphabet? 9) Where is the toilet? 10) Can I put a fridge on my cat when she's asleep? In addition to this, covert operatives were smuggled into the crowds to whisper solutions into passing ears—a technique that backfired as the customers lashed out at having other (assumed) customers giving them false solutions when the definitive ScotCall answers were all that was sought. Loudspeakers blasting out advice were raised alongside two enormous cinema screens broadcasting subliminal messages ("Please bugger off home!"). The last and most effective option was to hurl canisters of fainting gas into the crowds from the helicopters. The unconscious bodies were removed to special tents where upon waking the solutions were offered in orderly ways. This technique also backfired, as on their way back to their houses, the bemused customers would have a brand new query: *what the hell happened to us? Did you bastards just gas us?* It was certainly not an excellent PR move. Needless to say, I was happy in my safe haven.

The *Farewell, Author!* Conference

7

THE event organisers had witnessed many writer brawls, in particular the little-known fistfight between Gore Vidal and Norman Mailer back in 2007, where Gore emerged the victor after a vicious blow to the belly, ending Mailer's life (a press release lied that he had been undergoing lung surgery), and the bizarre bout between E.L. Doctorow and William H. Gass in 2015, resulting in a fractured tibia for Doctorow, and a 1000-page treatise *On the Vicissitudes of Violence* from Gass (never published). The safest option was to clear the area—the organisers knew that writers were the most cowardly, traitorous fighters out there, never averse to an attack from behind, or punching someone in their sleep, or shaking hands and calling a truce and stabbing through the navel with an icicle. In that vein, Muriel Barbery clobbered Paul Murray with a bag of frozen beefsteaks; Ben Marcus shoved Geoff Dyer towards an open freezer and, having failed to move him an inch, crouched down and begged "Don't punch me!"; Jáchym Topol kicked Claudia Rankine in the shins, and received a stunning slap in return; Warren Motte attempted a headbutt on Mark Haddon but ended up hurling himself at Lydia Lunch, who rolled him up like a carpet and fired him out the window. The scene of violence that followed does not bear rendering in another list form—to reduce these shameful acts to mere rote would be in itself a shameful act. I leapt up later to take the microphone and shouted: "YOU HAVE COME HERE TO DIE, NOT TO BRAWL!" This created the desired silence, and I followed this up with: "Did not Nabokov once say, 'Beauty is mysterious as well as terrorful. God and the devil are fighting there,

233

and the battlefield is the heart of a man'?" This caused an eruption of laughter.

"That wasn't Nabokov, you buffoon!" Jonathan Coe mocked.

"It's *terrible*, not *terrorful*. Terrorful isn't even a word!" Jhumpa Lahiri mocked.

"It's God and devil, not God and *the* devil. Did you memorise that from Wikipedia?" Agnès Desarthe ditto.

"That was Dostoevsky, you moron!" Toby Litt ditto.

"It is heart of *man*, not heart of *a* man. I can't believe you didn't know that!" Steven Poole " ".

"I fail to see the relevance of that line, are you saying you find us beating the shit out of each other beautiful?" Cynthia Rogerson " ".

"You are trying in some bungling manner to make us ponder a concept no longer applicable in the modern world," Georgi Gospodinov " ".

"You have proven to us all that you have no handle whatsoever on basic symbolic metaphor," David David Katzman " ".

"You stand proud on that stage, maintaining your ground, while inside that body beats the heart of a simple village dolt," Silvia Barlaam " ".

"I hate your words and the mouth responsible," Ever Dundas " ".

"How about this, then?" I tried again. "Did not Aeschylus once say, 'Be nice, for everyone you see is waging a hard fight'?"

"JESUS CHRIST!!!" Dan Rhodes " ".

"You are the largest fool I have ever permitted to speak before me on a picnic table," Geoff Nicholson " ".

"That was Jewish Egyptian philosopher Philo, not Ancient Greek tragedian Aeschylus!!!" Jim Dodge " ".

"There is a 500-year difference between the people you have confused and misquoted!" David Mazzucchelli " ".

"Your mere cardiorespiratory existence is a source of persistent bafflement!" Miranda July " ".

"Be *kind*, not be *nice*. As if an Egyptian philosopher circa the birth of Christ would say 'nice,' like some mum talking to her kids!" Daniel Handler " ".

"Everyone you *meet*, not *see*. How can one be kind to strangers on the street? Shoot them kind looks, or stop and ask them if there's anything they need? You, sir, are an inflated buffoon about to burst," Carol Ann Sima " ".

"It's *fighting* a *hard battle*, not *waging* a *good fight*. This laughable misquotation proves your IQ is several digits below an earwig," Frédéric Beigbeder " ".

"You are a boil on the neck of literacy," J.T. LeRoy " ".

"I have eaten bagels with more insight than you," Steven Hall " ".

"A few centuries ago, you would have been shot for such brain-buggery," Vanessa Gebbie " ".

"Your utterances transcend my otherwise prodigious capacity for empathy," David Shields " ".

"Scum," Scarlett Thomas " ".

"There are no words to describe you, although if pushed I would use 'pant-wetting fuckbudgie from hell'," Mary Roach " ".

"I could have quoted that correctly," T.C. Boyle " ".

And so, through my sheer idiocy, I had stopped the brawling. My intention had been to make them reflect on the meaning of the quotes, but the fun at baiting a writer for his mistakes had proven the stronger impulse.

Mhairi

8

As mentioned earlier, before my shouse was constructed, I had to share a sleeping bag with Marilyn Volt. This was one of the strangest experiences of my life, stranger even than sharing a glue bag with a ventriloquist (who offered his dummy some shit before inhaling). Marilyn is, in addition to a nutcase who takes far too many runs under false pretences, a delusional philanthropist, and a spandexed-up nincompoop, a sexual predator of the weirdest variety (and I have encountered a rich tapestry of weird and dangerous pervs in my time). Arriving in winter, where the ground floor is freezing at nights, and with no other sleeping quarters available (or so she lied to me), I was forced to squeeze into her tight sleeping bag, bumping uglies with her and enduring the unpleasant friction. "It can get very sticky under there, so I would advise sleeping in your underwear," she said beforehand. "I'm fine in these pyjamas, thanks," I said. She inserted her bronzed veiny physique into the sleeping bag and made a sliver of room for me, and I inserted my pale crack-ravaged physique into the sliver. I entered with my back to her, and she auto-spooned herself around me (there was no room to do otherwise), and I closed my eyes. Apart from the nervy, heavy breathing and the hand snaking along my right thigh, I knew something was amiss when her tongue worked its slimy way along my helix, down to my lobule, of which she took a horny bite and, meeting no resistance (I was in shock), she risked a squeeze of my left tit. At that point my shock ended. "What the fuck are you doing?" I asked. "Come on, relax and have fun with Mommy Volt," she said. That sent my psycho-radars into overdrive, and I struggled out the sleeping bag. In the end, I had to threaten her with the prospect of me finding somewhere else to sleep, and slightly pimp myself by offering the warm elixir of my body close to hers provided she kept her exploratory fingers and tongue to herself. Over the next fortnight, I had to chastise her for the following manoeuvres: wrapping her arm around me after protests of loss of circulation and probing a pinkie into my navel; breathing and drooling on the back of my neck; removing her bra with complaints of pain and squishing her breasts into my back (with erect nipples); pretending that her arms had fallen asleep and accidentally landed on my front or back bottom; muttering supposedly seductive endearments into my ears, such as "Come to me, honey-child" or "Let me *feel* you, darling babe"; deliberately wearing warm clothes, forcing me to strip to my underthings and have her touch my skin; and frequently stroking my legs with hers and claiming restless leg syndrome. One evening, I was so tired that I let her have a roam around my body, and in the morning I chastised her so viciously, she cried and promised to "have a long hard think about my foul ways." And she did, she had a long hard think about more ways she could be foul with me in that sleeping bag.

Writing into the future

I was hired by Ms. Volt to spearhead the ill-fated Writing Into the Future scheme.[1] I had completed a marketing degree at a nondescript college[2] five months before under coercion of the paterfamilias and, after a stint in the ScotCall Talent Pool, decided to swim into less shark-infested waters. The options for marketing graduates not being vast (nor the options for graduates from other schools), I was fortunate to chance upon the one non-ScotCall position in the *ScotCall Examiner*. Thanks to the last three decades of public paranoia and smear campaigning from politicians,[3] I was raised to view writers and books with suspicion. I suspected these supposedly criminal and dangerous "truth-fudgers"[4] of producing unpractical propaganda against the ethos of unlimited consumption that ScotCall promoted as vital to a pleasurable existence, and of attempting to dissuade consumers from turning to ScotCall to help shape and give their lives meaning. The sheer outrageous nerve! One month spent in the ScotCall impound cured me of this notion.[5]

I met Marilyn Volt who, after five minutes discussing her latest 20K marathon to raise awareness for puppies with cancer or doctors

---

[1]And, for the record, I was not responsible for any of the repercussions of this scheme. I would like to go on record stating Ms. Volt is not a resident in the same astral plane as the rest of us.

[2]Larton Community College. During my time there, one of the departments was always on fire.

[3]My earliest memory is of a Tory politician stamping on a copy of George Orwell's *1984*, saying: "Come on, we're beyond this." To rousing applause.

[4]Coined by Tony Blair on his deathbed.

[5]A cure helped in part by ads such as: "Freedom? Sounds nice! But how to be free, and how to maximise your freedom potential? JOIN SCOTCALL."

with the shakes or whatever,[6] sat down to brief me as to the post.

"The problem is Carol is this," she said, suckling a spout. She consumed about ten sports drinks per day.[7] "We're keen to keep The House going into the next generation. We need our writers to take an interest in procreation and propagating the writer species. No one has time to take an interest in this and consequently we have been unable to make inroads here. We can't afford to offer our writers childcare or time off for pregnancies. So I am looking to recruit a person who will be able to solve the issue for us."

"Uh . . . "

"Would you like the position?"

"Yes."[8]

"Good. Get to work!"

I was offered a cubicle inside Volt's maze of filing cabinets on the ground floor. Each cabinet contained receipts, accounts, manuscripts, medical records, and pictures of writers' teeth.[9] I had thought the complex maze between desks might allow me some privacy from Volt's panting progress checks, however I had underestimated her freakish skill (none of the cabinets were labelled and she knew the location of every file), and abandoned all attempts to obfuscate the maze in case I lost myself.[10] The first scheme I devised to solve the problem was to devise a HoW dating website. I naïvely believed that all the writers needed was a platform to express their repressed lusts and desires, so set up a free-to-use and

---

[6] All her "charity" money went into the doomed attempt to fix The House building.

[7] Later I discovered the money she spent on sports drinks undercut the "charity" funds by a considerable amount. If she drank tap water, she could have made fifteen times as many repairs over the course of three months.

[8] If she had asked me to construct a new moon made from rubber bands on the roof I would have still said: "Yes."

[9] You can be turned off an author pretty quickly if you happen to glimpse a magnetised still of their plaque.

[10] Since the outer layer of cabinets were not fixed against the wall, I was able to walk around the room and simply pull back one cabinet to gain access to my desk. Navigating the maze would have lost me an hour of work each day, and driven me mad.

basic website so writers could make love happen in their "breaks."

This was wrong. The site received no hits because creating a profile would have taken too long and eaten into writing time. Plus no writers wanted to waste words on something that couldn't be sold. Working in The House required an enforced celibacy. Becoming a writer required the eradication of desire, or the supplanting of one's desire into the manuscripts. I learned this when I asked a newish writer in the Westerns department for a date and spoke to him with frankness about having sex after.

"There's nothing we can do about this issue. Having a child means career suicide. It's not like at ScotCall where the pregnant people can answer calls in their beds or offer advice on the phone right up to the first contraction and two hours after having the child. Writing takes immense concentration and we have to deliver tens of thousands of words every week. Children don't fit into our set-up here," he said. I tried to override his stubborn practicality using seduction techniques. He was unresponsive. Even childless relationships were too time-consuming and even random sexual encounters were frowned on for draining too much energy, or for constricting the imagination when it came to writing romantic scenes. The act of doing narrowed the potential for dreaming.

So I had to find other things to do. I would meander from floor to floor conducting pointless surveys:

Q: How often do you think about sex? (*A*: Never.)

Q: How many children do you want to have? (*A*: None.)

Q: Who is your ideal partner? (*A*: No one.)

Q: What is your strongest goal in life? (*A*: To finish my (present) manuscript.)

Q: Do you think you would make a good parent? (*A*: No.)

and place them into shredders. I tried to interest the writers in parenthood with subliminal tactics—leaving pictures of adorable tots on their desks, scenting the air with talcum powder, mother's milk and fresh placenta, piping in lullabies and nursery rhymes to the offices, and in one case, borrowing a friend's baby to show around the building. The responses were predictable: rage at having their desks disturbed, their concentration broken, their nostrils diverted, the presence of an irritant in their offices. The act of writing for men had snuffed out their swimmers, locked their libidos; and for women, ostracised their ovaries and murdered their mothering instinct.[11] I tried to contrive romance between writers by leaving love-notes on desks. Failure. The writers merely sneered and hurled them binwards. At one point, I cornered a male in the lift and tongued his neck and seized his penis. He stood there blinking as I rubbed and said: "Have you finished? I have manuscript to go and write."

I feared being sacked. Volt would slither up and down the building in her soundless sneakers and catch me loafing. I was given an ultimatum—printed up on blue card reading *Ultimatum. Pull your socks up or I'll have to let you go. Love, Marilyn*—so I searched the building for places to lurk and hide. In the backstairs between the ninth and tenth floors I found a surplus cleaning cupboard. Behind the unused mops and dustpans was a small room where a group of dropout writers met to hide from their department heads. There were five when I found them on a settee, lying around staring at the ceiling. The room had a strong graphite odour. I soon spotted the pile of discarded pencils behind the settee, and that the walls had been covered in desperate scribbles. These were the Blocked Writers.

Having lapsed into complete indifference, turned their backs on their manuscripts, unwilling to leave and face the consequences, they hid in their graphite-scented room waiting for inspiration to strike, scuttling between floors and stealing food to survive. I was to become one of their kind. I openly admit I have no interest in writing. I took an interest in books to spite the politicians and their smearing. The first novel I read was the penultimate book from Zadie Smith called *Black Teeth*—a sombre novel about two families who lose their possessions in the Great Crash and have to turn to

---

[11] Peeking at some of the work these people were peddling, all I can say is . . . confiscate their laptops and knock 'em up.

hawking spare parts on roadsides to survive. I confess it depressed me. I value the comedic in literature more than anything else. We're put on the planet to suffer, so we may as well take a reprieve from this in our books. When I found myself bunking up with the lethargic Blocked Writers, I discovered that filling a blank sheet of paper with drivel is not as taxing as writers lament. I wrote a story about a disabled snowman who fought for his right to spend Christmas in a family's garden alongside the able-bodied snowmen. Paula, a Romance writer, perked up at my presence once she realised I might be exploited. She asked me to write a romance tale between two male builders. I made the first builder drop wrenches and things on the scaffolding below so the second builder would pay attention. When the second builder was brained into a coma by four bricks, the first writer stayed at his bedside until he healed. After exchanging various emotions the two got together and moved to Leeds.

I wasn't looking to be exploited, only I hated sharing the poky room with five moping writers. If I could produce plotlines, I could remove them from the room and have the settee to myself. Freeloading in The House was quite straightforward—writers didn't want to waste time eating so left most of their meals in the canteen. I would have some time to think things through before Volt found me. So I came up with ideas for Jo, Vivian, Paul, Jeremy, and Deborah and soon I had the settee to myself. Unfortunately, Volt found me lapping up someone's spaghetti in the canteen and sacked me.

This

8

A FEW words on the book blurb business. Blurbs can be purchased with ease in The House—ordinarily, a prawn sandwich
or a cup of lukewarm mushroom soup will secure you a burbling
blurb making use of trusty superlatives such as "timeless" or "evoca-
tive," and if you throw in a croissant, various hyperbolic statements
about one's novel etching a place in literary history alongside the
enthroned bones. I caught up with C.J. Watson who, having turfed
her Puff, was in a kindly enough mood to describe this novel, *The
House of Writers*, as a "labyrinthine satiric masterpiece . . . destined
for a place in the pantheon of eternal pleasures," and later I found
C.F. Milton who after a cappuccino and a triple chocolate muf-
fin, described my novel as "the hottest thing in the literary world
since Nora Barnacle's knickers," and for those who didn't understand the reference, "a gleefully sadistic romp through the byways
and sighways of this daunting edifice." In under six hours, I had
amassed a dossier of extravagantly insincere praise, written with
the prospect of warm pastry in mind, a fact that seeped into several blurbs, such as: "This novel is a crisp, buttery concoction that
tantalises the mind . . . a soft and mouthwatering crunch of pleasure tingling on the cortices and yumming up the imagination." To
redress the balance, I paid people in white chocolate cereal bars for
an honest opinion of the novel, paying four cereal bars per day, a to-
tal of ninety cereal bars per reader, causing a net loss of £59. Among
the blurb replies: "A ho-hum gallimaufry of stop-start narratives,
banal tangents, and boorish satirical pokes," "a towering inferno of
misrepresentation," and "the nadir of attempted comedy." I decided

245

to insert an equal volume of these verdicts into the novel, because the critical reception for the work would be nonexistent, and by building that reception into the novel itself, the process would be pre-complete (in the same way I am the only unpaid reader of this work).

The Trauma Rooms

8

"THIS is Frank Zemon."

"Hi."

"Yeah. Let me explicate. I had written my first novel, *Skeeter's Banks*, while bumming around Glossop on the last of my student loan. I emailed a tantalising blurb to Lamiel Burkan at Canongate. The novel was a heart-rending romp set in hostels the world over, with interconnecting tales of hedonistic kids from broken homes seeking a path in life, and finding one in their collective pain. I dedicated the novel to my then-girlfriend Marlene, not foreseeing she'd shag my brother between the final proofs and publication. I ended up dedicating a novel to a cast-iron bitch and the person I hated most in the universe. In the acknowledgements, I thanked Grant and Bill Wilthers, both of whom had proofread and helped the novel along. I had a falling out with the brothers when I slept with both their wives following an erotic round of Spin the Bottle. So the novel was dedicated to two men who hated me the most in the universe, and who I hated in turn for their refusing forgiveness. My next novel, *Whistling in the Window*, I dedicated to a more stable thankee—my sister, Erin Zemon. As the novel was sent to the printer, Erin wrote me a long letter explaining she had spoken to her psychiatrist and, after long week's soul-searching session, decided she could never forgive me for roasting her Barbie doll on the barbecue ("Barbie-cue"), and that she would not be seeking to be speaking to me ever again. My acknowledgements were to Brian and Graham Setplotter, both of whom turned against me for not checking if they wanted the final canapé at an event we attended. Another novel dedicated to people who no longer mattered to me! Forever etched in print, these wankers! I had to play things safe for my next book, *So You Think You're a Muslim Cleric?*, and dedicated the novel to my mother. Can you see what's coming? Yes, she disowned me! Cut me out the inheritance and prevented me from making contact ever again. She said that a character in my first novel had been based on her, and she knew I was making her out to be a "neurotic reactionary pinhead," so ended our relations. My acknowledgements had been devoted to my paid readers, both of whom sued me for poor treatment. I had wasted another two pages on people who hated me. That's when I hit upon a brilliant idea. I decided to have a sweepstakes as to who received my dedications and acknowledgements. I set this up on my website, www.thisiszemon.co.uk, and *Sprinkler's Matrix* was dedicated to Jan Rachaels of York, and I acknowledged Valerie Smite and Jed Brownimpings. This worked for a while, until I received a letter with a legal letterhead, claiming that as a dedicatee Jan was entitled to at least 25% of the profits. In two days, I received the same letter from Valerie and Jed. I pursued the case and lost, and had to cough up 75% of the book profits to these anonymous people. After agent's fees, I was left with -5% profit. For my fifth book, *Love is a Cinnamon Condom*, I decided to make the anonymous winners sign a legal waiver, allowing them no claim to the profits. The next thing that happens—the dedicatee, Liza Scrimmage, lawyers up, claiming *authorship* of the novel—that she created a fake name (mine), and set up the website as me, and that the whole idea of selling dedications was part of the fiction. It did so happen that the novel was about a writer who sells dedications (I was running thin ideas-wise), and because of that conceit, the lawyers were able to blur the true authorship to the point no one knew who had written what, and the all-male jury voted in favour of Liza because of her button nose and amazing bosom. As a result, she scooped all the profits. That novel became a bestseller, and Liza appeared on chat shows, discussing how she wrote the book as me and so on. I had been relegated to a character in a novel she didn't write, and of course, all my past novels were attributed to her by proxy, and my public attempts to claim authorship made me look insane. She contacted me a year later, offering me an insulting sum to ghostwrite "her" next novel. I told her to fuck her fat mother's ass, then a week later went crawling back and accepted her offer. Once the novel was released, who do I see mentioned in the dedications—Frank Zemon ;). That's right, she'd added an actual wink! As a final knowing little thing to make me feel like a proper stooge!"

"Cow," Erin said.

"Thanks for that, Frank."

"Yeah. Cheers."

C.M. Horvath's Almost Girlfriend

ONE of the most lucre-active floors is the fifteenth, a bustling workhouse populated by meekly subservient ghost-hacks taking orders from their hemidemisemi-famous subjects—a stoop of haven't-beens seeking to sell their hyperboiled tales to a handful of fans. I was assigned at once to ghost the autobio of one of West Region's most popular reality TV stars—Grenda Navel. Having stumbled to stardom in the programme *Posh and Dropped*, where photogenic upper-class socialites are deposited on a council estate to fend for themselves, she had branched into acting roles in medical dramas, and made numerous appearances on comedy panel shows. Her waspish tongue and take-no-prisoners attitude made her popular, along with her fondness for foul language, criticisms against the ruling classes, and championing of trash culture. She had tried her hand at a rap record, "Grenda's Agenda," a seven-minute unexpurgated rant against the losers who dared to 'dis her credentials as an all-around bad-ass-with-class babe.

In a change from the usual procedure—celebrities phoned in their requirements and had no further communication with their authors until publication date—I was invited to Grenda's abode in the West Region wilds. She lived in an ultra-pimped castle, a castle that was her inheritance anyway, that she tormented with the proceeds of her media appearances. Her conical spires were funked up with fake opals, arranged in a sequence of love hearts with shot-through arrows; her arrow-slit cannon ports were festooned with flags spelling out love banalities in purple and pink hues; her spiral staircases were carpeted in long tongues of pink fabric with salamanders kissing from stair to stair; her round-arched geminate windows were bedazzled with pink-power frillies including several pairs of love-me-tender knickers; her barbican was star-studded with statues of the finest pop singers throughout history, including a silver-plated monument to Lulu (four times her actual size); and her keep was where she kept her collection of gravity-defying 1970s platform shoes. I crossed the drawbridge and thumped the portal.

She appeared in a peach-patterned dress with a croissant in her hand and sized me up. "Writer?" she asked. I nodded. "Come," she said, thus establishing the faithful lapdog and master relationship to follow. I was taken to medieval dining table where she went straight to work. Despite the décor, her accent felt at home in the surroundings. "I have notes for the book. Firstly, I don't want anything that might besmirch my image as being down with the proletarians, I must appear to be on their wavelength at all times. Secondly, you must emphasise that my lifestyle is an ironic-slash-satirical squib against the upper classes and their wantonness, otherwise people might become suspicious as to my coveting my inherited wealth. Thirdly, I need you to talk up the importance of my musical career, dwelling on the artistry of my rap lyrics and so on, as that is the direction I will be heading in for the next round of my media blitz."

We thrashed out the disappointingly uneventful history of Grenda and the Navel family who, apart from Grenda's considerable media takings, the several mansions and other properties, had been rendered by kismet almost completely bankrupt. Born to a dim father with a fondness for the roulette wheel, and a mother prone to extravagant purchases such as plots of land on the surface of Neptune, a fleet of platinum-plated Mercedes-Benzes, an organisation running tours to museums for diabetic seniors, a collection of authentic spatulas from the Han dynasty, and so on, Grenda's future was looking insecure from the beginning. When she turned nineteen, she realised that an alternative cash pipe was sought to save her from the embarrassment of having to stay with relatives in a different mansion while her parents began their descent into not having enough to buy vintage wines for a few weeks.

I was taken to meet her entourage. Her personal advisor, Brian

Winston-Frye, was former publicist and spin doctor to Prince Harry, renowned for his adroit handling of the heroin affair, when the Prince was caught injecting the drug between his toes on the top of Buckingham Palace, shouting: "I feel free!" A polite man with expressionless eyes, he knew by instinct the correct manoeuvres to steer Grenda towards full media saturation. Her chef, Garland McVeigh, prepared her favourite meals—swan parfait with extra necks, doused in a crisis of violent gunge, a toffee apple suspended above an agitation of vegetable curry, a curlicue of wallabies in a nectarine coulis—and so on. Others included her political consultant Nigel Fromage, her hat appeaser Dana Trimble, her stocking selector Ian Gravy, her anecdote wrangler Bo Pringle, her nightwear specialist Oban Canny, her oboe trainer Juanita Crossroad, her candle snuffer Kay Horse, her horizontal waxer Jo Zander, her collar fluffer Liam Grim, and so on.

I spent the month scraping the barrel of her existence, plumbing her history for relevant material to include, alighting on anecdotes such as the time she raided her grandfather's liqueurs aged seven and devoured them all, falling drunk in the gazebo, and the time she accidentally shot a parachutist instead of the grouse on her father's hunting grounds, and the time she rescued three Jesus impersonators from a diamond mine (long story), and the time she emptied the contents of a porcelain vase (petunias and toenail clippings) over her nephew, and so on. I became quite close to her over the three weeks writing the book. Into the second week I reached over for an attempted kiss and she raised an admonishing finger and said: "Not, please." That was the end of the matter. I was paid my £19 for the book and she went on to a successful career as a hip-hop provocateur with a line in frankly odious tweenage cosmetics.

A Better Life

8

THUS began the slow dismantling of the ScotCall empire. Policing the crowds became a priority as the undirected and nonspecific anger rose in one long oddly rhythmical moan of incoherent slogans and songs. Including:

"We want now! We want now!"

"Here something please! Here something please!"

"When soon coming?! When soon coming?!"

"Know ours queries! Know ours queries!"

"Us mobilise unions! Us mobilise unions!"

"Got angry sounds grumble! Got angry sounds grumble!"

And the songs:

"This is the day that / we open yours and carrots / here's a horror sound / coming out the mouth / please prevent the something from not sure!"

"We are there to save them / open the door and lettuce in / a small mouse is approaching / and hasn't thought this through / and still we push on."

"Yellow and green and blue / ooh-wooah-ooh-yeah / green and apricot and sunshine / ooh-hooah-noo-waay / please be mine you lovely boy / ooh-hmm-well-never mind."

Millions were spent on providing cheap and barely digestible meals for those bivouacked in the grounds to save ScotCall from accusations of bastardry while the world's eyes were upon them. Humanitarian aid was flown in from Africa to provide for the customers, including a generous donation from Bernard Mugabe, president of Nigeria, who claimed to have personally packed all the foodstuffs himself, although Patagonian scorpions were found in the egg and cress sandwiches. The largest threat to the ScotCall was that people, by coming together, were speaking to each other at last and starting to find solutions to their problems without reverting to the hotline. Communities sprung up where people tried outlining nature of their problems in simple sentences, overcoming their vocal flops and stumbling towards sensible solutions.

An attempt to form a self-sustaining commune on the surrounding concrete flats proved to be a mistake. Spare parts from the stock-dump fields had been intermeshing over the last decade to form dangerous armies that were champing to beat up defenceless humans. A rusty battalion of quadrupedal warriors, known colloquially as the Microheavies, slowly edged forwards.

Using open laptops as splayed feet to advance clumsily and slowly across the landscape and to project images onto their monitor screen heads, the Microheavies tried luring suggestible customers nearer with hypnotic spirals, optical illusions, or the words HELP and ANSWERS flashing epileptically. Those who strayed into the range of the Microheavies were either blown up with the raging fireballs cooked up and spat out their washing-machine torsos, or were collected and taken to a secret pen where intricate surgical procedures were performed on them. Thus began the dawn of the first Microhumans. The humans were put to sleep and reanimated with several new features. Their brains were removed and replaced with Windows 14 processors and their stomachs upgraded to consume digi-pets and other scraps for dinner instead of food. Thanks to their inbuilt encyclopedias, the Microhumans were a superior race—the sort of perfect robot specimen humans had been trying to create for decades. The Microhumans, once several dozen bodies were refurbished, could reproduce quickly among themselves, and set about building a large compound from which they would devise their strategies for taking over the planet. Since they were using Windows 14 processors, however, the Microhumans constantly crashed and were caught in a perpetual loop of starting and restarting, so the swift global domination would never come to pass.

Another tribe eking out life on the concrete fields were the Macrohumans—to survive, their bodies adapted to the various half-animal half-mechanical creatures that had spawned in the fields and were used as food. These people became mere hunters, breeding sheep and slaughtering them for the carcass (reinstating haggis as the most popular dish—albeit haggis boiled through with bits of tungsten and plastic).

For the remainder of those straining to liberate the ScotCall Compound, a coup arrived swiftly, plunging the phone lines into anarchy. Callers from home and abroad seeking instruction on how to do basic things were instructed to shoot their brains out, and over two million suicides took place in the space of two weeks. Common were such exchanges:

"Where do the lemons live?"

"Shoot yourself."

"Does a blade of grass weigh more than William Gass?"

"Shoot yourself."

"Can a bomb be banned after exploding?"

"Shoot yourself."

"Where is the ointment?"

"Shoot yourself."

"If I were a carpenter, and you were a lady, would you marry me anyway, would you have my baby?"

"Shoot yourself."

"Can I use my oven glove as a scarf?"

"Shoot yourself."

"Is there nowhere on earth I can blend this pomegranate?"

"Shoot yourself."

"How far in cubic centimetres is it from Krakow to Dublin?"

"Shoot yourself."

"Open or closed or half?"

"Shoot yourself."

And so on.

The *Farewell, Author!* Conference

8

A PEEP at the clock: 11:50. The midnight suicide pact was approaching. The writers shuffled nervously, checking their watches, in some cases rewinding them or pretending the clock on the wall was wrong. Mumbled backpedalling followed. Damion Searls couldn't die as he was raising three mallards and a cockatoo in his Norfolk farmhouse and had to ensure their lives were not at risk; Daniël Robberechts had promised to attend a fun-run in Piccadilly Circus dressed as a chaffinch for the Bulgarian Repatriation Fund; Mati Unt was at present on experimental drug Flummox™ and could not spoil the pharmaceutical company's efforts with an entirely unrelated self-murder; David Nicholls was expecting triplets from his fourth wife, and wanted to make this, his fourth marriage in the UK, a success; Anna Burns had been implicated in a couscous-smuggling scandal—since the national shortage was declared, bootleggers had been smuggling in illegal and poisonous couscous from North Africa—and had to clear her name; Nicholas Currie was ranked third in the Regional Cribbage Championships and could not perish until he at least ranked second in the Paisley region; Chip Kidd had to acquire the latest album by The Fall, *Otex Horticular Drops*, to complete his 480-record-strong collection, despite this record being another compilation of B-sides and live scraps, and Mark E. Smith having been hooked up to a life support machine during the studio recordings; Andrew Kaufman refused to die without receiving a review minus the words "whimsical" and "cute"; Greg Boyd had booked a two-week vacation to the Andes where he hoped to retrieve the stapler he had left at the Aconcagua;

259

Deb Olin Unferth had not quite recovered from the bout of pneumonia she contracted in Toxteth and wanted to be fighting fit when she committed suicide; Tom McCarthy still had to explain to the world that necronautism had nothing to do with shagging dead pilots; Chris Bachelder was booked to appear on a panel discussing mimesis in torture porn movies in April; Christian Bök was close to completing the world's longest palindromic pangram in both Spanish and Malay; Ken Kalfus had to return a lost menorah to his rabbi or suffer forever in damnation; David Mitchell still had to beg forgiveness to the world for the "Sloosha's Crossin' an' Ev'rythin' After" section of his novel *Cloud Atlas*; Jonathan Safran Foer had left something outside somewhere, he wasn't sure what that thing was or where outside he had left the thing, only he wasn't able to commit suicide without retrieving the unknown thing from somewhere, and yes, he was aware this sounded like an excuse, but his wife had made him promise to retrieve the something from the somewhere, and he had promised on his life to retrieve the something, and since he had promised on his life, he would rather kill himself for having failed to retrieve the something rather than as part of a mass suicide, and if people still weren't convinced, he remembered now that the something was ovoid, that is to say, egg-shaped, and had been lost outside a large structure with two separate entrances, and no, he hadn't left an egg outside a supermarket, it was something more precious outside somewhere more prestigious, he would need to rattle his recall; Lydia Millet had to tick off the remaining items on her bucket list before she killed herself—shoot heroin, listen to a Robert Fripp solo album, tend bar for two years in Burntisland, Fife, steer a JCB into a bookmaker's, make a mashed potato mountain on a moat of beans and place a sausage at the summit, utter the word "glassblower" without sniggering, experience life in a Drumchapel tower block in winter after the heating allowance had been cut for those over 60, cease to be troubled when deranged truck drivers load their vehicles with explosives and drive into kindergartens; Jonathan Safran Foer had remembered that he had left one of those 1970s ovoid chairs outside a cathedral, and this item had been a present for their fourth child Resnais, who had taken an interest in 1970s culture and collected period furniture, and that this was his last chance to redeem himself in the eyes of a son who had long ago written his father off as a has-been, and without this chance, he might return to nursing his suicidal urges, and he couldn't kill himself before redeeming himself before his son and pleasing his wife; Nicole Krauss had to let people know that Jonathan Safran Foer was a fibbing bullshitter, that he had no children, nor wife for over three decades, and that he had spent the last three decades as a hustler on the streets, peddling extendible forks, cruet sets, matryoshka dolls, and fibre-optic lamps, and that he had been postponing his suicide now for over nine months, and after written and spoken promises, still hadn't produced the desired corpse. These excuses took over two hours, so the writers concluded that since midnight had long passed, perhaps it was a more sensible idea to put some minimalist techno or ambient trance numbers on the stereo and chill until sunrise, and see what the mood in the room happened to be then. Oriana Leckert had a copy of DJ Invernip's *Glucose Intolerant Melatones*, a classic in the chillambient category, played in nightclubs at 4am to mellow the hardcore beat freaks before they spazzed out on their E-fed rhythmic thrusts, so I cranked up the music and the room dropped to the floor to chill, remembered the roach-rats, and elected to chill standing up or leaning against the freezers.

Bizarro Tim

TIM had to flee the bizarro fiction department before a neon elephant in a cocktail dress sat on his face. To escape before a dominatrix attached seventeen volts of electric love to his nipples and spanked his swollen rump. To contrive an escape route over the vats of bubbling custard towards the two large raptors whose mouths functioned as lifts. To send an SOS to a small babe in Newark with two enormous brains under her sweater with the sexiest red nodes he'd ever tongued. To free her from the fluorescent amoeba in whose pseudopods she was ensnarled. To telephone the ostrich whose oestrus season was being broadcast on a satellite channel to subscribers from Nepal so the ostrich could send vibrations via his superconnected plumage. To ingratiate a paragraph. To dissolve an albatross in albumin. To suggest a viable method for transferring an asset-backed loan into the account of a squat Dundonian milquetoast. To locate the exact halogen-powered device that might rescue him from the kinetic molars of an alcoholic colander with cholera to be released into the smouldering lips of a sentence. To recall the exact moment he became trapped in thickets of bizarro prose. To extract his brain with pliers and offer it to the Council of Lumpen Delusions. To optimise the elders' cacaphonics. To swell up to the size of a balloon and circumnavigate the Outer Hebrides while tinkling on a tribe of fork-wielding farmers. To disclose a minor secret to the fortieth member of the Polish Air Force during a sluggish season. To correct a faulty surd on the silver wing of a polished pelican. To slip inside a slot and drip into a drot. To assault the badgers in their dens and make no apologies for the viciousness of Salt Garbald's empire. To chip-chop the theatre and wear flip-flops when it matters. To run out of time, money, energy, and the fear.

Mhairi

9

I HAD not expected, however, to become infatuated with Marilyn several months later. She began sending me emails about her life so far, discussing the torments she suffered in her childhood—having to endure Marmite sandwiches for dinner, long car trips to relatives' houses listening to a Beyoncé *Best Of* compilation on an endless loop, and continual taunts from her brother about her mostly male features. I read these with fatigue and left them unanswered, eventually replying with a request to refrain from the barrage, which she replied to apologetically. Somehow, from there, I found myself caring about her vulnerability, and I softened to the irritating qualities I previously despised, leading to an unexpected flowering of affection. Now we take runs together, make blueberry jam, write two-act plays about dreary astronauts, and make merry spooning in the sleeping bag as the winter months draw nearer.

This

9

IN writing this novel, I have suffered many delusions and break-downs. As I began, I entertained the delusion that the work would be received favorably by at least nine ecstatic readers, and that the novel would make me a folk hero in The House. The realisation that writing this novel for no monetary reward (not even the teeniest nibble on a mouldy brioche) was not destined to make me semi-popular, and that my peers in the building would pour scorn on me for choosing to spend my miniscule free time punishing myself by writing a reader-unfriendly piece of throwback basement fodder, caused my first nervous breakdown. Upon convalescing I continued to add sections to the novel, entertaining my second delusion, namely that this novel might bring me success via posterity, that I would two hundred years down the line be venerated as an innovator, an atypical genius in an age of the cynical exploitation of clichés. This was followed by the realisation that there will be no books in the future, no literature, no words printed on paper for readers, because once the present handful of readers dies, there will be no one to pick up the mantle, and The House of Writers will be demolished (if it hasn't caved in already), and narratives will play out on screens, flashily, stylelessly, feeding the viewer their steady diet of clichés, their warm syrupy feel-good portion of the bleeding obvious, and that I will be forgotten as soon as the final printout of this manuscript is tossed from the hands of the unwilling reader, that once the memory of this work escapes my own senile recall, the work will cease, and have forever ceased to exist. I had a second breakdown. And yet, I resumed writing the work. I resumed for no reason I can conceivably fathom. Here I sit, tapping these sentences onto the page, squeezing out my melancholy thoughts even though my hands ache, my fingers are stiff from repetitive strain, and my body slumps over in this stiffbacked chair, utterly depleted of energy, and yet, I limp towards the end of this project . . . the only thing that guides me towards an ending that I will have made something . . . that I will have written, and been heard, albeit ricocheting in my own cranium, that I will have said something, albeit incoherent and directionless . . . that I will have expressed my incoherent and directionless message with passion, determination, and a grim desperation to make words on a page matter again.

The Trauma Rooms

9

"**A**ND in a similar vein, meet Hank Zepon."

"Hi."

"Yeah. Let me explicate. I was struggling to fend off the taxman while writing novel number four, *Gertrude's Garters*, a pornophantastical hallucination involving Ms. Stein, so I invited donations in return for a namecheck in the text. I received £5 donations from a thousand people, so £5000. This was enough to survive for the next year, allowing me to complete the novel. I chose to insert the names during a hallucinogenic episode, where Gertrude recalls all the people she had insulted over a six-month period. This proved a lucrative method of reader sponsorship. You can't trust readers to actually buy copies of your novel. Even your most admiring fans will wait for the library stock, or borrow from friends, or torrent ebooks, when that was still an option. I'm told all the computers have exploded outside, or some such bollocks. Anyway, my next novel, *Kafka's Pantaloons*, was an eroticophilosophico exploration of the sexual kinks of Franz. This time, 689 people donated. I think some people felt cheated by my long list of their names, expecting a more subtle insertion. So this time I had the names more casually inserted in such passages as: "Felice strapped on her dildo and, approaching Franz's parted buttocks, noticed out the window her friends Paul Thompson and Linda Stewart walking past." And: "Dora lowered herself on to Franz's rigid cock and asked whether he had written back to Julie Driscoll and Nigel Parsons before jiggling into penetration." This proved more successful. For the next novel, some 300,000 people had donated, meaning I had some work to insert them. I had to write a novel in the manner of Perec's *Life A User's Manual*, rife with lists, so I wrote *The Hopscopalypse*, about a plague that descends at random on various towns, including several pages listing the dead in each chapter. The novel was panned by Adam Mars-Jones in *The Telegraph*, who wrote: "Zepon's latest reader-funded production drowns in its own making." Meaning: too many names. I had made the cardinal mistake of becoming too avaricious. My next novel received 69 donations. This made no difference, as I had made £150,000 with the previous, allowing me to survive in luxury for a long time. I wrote *The Full Sixty-Nine*, a sequence of pornohomoeroticophilosophico tracts interspersed with hardcore fucking. This proved so popular, 3,382,818 people donated £5 for a namecheck in my next book. I made £16,914,060. All I had to do was write this novel and retire forever. I had almost three and a half million names to insert into my novel. These alone, providing each consisted of two names, would take up 6,765,636 words, longer than *Artamène ou le Grand Cyrus*, *À la recherche du temps perdu*, *Zettels Traum*, *Clarissa*, and *Poor Fellow My Country* combined, with room to spare for an *Infinite Jest*. I made things easy for myself by writing a meta-novel about a writer attempting to write the longest novel in history (this endeavour minus the creativity had been attempted in halfwit conceptual artist Nigel Tomm's *The Blah Story*, where the artist had cut and pasted 'blah' in various permutations over 23 enormous volumes), so I could include the names as lists for a few pages without provoking the reader's ire. The whole thing took over five years, during which time I suffered a nervous breakdown. I wanted to write a work of art and not be written off as a cash-hoovering has-been. I was up to 7,181,819 words, with 2,639,182 names left to insert when I collapsed in the street, the millions of names rolling in a permanent tickertape in my brain, causing me to haemorrhage cerebrally. I recovered a month later to discover some supporters had withdrawn their monies, forcing me to search and replace them with another. A million people believed I wasn't able to complete the work. I had to prove them wrong. Two years later, I delivered the finished novel, entitled simply *i*, to be published in thirty volumes, one volume per month for two-and-a-half years. The publisher predicted astronomical sales, but the poorly received first five books led to the novel being shelved. The subscribers demanded their cash back. I had to return a fortune and privately publish a revised version. I cracked up when one subscriber ranted at me on TV for 'failing to deliver.' I punched his face to Picasso. After paying £500,000 bail, I fled for Switzerland. I came here to try and sell the original version of my novel, and finally be recognised as a genius. This didn't happen. I ended up in this ward for nutsos."

"That is not the word we use," the doctor said.

"What happened?" Erin asked.

"Other writers stole sections and sold them as their own novels."

"Of course."

"Thanks for that, Hank."

"Yeah. Cheers."

A Better Life

9

PETE and Rob, having picked up the pertinent information that I used to be a writer, struggled through the throng to The House. Starting on the first floor, they Tweedledeed and Tweedledummed around looking for me and making brattish diversions. Their inquisitiveness took them to my desk as I was typing out part of my space western. Pete, in his Swiss-cheese boots, and Rob, still resplendent in his sweat-drenched bus driver's shirt, arrived like two flairless hobos at my desk, attracting the shifty-eyed contumely of my colleagues, who looked up from their intergalactic saloon shootouts to flash their aggrieved miens. Pete launched my stapler towards the ceiling and leaned over my manuscript, making exaggerated sniffing sounds and a peee-eeeew gesture. He read aloud:

" 'Terence stepped out the ship with luck in his loins and lions in his underpants.' People pay to read this crap?"

"That's my lions-in-the-underpants scene," I said. This didn't recapture my dignity.

"Miss us?" Rob asked.

"You know, my grandfather and great-grandfather were writers," Pete said. I had read the work of Gilbert and Christopher Sorrentino with admiration and found it hard to believe Pete came from the same genes.

"Yes."

"I bet I could write a better novel than you, using my writing genes."

"Nope."

"Pass me a sheet of A4."

I plaintively obeyed. Pete kicked C.G. Higson from his desk to free up space and began his novel as C.G. blankly continued scrawling his Klingon orgy on a Post-it. Rob went off to kick chocolate bars from a vending machine. I sat staring out the window at smog clouds as Pete wrote feverishly, using up my A4 and laughing at his inherited wit. Fours days later, with only two breaks for food and sleep, he showed me his manuscript, detailing the third life and second resurrection of Antony Lamont from Gilbert Sorrentino's *Mulligan Stew* (foremost of Flann O'Brien's *At Swim-Two-Birds*), after moving into a hack novel written by, surprise, yours truly. Lamont, having escaped the scourges of *Guinea Red*, ended up in a devastating parody of my space western, brimming with parodic dialogue and mock-terrible writing. I read the completed manuscript wincing and laughing at the same time, kicking the fates for making this asshole Pete into a splendid comedic writer like his forebears, and making a mental note of some ideas I could steal for my next book. I took comfort from the fact this novel was too niche to ever find readers and so handed it back safe that my job wasn't under threat.

"You know, you should consider working here," I offered.

"I don't have time for that shit. Literature is piss. In fact—" he produced a lighter and torched his brilliant novel, extinguishing the fire with a piss cataract. As I watched a man burn a manuscript ten times better than anything I could ever write, and cackle hysterically, and kick over my desk, and call everyone in the room expendable cunts, I contemplated whether saving the world from ScotCall had been a sensible manoeuvre. He masturbated in my bed and drank all the milk in the canteen.

The *Farewell, Author!* Conference

9

INDING nothing else to do, with the night dwindling to mere hours, and the horrible threat of the morning on the loom, the writers cuddled, nuzzled, tickled, touched, stroked, licked, sucked, kissed, and poked one another, on and against the freezers, and afterwards, promised to protect and love one another until the end of time, surrendering to the tantalising delusion of mutual support in an age of self-preservation, mouthing their meaningless words of love which, coming from writers, were far more poetic and cribbed subconsciously from Shakespeare, fighting the sleep that would lead them into the unwanted daylight. I curled up with Linda Tunnet, whose novel *A Bee, See?* won the Adair Prize in 2039, praised for its skill at "using clichés in a such a manner the reader is momentarily duped into believing the novel has something original to offer," and mouthed romantic lies into our mutual ears. "I will hold your hand like this until you are a wrinkled old prune repulsive to the eyes," she said. "I will touch your knee like this until your skeleton is bursting out your flesh," I replied. "I will squeeze your penis in this manner until the heat death of the universe," I said. And so on. Following on from this, the writers entertained the delusion that they still had futures, and further works to write, and proceeded to describe their upcoming novels. Joanna Ruocco outlined her novel about a man obsessed with the curliness of kale, whose mania unlocks deep ontological questions and forces us to consider each individual Atom of our very Humanbeingness; Naomi Alderman her novel about a school teacher combating her depression and love for a female pupil and her unfortunate name "Miss Butt" that

275

forces us to consider the plight of the Other in the age of the Self; Ned Beauman his novel about a scientist who invents the controversial pneugenics theory, whereby those taking up precious oxygen with pointless blabber or breathing were deemed more suited to termination, that forces us to consider Compassion and Trust in a world with dwindling room and resources; Shane Jones his novel about a clown whose left testicle swells to spacehopper proportions during a performance, and the ensuing media furore about his accidental exposure in front of children that forces us to consider how the Truth is distorted in the era of Viral Media; Joanna Kavenna her novel about a ukulele player with jaundice who is thrust into the limelight on a TV talent show and struggles to cope with the ensuing fame, and begs for a return to his poor life that forces us to consider the Price of Fame in a Transient Age; Brian Oliu his novel about a computer virus that uproots an internet user's mental landscape, causing him to return pointlessly to shops where he had no further business to conduct, to return to concluded conversations to see if they might have anything else they wished to say to him after their meetings had concluded, and to stumble with no purpose into shops and buildings with no motive but to distract or lose oneself in the maze of distractions, that forces us to consider Technology's impact on the Mind and Body; Kamila Shamsie her novel about a secret sect formed during WWII to make unkind remarks about Catholics in addition to the Jews that forces us to reconsider the Parameters of Evil; William Seabrook his novel about a packet of crisps elected Prime Minister of Britain that fails to live up to its promises of 100% more starch content in the House of Commons, a beef 'n' onion flavour resurgence, and the promise of 20 new combos—caramel 'n' hops, pear 'n' lava, lemon 'n' cardboard, pesto 'n' ink, banana 'n' turmeric, olive oil 'n' brine, Benylin 'n' peach, hazelnut 'n' sweat, avocado 'n' sapling, aspic 'n' oregano, Polyfilla 'n' nachos, sports sock 'n' pizza, s'mores 'n' elbows, pickle 'n' toothpaste, oak 'n' tulip, lime 'n' stubble, cream 'n' wool, horse 'n' halloumi, snot 'n' air, hair 'n' time—that forces the reader to consider the Power of the Democratic Process in a Cynical Age; James

Yeh his novel about a professor of mathematics obsessed with the *mise en scène* of Jim Jarmusch movies who beats his drinking problem through the snugger drug of independent cinema that teaches us to appreciate the important of Radical Thought in an Age of Prescriptive Thinking; and Ross Raisin his novel about a murderous stereo that instructs toddlers to slice up their parents and deposit their remains in a sewage pipe that teaches us the importance of Love and Understanding and not listening to Immoral Voices that will Lead Us Astray.

THE HOUSE OF WRITERS

The Two Poems of Archie Dennissss

HAROLD Impugns woke to a vexing reality when celebrated poet Archie Denissss arrived at The House upon his 75th birthday. Archie Denissss had written the world's most popular short-form poem (a senryu—the non-pastoral form of the haiku) called "Hope," an overly sentimental blip that became every citizen's number one favourite-of-all-time example of the redeeming and hopeful function of the poetic "arts." The poem:

> *Tomorrow is here*
> *Let the sun into your heart*
> *and your life begin*

Archie had written the poem as a Media Studies student at Napier University and published it in the irritating arts journal *PoeEatTree* alongside Harold Impugns's first poem "Fitzwaller's Disgrace," a deeply moral and metrically daring exculpation of shamed opera singer Harvey Fitzwaller—rendered in a complex scansion of double dactylics with a sonorously emphatic spondee on each third word, Harold's nine-line poem took over nine months to compose in comparison to Archie's ten seconds. Thus began Harold's deep hatred for the "work" of Archie Denissss—a vast corpus encompassing that one mawkish and meaningless poem printed and reprinted in every popular anthology for the next six decades while Harold composed technically ambitious works of increasing depth and power second to John Ashbery and Edwin Morgan and struggled even to publish in obscure university magazines.

Archie's poem was reviled among critics for its cheap heart-tugging and the horrible clumsiness of the final line. It made little sense when scrutinised. How could tomorrow be "here" when

279

tomorrow is always the next day, no matter what the time of day? At 00:00:00, the tomorrow of 23:59:59 becomes the next day and yesterday's tomorrow's present—tomorrow can never backslide to the present tense. As a poetic construction, "Let the sun into your heart" fails because direct sunlight is harmful to the skin and to exposed cardiorespiratory organs. The "poet" was straining for a hopeful message, but the sun is a relentless death-ray that burns up everything in range. Some critics loved the "ambiguity" of this image, suggesting light or dark. This "ambiguity" lent the poem gravitas among its apologist anti-elitist critics, and among the high, low, and nobrow populace.

A mediocre Media Studies student, Archie was happy to dine out on this one senryu his whole life, earning royalties for the endless reprints and special book versions (including a famous woodcut with one word per page, accompanied by an illustration from artist Debbie Nimmo). He read his poem at Buckingham Palace, 10 Downing Street, The White House, the European Parliament, Tom Cruise's funeral, and various venues where VIPs cumulated across the world. A new school of so-called Denisssesque poetry sprung up—a term to describe poems that dealt with hope in an "ambiguous" way for both the masses and the eggheads. To his eternal shame, Harold wrote a Denissssesque poem in an attempt to finagle a couple of schmaltzy billions, but was unable to publish due to the upsurge in imitators. Archie wrote nothing new for sixty years.

When writers became irrelevant to public discourse, Archie's tours dried up. He lived on his royalties and Monte Carlo hedge-funds until the funds were hedged by gross inflation. He was forced to scrape a living in The House, working on a long-awaited second poem for his ten fans. Harold revelled in seeing his old nemesis reduced to paupery, and his festering lifelong resentment and ever-raging enviousness made a reconciliation impossible (and undesired). Archie failed to recognise Harold, as they had only met fleetingly on the Napier campus, and Archie quit his degree to be an international star in his third week of the first semester. Harold kept his distance at first, plotting the means to slight or humiliate his nemesis, until one afternoon, Archie came to Harold with a request to help him write his second poem. "I haven't written a poem in almost sixty years. I never thought I'd have to," he said. Harold set about his plan of destruction. "What you need is a change of direction," he suggested. Archie was bewildered as he read Harold's offering:

> *Fuck all you cuntheads*
> *drown in your mass delusions*
> *I'll see you in Hell*

"It's a little, er, strong compared to my first poem. What worked about that one was the ambiguity," Archie said, as though convincing himself.

"Yes, exactly. This is a more startling direction for you. No one will have expected such a radical departure from the hope etc. That's what so marvellous."

"And you're sure I can take this from you?"

"My gift. I've been a huge admirer of yours for years."

"Thank you."

Archie sold the poem to his ten eager readers. Their initial response was confusion and fear at this startling new direction. However, as disciples of the great poet, they chose to stick by him and purchased "his" next:

> *No seriously*
> *I hate all you fucking cunts*
> *I piss on your graves*

His readers were soon electrified by this *startling* new "direction" and believed his bleak and violent imagery was a necessary reflection of the harsh and unremitting post-capitalist world. Harold wearily forged ahead:

> *I mean all you lot*
> *reading this now—fuck yourselves*
> *and your mums and dads*

His readers adored the meta-mention of themselves and the dark humour in this one. Despite feeling an incredulous rage that people were swallowing this drivel, Harold was in a position to earn more ghostwriting Archie's comeback poems than his own works, so continued to write sweary fuck-yous in ten seconds for his supper over his own knotty constructions. He put together a chapbook of these in a deluxe edition and charged a fortune. Meanwhile, Archie managed to write his second poem:

> *Yesterday has gone*
> *the sun giving way to rain*
> *life nears its dour end*

Despite being a far more appropriate "career"-capper, his ten readers reacted violently to this poem, "a saccharine retread of the first," and refused to cough up a penny. Archie never wrote another poem again and Harold continued to bankroll his fallen enemy, conning his public with random abusive poems in ludicrous abundance. His fans viewed this as a "late spurt" in his career, and paid upwards of £2000 for what was seen as his crowning opus:

> *A late spurt my arse*
> *these poems are fucking shite*
> *you're all clueless cunts*

This is the poem Archie would be remembered for when he died two years later from a vitamin deficiency and a general air of abstracted melancholy. Against his wishes and at Harold's behest, it was chiselled on his headstone.

AD FROM SPONSORS

WE are also recruiting team leaders. Are you the sort of person who could motivate an office of 200 operators into upping their daily targets by 5%? **Which of the following speeches would you use to motivate your workers?**

Speech 1

"We are behind on our targets, people. It would be really nice if we could hit a target of 400+ inbound calls this week, what do you say? I am sure with a little coffee and pep we can do it!"

Speech 2

"Right, you telephonic runts, time to up the ante! I want an extra thousand calls answered this afternoon. Keep your advice concise, no flimflamming about with maybes and don't-knows. You know what happens to the slackers: we sever their arteries and feed them to the vultures. Not really. But you know what I mean. Now let me tell you a story about The Little Boy That Couldn't. Everyone got so fed up with his moaning about can't-do-this, can't-do-that, they kicked him out the village and he fell into a life of alcoholism, hard drug use, and depression, and ended up blowing his brains out under a bridge, having caught syphilis from a fifty-nine-year-old prostitute. You might find the moral of this fable instructional as you hit your targets this afternoon. Remember, we are The Little Boys and Girls Who Can. Up and up, people! Let's punch those slackers in the face with our 500+! Answer them phones!"

Speech 3

"I am very disappointed at the slackness in this office. I thought you were really super-dooper phone-slingers capable of at least 450+ inbound calls, but I suppose I must have formed the wrong impression. I thought you were all cool dudes devoted to excellent customer service and helping to deliver an A plus plus experience. Oh well."

Speech 4

"How do you think we're going to out-perform our rivals with this kind of performance? For God's sake, are you all inbred bumpkins with fifty sister-mothers living in a barn? If this kind of laziness persists, I am sacking one of you useless turnips one per hour on the hour. I have had it up to here with your timewasting and dummkopfing."

Is this *you?*

SCOTCALL.

YOUR FUTURE.

Recruitment Line:

0800 717 717

This

10

ONCE again I am not writing this novel, *The House of Writers*. I am not writing this novel (as stated in the previous sentence, and again, pointlessly, in this sentence), because the prospect of writing this novel (title: *The House of Writers*) fills me with apprehension and fear, and in addition to these formidable blocks, I am laziness personified. I am not a punctual or reliable (or handsome or prolific) writer, I am a deadbeat internet addict with a penchant for slouching back into bed to read better works than mine (works that deepen this apprehension and fear and laziness), or to listen to another indie rock LP while surfing the net to peruse books better than mine, because these books transport me from this mundane life of bed-slouching and never-ending blank pages calling out to me to be filled with words on a par with those I read in those aforesaid published volumes I covet so dearly. You might think that with this sort of defeatist attitude, I should be fearless in the face of the blank page, that I adopt a nihilist nothing-new-under-the-sun aesthetic, but this would be a naïve assertion, as there is no such thing as a nihilist nothing-new-under-the-sun aesthetic when the writer (me) lives in the permanent shadow of a thousand nihilistic nothing-new-under-the-sun innovators who have proven, in fucking outstanding prose (better than mine times like a million), that there is nothing new under the sun, so let us rave it up with divine demonstrations of literary prowess instead. The novel I am attempting and failing to write, *The House of Writers* (I repeat pointlessly, as I repeat this pointlessly, and this, and so on—hoping to fill up space and cribbing some cred for Stein-influenced repetitions [I

285

hate Stein]) aspires to the incomplete, to the self-terminating void in the manner of other fictions by this author (me), whose entire corpus so far is an attempt confront the sheer pointlessness of new fiction in an age when books pour from every orifice, that all the Great Books have already been written, but battling on regardless, knowing this was the feeling in 1960, 1930, 1900, and that if his own drivel might in some small way contribute to his beloved Babel bookpile (Borges reference), then he will have done his work, despite that work consisting merely of comments about him not writing his work, and so on until you cannot take another sentence like this, where the author once again repeats the title of his unwritten novel: *The House of Writers.*

The Trauma Rooms

10

"WELL, here we are at last!" the doctor said, cupping Erin's shoulder for the final time, nudging her into a vacant room.

"Whose room is this?"

"Yours."

"Repeat that?"

"Your room. Do you not remember? You went on a mad rampage throughout the building, braining writers with staplers, stapling their anuses and lips shut."

"Erm, no . . . I was looking for a stapler on the sixteenth floor."

"Take a seat, Erin."

Erin sat on her mattress, scanning its items: sugared apple scented candle; 32″ × 48″ canvas art print of Terence Stamp in *The Limey*; a nine-cassette VHS boxset of *Dawson's Creek*; a photo of Auntie Loretta Grahams in a pearl-studded fame; a plasticine rendering of the Sistine Chapel; various receipts on a kebab skewer sellotaped to an urn lid; a necklace monogrammed "Ayran" from her prankster ex-boyfriend; a thoroughly dog-eared copy of Joel Norst's *Mississippi Burning*; a signed poster of '90s one-hit-wonder Shanice; a cheap replica of a Turkish *seccade* Islamic prayer rug; a spanner in a plastic box marked "spatula"; the northwest corner of a ticket stub from a Republica concert with noticeable lipstick smear from Saffron; a bronze statuette of Olympic pole vaulter Renaud Lavillenie; an uneaten packet of fig rolls; and a wall-spanning series of photos showing a Sudanese tribe quizzically confronting a Volvo S70.

"Yes, these things remind me of me," she said.

"Let me remind you. Two months ago, you worked on the four-teenth floor, where periodically people would pinch your staplers when you needed them to bind your manuscripts for prospective readers. Your manuscripts were sent to readers unbound, causing rage and cancellation of commissions. On one occasion you wrote a whole novel for a reader, and your stapler was filched, so you sent the chapters loose. The reader called you a flaming disgrace, accused you of slovenly presentation and withdrew her $50 cheque. You were unable to sell the novel to another reader. A week's work, wasted. This regrettable cycle continued, with entire novels being refused and re-*f*used. You were struggling to afford a pack of mi-crowave noodles. You opted to spend your nights prowling the of-fice to reconnect with your missing staplers. Some writers placed forcefields around their staplers, harnessing the power of magnetic particles to prevent a midnight attack; others set up laser beams, causing powerful skin-flaming damage to invading hands; others chained malnourished guard dogs to their desks; some slept with their staplers in intimate places; some hid their staplers in secret compartments in their desks, and so on. You chose the path of direct physical attack. You raided the stock-dump fields for a weapon to use against the thieves. Finding an old panini sandwich press that heated and fired flaming rocks at targets, you launched an assault on your fellow writers, braining them with rocks and stones at temper-atures over 200°C, hoarding the staplers in your desk. You placed a barbed wire fence around your desk and attached mini-missiles to staplers and rigged up hole punches to squirt acid. When the office mounted a collective attack on your defences, you fled with your staplers on that aforementioned rampage, killing over seventy writers from the Sports Thriller department."

"No great loss."

"Ha! Quite. You managed to escape your room through an air vent that has now been stuffed with asbestos."

"I thought I was looking for a stapler."

"Yes, you have moments where you regress back to your earlier trauma. Sometimes, I will let you hold a stapler if you require consolation."

"Oh."

"Well. I will see you later."

"Thanks."

"And that concludes the tour!" He smiled.

"Ha." She frowned and lay back on her mattress. She stared into the intense peepers of Terence Stamp. She opened the uneaten packet of fig rolls and popped a fig roll into her mouth. She ate the fig roll. From under the bed she heard the words: "Hello again." A man rolled out. The man was the maniac who hated bios.

"Oh no."

"Yes. I know about your bio. Let me remind you: 'Erin Grahams writes soap operas featuring the occasional cannibal nurse. She has a fondness for escalators and have-a-go heroes. Her two kittens think she smells.'"

"I can explain."

Erin had no time explain because Gerald had already begun to do his murdering.

Writer Portraits

The Beekeeper

I RESIDED in Lavelle in Southern France—a serene hamlet responsible for two hundred eclogues and thousands of middling watercolours. Having retired from four decades teaching nippers the alphabet and basic sums, I chose to settle there for the famous stillness (no falling leaf exceeded 0.002dB). I had endured hardships as a school teacher: the unwanted milk siphoned into pockets, blazers soaked in snot and tears, and shoes gummed up with play dough; in addition, I came to the realisation that I would forever be remembered for my occasional stuttering blow-outs, when I would leap from the chair to shout at troublemakers, waving my arms around madly, failing in anger to pronounce words while the kids laughed and taunted me. To teach for four decades is to open oneself up to the insatiable cruelty of the pre-tween mindset and endure persistent humiliations that no other professionals have to suffer. This is why I felt equipped to become a creative writer. I had no problem with being mocked or humiliated on the road to success. However, one incident forced me to retire from the peace I had cultivated.

In Lavelle, I bought a cottage with a small plot overlooking an orchard. I made the room overlooking the orchard my library and study, where I would retreat each morning to write fiction. I began writing childhood reflections about my upbringing in Norway, my relocation to Ruislip, and my time at school and so forth . . . nothing of particular interest to the common reader, but material I might be able to reshape into a novel. I wrote by hand as the twitter of birds and rustle of branches provided the backing track for these deep excavations of my childhood recall. Once, when composing a passage on my first kiss, a bee buzzed in through the window and landed on my middle finger. Before I could flick the bee clear, the blighter stung me and fell insensate on my notepad.

I went to the bathroom to cool the sting and upon returning noticed no bee. I scoped the room for rogue bees then resumed. Where was I? Ah yes, "I placed my wet lips . . ." Two bees landed on my notepad. One flew into my face and the other sat on the paper, alternating this process four times. I leapt out the chair to swipe the newspaper, chasing them out the window in a huff. I returned. "I placed my . . ." Where had my wet lips gone? Bemused, I headed out to inspect the garden, observing a busy beehive in a tree in the orchard belonging to a local farmer, and returned to the study, curious as to why the bees had ventured into my window when there were no flowers nearby. I kept my window open until more bees arrived and the hassle continued. I returned again to my notepad to notice the preceding sentence was missing. These bees were harvesting my words!

Over the next two days, I had to fend off dozens of ambushing bees at a time, sucking up with violence the words I had written on my notepad, and taking them back to their hive. I tried closing the window, but the summer heat was unbearable, so I hung a light curtain to prevent their incoming. Next, I inspected the beehive. I am not the sort of man who surprises a beehive unprepared . . . I wore my old fencing outfit, and pondered how to penetrate the hive. A loud English voice boomed: "Hoi! Hold on there!" The Englishman was a bronzed creature with several planets orbiting his hips. His face was not a kind one. "You messing with my beehive, are you?" I retreated. I looked absurd in the fencing equipment. "Hello there. No, I wasn't. I've been having a problem with bees, you see . . . flying in my window," I said. I could not explain the next section without sounding mad. I trailed off. "Keep your hands off my bees. Get back on your own property. First warning, OK?"

I returned in poor spirits. I had hoped for a retirement free from the unpleasant sorts I had encountered in bygone days, and to make some new friends in the region. This bellicose Englishman was the closest person to me in a two-mile radius, reminiscent of the one teacher in the block I shared in the 1990s: never a pleasant hello exchanged. I returned to my notepad the next morning alarmed to see the whole page I had written the previous day was missing and that someone had torn a hole in the curtain. I contrived useless solutions. I left books open to see if the bees might feast on pre-printed words—a sticky glaze was left on these pages in protest. I wrote nonsense on second notebook—only the sensible sentences were harvested. Panic ensued. What was I supposed to do in this situation? I wanted to write in my study, not the kitchen or my bedroom. I had the right.

I spied on my neighbour and, one morning when I saw him drive away in his Land Cruiser, sneaked back towards the beehive. I had never dismantled a beehive before, but found out on the internet that to "smoke" the bees beforehand to make the bees gorge on honey was the best approach. I had ordered a handheld smoke machine, which I took towards the hive. I pumped smoke into the hive first, and broke a small part with a chisel to inspect. Once the smoke cleared, the bees launched themselves at my face, trying to obscure the view of their hive. Batting the pests aside, I peered inside and observed that each hexagon of their hive housed a different one of my words. I noticed "I placed my wet lips on her peachy lips" along the back of the hive and, scattered, other sentences from the novel-in-progress that had been eaten. I returned to the cottage to ruminate over my actions. I simply had to have this out with my next door neighbour, now there was evidence to show him.

I needn't have worried, for an hour later, the raging Englishman next door barrelled towards me in his huge clodhoppers. "You've been at my beehive again!" I faced up to the brute and his clod-hoppers. "These bees have been menacing me, buzzing in my window, upsetting my writing time." The man smiled, revealing two browned molars. "You're a nutbag. This is the French countryside, if you don't like bees, buzz off back to Jockland." I retreated. Returned to composing the novel. Fought the bees. All the while, I kept a camera trained on the beehive. One morning I caught the farmer raiding the beehive, returning inside with its contents in a sealed box. A month later, I read a story in *The New Yorker* where each of my words had been used in a different order—the author Simon Tremaine, who "spends his time in the South of France with his two dogs tending his orchard."

I searched Tremaine on the internet, discovering that he had been sued amid rumours of plagiarism. During his time in London, writers living in the same tenement had accused Tremaine of "hiving off" their creativity, and reassembling their words in his own formations to produce his works. His weapon of attack became clear to me. He had been training his bees to steal the words, and these super-intelligent insects had rearranged them into successful pieces of original and marketable fiction.

I considered my options. I could sit in the house attempting to write fiction while the bees stole my every word, helping Tremaine's career; I could move house to another part of France . . . or, since I knew Tremaine's secret, I could steal his beehive and flee the country, making a name for myself using his brilliant bees. This was my only real shot at literary success in my late sixties. I waited one night when Tremaine was active with one of his random lovers, and sealed up the beehive, chiselled free from the tree. I made a swift hotfoot from Lavelle, having put my cottage up for sale, and sped towards the Channel Tunnel. I made sure the bees survived by punching a few airholes in their hive, where I poked a few pollinated roses for them to lap at during the long drive back home.

I arrived at The House of Writers and signed up to write memoirs, keeping my beehive in a briefcase. Once installed in The House, I set up the beehive in my room and waited until the writers had retired to bed, releasing the bees into the office, where they scavenged for words from open notepads, or for those using computers, print-outs. The words were rearranged in the hive and published by me as original work. I kept the bees going like this until I had completed three books. Unfortunately, I had failed to be as attentive to the bees as I should have been, and the insects, having had no time to lay their eggs, died without having produced enough offspring to keep my career going. As I write this, I have no means of writing my fourth book, a room full of dead bees, and Simon Tremaine said he knows I stole his bees, and is coming for me. This is not a happy time in my life.

A Better Life

10

My final attempt to drop the scurrilous duo Pete and Rob, and escape The House forever, took place one winter morning upon completing my final paid commission—a psychosexual thriller set in the Balkans—and pocketing my last few pounds. It was the coldest winter in decades, and The House had contracted chronic pneumonia—raindrops froze on contact with the window-panes, breath clotted into clouds to form scalp-stabbing icicles in mid-air, pipes required a thorough blowtorch to produce water. The building itself was wrapped from bottom to top in a glacial coat, resembling the tip of an iceberg rising from a vast Arctic ocean. The heating had malfunctioned, so the writers were expected to deliver their manuscripts at subzero temperatures while lapsing into the incoherent chattering death-rattle of hypothermia. This was, even to the dimmest observer, the end. I had arranged for a pack of huskies and a sled to be delivered to the front door with my final earnings, and hoped to make my escape into the sprawl of neck-deep snow that smothered the periphery like some blank page rising from a writer's nightmare.

Pete and Rob had been stalking me for weeks, relying upon my survivor's cunning to help keep them warm. Their one notable characteristic—brattish disrespect (mostly for me)—turned to pan-icked servitude as their noses ran and their blood cooled, and to humour them into thinking a full life existed the other side of winter, I helped them staple extra layers of carpet to their bodies and milk the plug sockets for electric shocks. On the morning of my departure, I dawdled around the ground floor. Mhairi and Marilyn were wrapped inside a blanket, "hibernating" until the winter ended, subsiding on licks of frozen water and a hidden stash of pickled onion crisps. This Great Freeze was to be the end of my colleagues, to be the end of the writing industry—Marilyn and Mhairi would survive with icy saliva and a lifetime's stale oniony breath.

The huskies and sled arrived as ordered from Tuktoyaktuk Imports Affiliated, signal-barking as per the agreement as I walked to the first floor, where I had to exit via the window due to the snow's volume. I wasted no time in shattering an ice-glazed window with the Man-Blaster I had constructed in my spare time, and coldfooted it to the sled. People attempted to raise their eyebrows as I fired a toaster at the window, terrified at the extra bite of coldness and hoping to utilise some of the created energy. I hopped on the sled and mushed the huskies onward into the Crarsix wilds. The Scot-Call compound, having been built on a flat plane, had been buried in snow, and the temporarily impressive Microhumans and Microheavies had all frozen, leaving nothing alive in an undetermined radius, and I powered on despite the frostbite, until I alighted upon a hotel. Inside, warm cups of coffee were being served, and a warm fire stoked. No one says a word, and everyone basks in the comfort of the fire. There you can stay as long you like, and everything is free.

Or, at least that's what I hope might happen as I sit here and wait for the huskies to arrive. They are several hours late, and I'm starting to wonder if I ever placed the order, or I merely thought I had since I wrote about it happening . . .

The *Farewell, Author!* Conference

10

THE sun shone, having no alternative, on the writers who could produce nothing new. It was time to abscond. The diggers had arrived, their wrecking balls poised, eager to demolish the Fossilfoods and open the first ScotCall compound in Cumbernauld. The writers, their literal and metaphorical hungers still unappeased, began the short trudge to oblivion, having failed to commit suicide en masse and reach their final Full Stops. Their collective hope that out there, somewhere, nestled a sentence that might sum up this sinking world, taking them to that place of pleasurable transcendence—the perfect phrase—kept them trudging on. Andrea Kneeland, speaking in tongues about Beckett's Second Coming and the Rapture, stumbled along the B8054 towards an active golf course, where she inserted herself into the fifteenth hole and cosied down to her eventual starvation; Sunjeev Sahota boarded a train at Greenfaulds, derailing into Bog Stank, where the survivors formed a primitive cult around the worship of mangled locomotives, ending his days dancing around a rusted engine and an effigy of Richard Trevithick; David Szalay was hunted by a ScotCall recruiter and smoothtalked into signing up for twelve hours per day on the phones, the perpetual ring-ring and prattle of the yokels soon erasing his history as a writer; Zach Dodson took a wife in the borough of Kildrum and sired three Scottish kids—Anchor, Albatross, and Deadweight—reminding them hourly that their existences had stripped him of his freedom as an artist, and the best he could hope for them in life was a permanent kick in the nuts; Angel Ivov ate the mushrooms in the Ravenswood forest and ascended to the heavens on a prism of light, arriving at nirvana to be met by St. Peter Cook, who led him to a room where wit zinged from corner to corner, and the Purpose of Life was revealed as Vonnegut had predicted—To Fart Around—and was found by the police licking a tree in his pants before exploding with happiness in a controlled environment; Tahmima Anam sheared as many sheep as she could in nine hours to amuse herself, and entered the world Sheep Shearing Championships, where she came twelfth; A.L. Kennedy opened a vein with a disposable razor and noticing she bled pound coins not blood, went to homeless shelters where she offered a sample to everyone, until she collapsed from a pound shortage and had to have pounds inserted into her body, and since no one was kind enough to donate their pounds to her, she died in her sleep; Christina Kloess repopularised asparagus as a vegetable after several decades in the wilderness of neglect; and R.M. Berry kept rubbing his chin in contemplation and wore the skin away, waking up one morning to an ant colony sucking on his bleeding chin, and after months of resistance and frustration, came to accept his chin ants and their thriving colony, before collapsing from no blood soon. I, meanwhile, ambled around Croy, the Barhill Wood, thinking on the future, surviving on acorns, before making the resigned trek to The House of Writers, where I reside at present, writing *Star Trek* fan fiction. To cut this story short, I wish I had killed myself that night. My future lies in a coffin.

The Corridor of Closing Lines

ALL things were lost, that being the way of all things. I have none but this table has legs remaining. "So you see, Candice, the pastime of philately might be twice as illuminating and filled with the potential to perplex, amaze, stun, and confound as you previously thought!" He paid a terrible price for doubting the word of Alvin G. Bingle. Nicola snuffed the lamp and crawled back under her well-hewn quilts of eiderdown. Godard is not our master, but I think I have mastered Godard. Perhaps I will eat this salad—perhaps not. The klaxon ringeth. The ochre is blinding. "Yes, Gregory,

G

O

O

D

B

Y

E

THIS ipod is meatier than we expected. The drought lasted for a wee bit longer than the ecologists had predicted. Invisible arcs are not as effective as visible arcs. "You know that lobster we ate for supper, Rico . . . I have a confession to make: that was no lobster . . . . that was your father!" Coming soon to a theatre near you: the plague! There is no problem that cannot be solved with frenzied masturbation. "Aztec pottery, Edwardian calligraphy, Victorian architecture . . . balls to the lot!" shouted Simon while admiring his penis. Rest assured

I *can* see the advantages of a smaller sprocket but in this instance I prefer the maxi doodad." "Pomade is *not* a drink consumed by Brits in Australia," Ana remarked with a furious determination. The suicidal kitten returned to his cave and contemplated the mess he had made of his lives. Next time I will end at the beginning. The first time I met Nora she smiled and called me a funky ogre. "Oh!" said Ian. Luckily the whole thing was solved with a handshake and a lifetime's subscription to *Penthouse*. Beluga caviar was not on the menu so I shot everyone in the restaurant. I peered into the middle distance and observed a Panzer tank alongside the fifth German battalion approaching and thought: perhaps now is a good time to write that opera I had been planning for decades. The leaves were rustling and Tim thought that the

that the rest is insured. Follicles appeared from nowhere. The rest is history, starting with the Early Pleistocene period. Asphalt! "Great things are going to happen not to you, but to everyone you know, so that's something at least." Demerol, sir? I met a lonesome man who loaned me a yurt. "The Arctic roll is *not* the same as the buttered pineapple, and I can prove it!" shouted Nira. Four cooks spoil the broth, three make a delicious consommé with veal and parsley, and two insert their seminal fluid into everything. "There is something about a child's energetic yelps that reminds one of the lustful screeches made during intercourse," Klaus said, emptying the room. A wasp in the washbasin is a reason to weep. Carol singers in the dungeon, olé! Carol Singers

FROM THE HOUSE

leaves were rustling and Anna said, "Hey, those leaves are rustling." I demand to be removed from the blacklist. "This is a dull performance of Bizet's *Carmen*," Todd remarked. The ideal novel should be like an art exhibit one walks through gleaning only snippets of inspiration while otherwise absorbing nowt and pondering what to have for lunch. We can but hope to shuffle off this coil with love in our loins and hope in our hearts and sick in our stomachs. Does the patio furniture squeak when immolated? Forward thinking or backward drinking?

O F W R I T E R S

in the dungeon, *O sole mio!* The path to success is littered with the corpses of kind and gentle souls. "You can always go back and edit," she said with a conspiratorial wink. "Two to a bed or one to a shed?" I said. This novel contains blasphemy, goddamn it. "You know the way out, Sally." In the beginning there was the word, and the word was surrounded by streams of other, stylelessly used words, rendering the business of making literature redundant through the systematic abuse, raping, and butchering of the language. Meow.